GET READY TO RUMBLE

D'ekkar Han Valoren. To others he might command respect, fear even. But he wouldn't get any of that from her; not anymore. True, he was Prince Kyber's half-brother, tied to one of the world's most powerful monarchies. But to her, he was just Deck—bastard son, black sheep of the royal family, and all-around rebel without a cause. Oh yeah, plus the worst unrequited crush she'd ever had. But that was then, and now was turning into . . . who the hell knew?

"I need you to come with me. I'm not going to discuss it here." He quickly surveyed the high-rises around them. "We've been in the open long enough."

She could see his patience giving way, and couldn't help but push him to the edge. "I've been living in this dump for two years, and now the . . . the freaking royal brigade miraculously finds me and I'm supposed to drop everything and follow you? Why the hell should I?"

He took out his gun and pointed it at her forehead. "Oh, I don't know. Because the food's better where we're going?"

Holy hell. She swallowed hard, then rolled her eyes, making a big show of moving the muzzle with her forefinger and scratching the spot it touched. "Okay, it's a need-to-know basis. I get it. Just one thing . . . what's in it for me?"

THE Shadow Runners

Liz Maverick

LOVE SPELL

NEW YORK CITY

LOVE SPELL®

June 2004

Published by

Dorchester Publishing Co., Inc.
200 Madison Avenue
New York, NY 10016

ISBN 0-505-52589-5

The name "Love Spell" and its logo are trademarks of Dorchester Publishing Co., Inc.

Printed in the United States of America.

Visit us on the web at www.dorchesterpub.com.

THE Shadow Runners

This one's for the girls.
Especially . . .

For Susan Grant. You totally get it.
You *are* a kick-butt heroine.
Thank you so much for everything.

For Cathy Yardley. You can say I told you so now. Thanks, Moe.

For Laura Bradford. Day 1. Thanks, Pickle.

And special thanks to Carolyn Jewel and Gabrielle Pantera
for their Regency-era insights. Any (unintentional) deviations
from historical fact are mine. The intentional ones are
definitely mine, too, but . . . well, you'll see.

Chapter One

The Macao slums, 2176

Nobody lived like this if they didn't have to, but it all depended on what you were willing to do to get out. Jenny changed her mind a lot on that score. It was amazing how easily real life could mess with your standards.

The vendor in front of her cleared his throat impatiently as she considered his offerings. She ignored him, using the muzzle of her stun pistol to lift the bread and examine the small slab of *bloni* underneath. Meat substitutes on Macao were a bit dicey these days, but she'd had her last round of innox shots pretty recently and she needed cheap fuel.

She'd been trying to get out of places like this all her life. Except for that one year at the palace, but . . . frankly, when the grass was really greener on the other side, it was better not to be able to see over the

1

fence. She poked at a second sandwich. Yeah, ignorance was bliss, for sure. Especially when it came to synthetic meat.

She held up the forefinger of the hand holding her gun. "I'll take those two. And don't even try to rip me off."

The vendor scowled, his eyes flicking from her pistol to the coins she held in her opposite palm. "You got any other kinda value?"

"No. Do we have a deal, or not?"

He grunted, chose the coin that looked brassiest, and dropped it into a grease-smeared apron pocket.

Jenny wiped her hand down her vest, then realized the vest wasn't any cleaner. With a shrug, she replaced her stunner in its ankle holster, picked up the sandwiches, and stuffed one in her mouth. She chased it with a quick shot of alcohol mixed with antibiotic from a flask, both to kill off any newer forms of bioinfection and any flavor.

She ate quickly, an iron grip on her messenger bag, her eyes focused on the people milling about in the square, her ears listening for unusual variations in the droning sound filtering down from the built-up highways and skyways above. The nagging feeling of being watched followed her everywhere.

Of course, people around here watched any female who appeared to have all relevant body parts.

She turned slowly in a casual circle. *Observe carefully and pretend you see nothing. And if you do, just keep it steady . . . keep it steady. . . .*

Okay, who's that?

The guy was too clean for the area. Too fit, too well fed. And his weapons were way too new.

Her second glance was quick, practiced, and if he hadn't already been staring straight at her, they would never have registered eye contact at all.

Jenny's mouth went dry, but she'd overreacted and made a fool of herself before; she wouldn't do it again. Paranoia was a disease down here, blooming out from one person and infecting a crowd with deadly consequences. She stopped turning and stood motionless in front of the sandwich kiosk, only half aware of the bread squeezing under her nails. Her mind skidded through a list of jobs she'd had over the past year. Whom did she know ... whom had she worked for ... what jobs were unfinished ... had she screwed anyone over?

It could be anything, but she always came back to one likely possibility. Parliament. Had they come for her at last?

Well, in all fairness, she'd gone and killed one of them. A man. A very particular sort of man. And if it were her on the flip side, she'd still be looking for her, too.

Members of Parliament rarely stepped outside their realm of influence, even to square up a dispute but—Jenny chewed nervously on her lip—in her case, maybe murder was worth the trip. From a strategic point of view, making an example of someone like her was a reasonable way for them to keep order, to keep Newgate—hell, to keep the whole of Australia—for themselves.

She shuddered as she thought of that place, those

men. Hardly men, really. They were more like empty souls, burnt-out husks using opiate to make their sick reality palatable. Creepy men posturing as aristocrats from a time made moldy in memory: the English Regency. And though the members of Parliament had little power in the rest of the world, they ruled with an iron fist clamped around the throat of Newgate City.

And now, just when she was ready to believe they'd forgotten about her, that they'd decided she was small potatoes, that they'd never send anyone out from Newgate just to snuff her . . . Well, she always seemed to find a reason to keep looking over her shoulder for them, didn't she?

At the edge of her consciousness, she could feel a change in the atmosphere, the negative charge as the crowd slowly emptied from the market square behind her. A bead of cold sweat trickled down between her shoulder blades. The vendor stared straight in front of him, almost catatonic, as if he could make himself invisible through sheer will.

Jenny made a sound; their eyes met, her look a question. If there was one thing the slummers of Macao had in common, it was a mutual distrust of outsiders.

The vendor's gaze flicked quickly over her shoulder. He nodded almost imperceptibly; then he picked up an empty sandwich tray from the counter and bent down with it, scattering food as he shielded himself below the table.

Jenny took a deep breath and split to the left, into the crowd. Pushing through bodies, she hurled herself over the concrete slab that demarcated the boundary of the marketplace. Balancing herself with a hand to the ground, she hardly felt the cement scraping her palm. She moved to snatch the stun gun from its holster as she ran, but bobbled the grip. It skittered away across the pavement. Pausing to grab it, she reared up and accelerated into a flat-out sprint. She knew these alleys like the back of her hand and was fairly acclimated to the pollution; there was no question she could lose such a big guy with just a bit more lead.

Her damn messenger bag thumped against her back as she ran. She could unlock it, drop it, but not unless she had to. It held everything she owned: some ratty clothes, first aid, random ammunition—nothing that could help at the moment. She had a couple of low-grade explosives, but she'd run out of ignition clips.

Still running as fast as she could, she glanced behind her to see her pursuer jump the concrete barrier with surprising ease. A double take revealed he was talking into a comm device. Not good.

She ducked down another side street and flattened herself against the wall, sliding awkwardly across the slimy bricks.

Footsteps thundered toward her. "Don't run!" came a call.

Don't run? Yeah, right. What's the one thing you do when some huge bastard with a gun warns you not to run? You run like hell and hope you're a better shot. Jenny flipped herself face-first against the bricks, took a second to try and control the shaking of her hand from adrenaline, then fired once around

5

the corner. Her stunner flared halfheartedly, then sputtered and died.

Cursing a blue streak, she slammed the side of her hand against its muzzle, shook the gun almost desperately, then tried again.

"Jenny Red!"

The stunner worked this time, sending a flare straight down the alley. Bull's-eye. The heavy grunted and reeled back, losing his footing and falling to the ground. But it wouldn't stop him for long.

Jenny stared up at the traffic-congested sky, if not expecting a miracle, at least a little inspiration. The sun was already beginning to go down, and against the backdrop of electric-pink and orange neon clouds enhanced by the chemicals in the smog, Jenny could see a copter circling above. There was probably a launch pad on the building. She'd just have to throw herself on its pilot's mercy.

Swinging around, she looked for the rooftop ladder access for the high-rise behind her, and when she found it she ran, leaping onto its rungs. Halfway up, she looked down. The heavy was already on his feet, shaking his head like a dog ridding its coat of water. Okay, so much for stun. She slammed her pistol back in its holster and just kept climbing.

"Don't run!" The man stopped abruptly, clearly under the mistaken belief that if he gave the impression of retreat, she'd somehow interpret him as a friendly. Not likely. Not even close. Although, for a nanosecond, she did almost consider surrender on the grounds that it might get the idiot to quit screaming her name at the top of his lungs for every bounty hunter in a five-block radius to hear. For all she knew, Parliament might literally have put a price on her head.

"Jenny Red!"

Okay, okay. So he knew her name—or lack thereof. She'd lost her given name what seemed like eons ago, after it stopped mattering who her family was. Well, she'd barely had a family, anyway—a father, mostly in name, who had probably only dragged her around with him to facilitate his scams. "Red" was her surname now, given to her by a couple of slum pals because of her hair color.

"Jenny Red!" The heavy's dogged pursuit sent chills up her spine, and he ran the length of the alley in what seemed like record time. Jenny just kept moving up the endless ladder.

She was at least seventy-five pounds lighter than him, and gasping for air. Given his size, that this guy could move so fast in this kind of atmosphere meant he had access to oxygen poppers. He obviously worked for someone with a lot of value, to be able to afford that stuff. Definitely not good. Made the idea of trying to kill him a less appealing investment in the rest of her life.

Sweat ran down the inside of her bulky protective gear. Clearing the side of the building, she stepped onto the rooftop and battled a wave of nausea from the combined altitude and pollution.

The rhythmic clang of boots sounded on the ladder below. Jenny focused on the copter resting in idle on the launch pad. The pilot opened the door, and Jenny pulled her stun pistol again. Glancing behind her, she saw her pursuer step off the ladder and onto the roof.

She trained her gun on him, gasping and gulping for air, her finger slippery on the trigger. The heavy stopped in his tracks, obviously unsure, and she finally got a good enough look to realize that he didn't have the stamp of Newgate on him. It was just a gut feeling, unprovable, and it didn't provide her any sense of relief. He could have been hired by Parliament through a middleman. Given his obvious Japanese descent, he was likely a local. Closely shaved black hair, angular face, eyes narrowing as he stared back at her—none of that caused much concern. What worried Jenny was that the guy was built like a tank. Taking a hit from one of those fists probably felt like slamming into a side of beef.

Slowly, he raised his gun. "I'm—"

She didn't wait. Swinging around, she ran toward the copter pilot. Shit, she was going to have to go for a hijack.

Suddenly the heavy was right behind her, and she was flying face-first into the ground. Her gun went airborne. She raised her leg up, bent her knee, and bucked her boot violently behind her, a cry of pain indicating she'd hit her target.

He flattened her anyway. "You keep using up your oxygen at this rate, you'll be delirious within five minutes," he said into her ear.

He was right, and she stopped struggling.

He sighed. "His Lordship's going to be pissed."

His Lordship?

Jenny turned her head toward the copter.

Its engine kicked up swirls of filthy air as its pilot strode toward them, charcoal-colored trench coat billowing out behind him. Polarized shades obscured his face, but he looked tough, nasty . . . and familiar. The Han royal emblem snaked around the upper arm of his coat. Traditionally affixed in hammered platinum, this was fashioned in the raised black leather she'd seen only on one person before.

Holy hell. It was Deck.

D'ekkar Han Valoren, former prince and scion of the Han monarchy, walked up to the pile of body parts that comprised Jenny and his heavy smashed into the concrete together, cocked his head, and removed his shades. "Jenny Red. A pleasure."

His eyes were as hard as she remembered, but his voice still seeped under her skin in a soft growl.

"Sorry, sir," the heavy said regretfully as he peeled off of her. "She ran."

Deck held out his hand, sheathed in a glove made from the finest armored fabric Jenny had ever seen. Still working to catch her breath, she let him help her up and squinted at him through the smog.

"You know, you could just . . . I don't know, send a letter. Make a call. What's with the theatrics?"

The heavy shifted behind her; Jenny could actually feel his breath on her neck. Lovely. He clearly didn't like her taking such a casual attitude with his boss. Well, that was just too damn bad. She'd spent enough time at the Han palace to know that the trappings of royalty might be special, but the royals themselves were no better than the scum who lived here in Macao.

To others, Deck might command respect, fear even. But he wouldn't get any of that from her, not anymore. True, he was Prince Kyber's half brother. He was tied to one of the world's most powerful monarchies. But to her, he was just Deck—bastard son, black sheep of the royal family, and all-around rebel without a cause.

Oh yeah, plus the worst unrequited crush she'd ever had in her life. But that was then, and now was turning into . . . who the hell knew?

Deck took her hands and turned them over. One palm was pretty much okay. The other was a scraped-up, bleeding mess. He managed to pick a piece of gravel out of her flesh before she pulled away.

"Nice manners, your guy," she said roughly, nodding toward the heavy to mask her confusion. Behind the palace gates, you couldn't so much as lay a finger on a member of the royal family—and vice versa wasn't so good an idea either. He'd only ever touched her one time before, at the last.

"Jenny, allow me to present my associate, Raidon. Raidon, my old friend, Jenny Red."

"That's helpful. I make it a point to always know who's lying on top of me." She touched her fingers to her nose; they came away red with blood.

"Old friend, huh," she noted absently as she searched in her pockets for something to clean herself up with.

"Still leaping before looking?" he asked.

"Still alive," she countered.

Deck's hand slid toward his breast pocket, and

10

Jenny flinched out of habit. He raised one eyebrow, then simply pulled out a crisp, white handkerchief.

She had to laugh. *Jenny, you are so torqued.*

She took the handkerchief. "Ready for surrender at a moment's notice?" she teased, instantly destroying the fine lawn square with the blood and dirt on her hands and face.

Deck snorted. "To whom?"

"Not me, clearly," she grumbled. With a rueful look in the direction of the ever-watchful Raidon, she held the mottled cloth back out.

Deck shook his head. "Consider it yours."

Jenny stuffed it in her pocket, a corner of her mind already calculating how much value she might get for a stained handkerchief made of the finest natural fiber and monogrammed with the initials of a Han prince. Maybe she could get something for it as a novelty item. Maybe not.

"Well? What are we doing here, Deck?"

"We're picking you up." He nodded toward the idling copter. "Ready to go?"

She widened her stance and looked up at him through narrowed eyes. "Sorry. Doesn't work that way. I don't just go with anyone who asks. What's on your mind?"

He sighed impatiently. "Two things. One, I need to talk to you, and, two, I would really like to conserve what fuel I can."

She glared at him in stony silence.

"I need you to come with me. I'm not going to discuss it here." He quickly surveyed the high-rises around them. "We've been in the open long enough as it is."

She could see his patience giving way, and couldn't help wanting to push him to the edge. "I've been living in this shit hole for two years, and now the . . . the freaking royal brigade miraculously finds me and I'm supposed to drop everything and follow you? Why the hell should I?"

He took his gun out of his holster and pointed it at her forehead. "Oh, I don't know. Because the food's better where we're going?"

Even Raidon jerked back in surprise.

Holy hell. She swallowed hard, then rolled her eyes, making a big show of moving the muzzle of his gun to the side with her forefinger, and scratching the spot it had touched. "Okay, it's a need-to-know basis. I get it. Just one thing. What's in it for me?"

He looked her up and down. "A bath to start."

She flushed. "For a prince, you always did make a lousy gentleman. A bath, food, medical supplies, ammunition . . . all the water I can carry. And that's just to come with you."

"I'll throw in tantalizing conversation for free. You have a deal."

She held out her hand.

"I trust you," he said.

"I trust me, too. It's you I have issues with." She wiggled her fingers. "Put 'er there, Deck."

The corner of his mouth quirked up in a smile. He met her in a handshake. "A gentleman's agreement."

Raidon led Jenny to the copter, with Deck following behind. "Are we going far?" she called over her shoulder as the heavy hustled her into the backseat.

"Not that far."

"How long is this going to take?"

Deck settled himself in front of the controls. "I only have one major question to ask you. How long the rest takes depends on your answer."

She frowned. Raidon strapped her in beside him as if he were tucking in a small child. "Well . . . tell me the question, and I'll have an answer for you by the time we land."

Deck looked at her in the rearview mirror. "Have you ever heard of Banzai Maguire?"

He hit the accelerator, one eye still watching her. Jenny hoped he would assume it was the gravitational pull that drained the blood from her face.

Chapter Two

Deck stared out the bulletproof window at the Macao skyline. Between the cookie-cutter rectangular skyscrapers and the lasers illuminating the city's public flight paths, thick black smoke rose up through a huge network of purification tubes into the stratosphere. It was an effort to keep the street-level pollution under control. Red, pink, green, blue, and yellow lights glanced off the tubes from enormous blinking neon billboards, sending rays of color to illuminate the swirling particles being vacuumed upward. This public work he knew well; he'd helped plan the logistics for the test project. He'd still been a prince, then. The House of Han had not continued implementation, but Deck had no idea if it was because the project wasn't economically feasible, technologically sound, or whether Kyber had simply lost interest.

He sighed and rubbed his eyes. How long ago it all seemed.

Raidon cleared his throat, and Deck swung around. "Is she out yet?"

"I called, sir, but she didn't answer. I think it's been a while since she's last had a hot bath."

Deck stared at him. "You're already coddling her." He should have known his right-hand man and personal bodyguard would get emotional about the girl once they were face-to-face. Hell, Raidon had spoken of Jenny as he would a pet or a little sister since the day he'd been assigned as her tail.

Raidon donned his stubborn face. "We have plenty of time to make the transport."

"Don't give me that look. We still need to get her fitted out before we go."

"Speaking of which, it's bad enough we're stuck with junk weaponry to defend ourselves, but to be further constrained by other things we can bring in? Sir, I'm really not comfortable with this level of security."

Deck scrolled through the to-do list carefully programmed into his organizer, trying not to let Raidon's rant grate on him. He was aware he still had much to learn about Newgate, Australia, but one thing everybody knew was that anything beyond late-twenty-first-century technology was banned in the penal colony. And that included weapons *and* defense technology. Which made sense if the rest of the world wanted to make it impossible for residents to escape.

He'd probably feel differently once he made it to Newgate, but the idea of being constrained to the historical, to the obsolete, no less, was intriguing. At least it allowed for a predictable playing field.

"The goal is to enter Newgate with a minimum amount of notice," he snapped. "Now let's just do what we have to do, all right?"

His heavy chuckled. "A little testy, are we, sir? I can't imagine why." He continued checking over a supply chart.

For some reason, Deck couldn't let it go. He threw his organizer down on his desk in disgust. "Look, it had to be done, you know. Jenny is stronger than you realize."

It was ridiculous. He'd been blathering about this for the last hour, and he knew he was beginning to sound the fool. But seeing her condition was a shock he hadn't anticipated. Guilt was not a pleasant emotion, and it was one that Deck usually avoided with success.

Unlike his heavy, Deck was good at taking emotion out of the equation. He'd actually managed to completely forget about Jenny for long stretches of time. And when he did think of her, he didn't do so as she probably was: living hard on the bad side of town.

We rich don't like to think about the poor, he thought detachedly. He'd only seen Jenny three times over the last few years, whenever Raidon reported an emergency. They'd been clever; she wouldn't have known she had a guardian angel. Of course, her guardian angel was playing both sides of the game.

"The ends justified the means in this case," he argued darkly.

Raidon stopped what he was doing and looked up in mixed exasperation and amusement. "Who are you trying to convince, sir?"

"Raidon."

"Yes, sir."

"*Stop* calling me 'sir.'"

His bodyguard shook his head, one eyebrow raised.

Deck hated being called sir, like he hated most reminders of his link to Prince Kyber and the House of Han. "Highness" was out of the question now that he was illegitimate, but his heavy simply refused to stop using "sir" out of propriety, and occasionally still paid Deck the dubious compliment of referring to him by the questionable title of "Lordship." But, then, Raidon had earned the right to a little latitude from Deck. He couldn't say the same for anyone else.

Well, there was Jenny. But she was a special case.

The first time he'd seen Jenny was behind the palace servants quarters. He'd gone out there to take a break from staring at holoscreens and to get away from the palace, as was his custom, and he'd found a group of servants tinkering with some discarded engine parts. They'd all greeted him politely, with deference as usual, but it was the new girl with long, red-blond hair who'd got his attention.

Leaning against the gate, he'd watched her over the top of one of his tiresome protocol manuals. She'd glanced up, ice-blue eyes catching his gaze. They'd stared at each other, a contest of wills, the tiniest corner of her mouth quirking up in amused challenge.

He'd won, of course. But mostly because one of the others nudged her hard in the shoulder and hissed, "Quit staring at him. Don't forget who he is."

It shouldn't have come as a shock that she was no longer how he remembered her. She was filthy and exhausted now, in disarray. Her arm and leg protectors were mismatched, her clothes old and worn. She sported the old-style bulky high-collar armored jacket and outdated leather pants, which explained why the majority of her rather sorry arsenal was strapped to the outside of her body, giving everything away. Only her body language didn't spell defeat—Deck had been pleased to read mostly defiance there, instead.

She seemed . . . harder. Certainly she'd already been damaged when she came to the palace, having been dragged from slum to slum by her ne'er-do-well father who'd eventually managed to wreak his havoc on both their lives. But there'd always been a sweetness, one that now seemed faded and worn. She was bitter, most likely. Disappointed. He didn't blame her. When you finally realized what life had to offer, and that it wasn't going to get any better . . . well, it wore down even the strongest. He suspected it was the only thing they'd ever have in common: that feeling of being suffocated by their own lives.

Class distinction had rendered them fundamentally incompatible from the beginning. It was the burr in a friendship that had started as an act of rebellion and become something of a necessity for him, for reasons he didn't wholly understand. Jenny had always made it clear she thought he was crazy not to embrace the trappings of royalty; but then, she didn't know what really went on inside the palace walls. He'd preferred to keep that to himself.

"Sir? Did you say something?"

"Hmm? Oh." Deck ran his palm over the stubble on his jaw. "I think it's perhaps best if we not mention to Jenny that we've been watching her so closely these last two years. I can't imagine she'd appreciate it."

Raidon gave a wry grin. "You may be right, sir. She's pretty independent. But you've saved her life a couple of times, that's for sure. It might help the bargaining process if she knew she was indebted to you."

Deck waved off the suggestion. "She doesn't need to know. Not now, anyway." He added under his breath, "Besides, what's the point? She'll never forgive me—but that's not really necessary, is it?"

Raidon pursed his lips. "No, it's not," he agreed. He cleared his throat. "Sir, did we ever have that discussion about mixing business with pleasure? If you're concerned about the girl's future safety, I want you to know that I will be looking out for her as I always do. I'm not one to meddle in your personal life, but Jenny's—"

Deck silenced the man with a look. "What time is the transport again?"

With a sigh, the heavy answered, "Five hours, sir."

"Are we ready?" Deck punched in a few keys and studied his organizer. "Do I have everything?"

"Everything but the girl, sir."

Chapter Three

Jenny soaked in a bath, bubbles up to her neck and her eyes closed, trying to relax and not even coming close. So, Deck wanted street information. He wanted to know if she'd heard of Banzai Maguire, which meant that he was somehow involved in this revolution business that was making people so edgy these days. Well, she'd heard of this Banzai, the so-called "Spirit of the Revolution"—and of the broadcasts by a "Voice of Freedom," a "Shadow Voice"—but that was about it. Of course, those things were still more than she cared to know. World politics bored her.

Of greater interest was why a man who could still probably buy Macao with his fortune, in spite of his estrangement from his royal family, would be interested at all in a commoners' revolution. Was he for or against it?

Probably for, knowing Deck.

Jenny breathed slowly and deeply, letting the perfumed water sink into her pores and take over her senses. The scrapes on her palms stung like holy hell, but the pain was worth it, and the nanomeds were already working their magic. It occurred to her that Deck could've given her a drugged scent. No. It wasn't that she trusted him not to; it just wasn't his style. So she dumped a ton more bath stuff in the water, and man, did it smell good!

The door unlocked and Deck stepped in, switching off an electrorod he'd used to jimmy the lock. He leaned against the sink and crossed his arms over his chest.

Jenny's mouth dropped open. "Who exactly do you think you are?" She gestured behind her to the screen-covered wall. "You could have used the hologram at least."

"Raidon's been asking you to get out of the bathtub for an hour."

"I couldn't hear him from in here," she lied sweetly.

Deck walked toward the bathtub, stepped up on the riser, and crouched down at the end of the translucent porcelain tank.

Jenny jerked back involuntarily, sloshing water and bubbles onto the floor.

"Haven't you ever heard of personal space?" she shot out, trying to cover her confusion and the flutter in her heart with a heavy dose of grit.

Still locking eyes, he reached down with both hands, gripped the sides of the tub, and leaned toward her until his eyes were level with hers.

"Can you hear any better now?" he growled. His eyes darkened, flickering with potent suggestion. "Or shall I get a little closer?"

Aware that her body was still mostly camouflaged by the perfumy clouds of bubbles, she regained her composure—hoping Deck hadn't noticed she'd lost it in the first place. "Are you trying to prime me for a favor? 'Cause if you are . . ." *It's definitely working.* "It's definitely not working."

He moistened his lips and looked down at the bubbles. "A shame. I'll have to stick with plan A."

"If plan A involves getting any closer than plan B, you're going to come out of this missing some body parts."

He smiled rather sardonically, slid backward and stood up. "Get out." He tossed a towel at her face and she caught it neatly just above the water.

"I'm done anyway." She boldly stood up and purposely flashed him before wrapping the towel around herself.

He didn't look away. Just gave her a long, hard look that turned the situation upside down and made her wish he'd been a little more specific about plan B. Jenny silently cursed her fair skin as a hot flush crawled up her neck.

Deck cleared his throat. "Raidon is waiting for you outside. He'll bring you to my office."

She waited for him to leave, then walked into the adjoining bedroom, not bothering to wonder if she'd actually get to sleep in the princess-perfect bed tonight. Her worn belongings were laundered, folded, and sorted on the mattress, contrasting horribly

23

with the incredibly sumptuous silk comforter and multicolored pillows. She grabbed her clothes and dressed, stuffed everything else back into her messenger bag, then stepped outside and ran straight into the back of Raidon. The man smiled at her and led her to the office.

The room had Deck written all over it. Severe with dark colors, but expensive and tastefully appointed, it was about as far from the white and gold opulence of the Han palace as you could get.

Jenny settled into a black leather club chair, eyed a plate on Deck's desk piled high with bonbons, and shook her head with amusement. Deck apparently remembered with whom he was dealing.

"Want some candy, little girl?" he purred with a teasing grin.

She snorted. "You're a real menace, Deck." She carefully picked up a tiny pink square with a blue icing bow and bit in.

Sugary raspberry exploded in her mouth. It tasted like nothing she'd eaten in a long, long time. Deck didn't rush her, just gazed boldly at her lips as she licked the sugar off. Jenny stared pointedly back and roughly wiped her mouth with her sleeve.

He chuckled to himself and rubbed his eyes. Come to think of it, he looked really tired. She hadn't noticed the dark circles under his eyes.

He steepled his fingers and finally said softly, "Help me out, Jenny. I'm holding up my end of the bargain. Tell me what you've been hearing these days."

"About what?"

"I know there's been buzz on the streets."

"About what?" she repeated.

"Revolution, Jenny."

She shifted in her seat. "I should think you of all people would know everything there is to know. You can buy as much information as you want."

"I know a version, and now I'm interested in hearing yours."

"Don't know what makes mine so special." But she knew exactly what made her knowledge special. That was the trouble with living under the radar with the rest of the slummers. Secrets like this got around. Things you didn't want to know. Even criminals and rabble-rousers needed someone to talk to, and they weren't going to punch up the palace on the fiberoptics for a confessional. And Deck knew her, and knew he could trust what she told him. Or, he thought he could.

She picked up another bonbon and gestured with it to her surroundings. "Whose place is this? This yours?"

He cocked his head. "Why do you ask?"

"What I mean is, is this part of the Han holdings or is it secret?" Impatiently, she went to the point. "I'm worried it's bugged, okay? Because if it's bugged, I'm—"

"It's one of my safe houses. It has nothing to do with my family. I give you my word it's not bugged."

His word? Like that was supposed to mean anything at this point.

"Why should it concern you, anyway? I've personally invited you here."

25

She glared at him. "You're talking to me about revolution and you have the nerve to ask? Treason would be on my list of concerns, to start. Sedition."

He remained silent, waiting.

"Fine. Whatever. The word is, anyone who gets a rep as knowing too much about all that revolution stuff gets disappeared."

"Disappeared?"

"Yeah, they say some group or another is systematically 'disappearing' people who might be part of this 'groundswell,' or whatever, of revolution. Maybe it's Kyber. Maybe it's the UCE. Maybe it's all just a rumor. I would have figured you'd know."

His hand crept up to his collar and loosened it. "Kyber and I never had much in common," he said obliquely.

She shrugged.

"What else are they saying?"

She shrugged again.

"Have you ever seen any of these revolutionaries? I suspect that when you're trying to lay low, these slums are a good place to do it. What do you think?"

"I don't think slums are a good place to do anything," she grumbled. "Look, I've got plenty of problems as it is. I don't need to add treason to the list. Macao is still part of Kyber's monarchy, whether he takes an interest in it or not. And you aren't exactly the poster child for commitment to the royal agenda. These questions are a little sticky, if you can appreciate what I'm saying."

Deck sighed and ruffled his hair in exasperation.

"Patience was never your strong suit," Jenny commented blandly.

"No, it isn't," he agreed. "So, do you know anything at all about Banzai?"

"No."

He seemed to hesitate. "What about a group called the Shadow Runners?"

"The Shadow Runners? No. Honestly. I know nothing specific. In fact, some even say the woman's just a fake, and the Shadow Runners are just another gang. I mean, maybe the stuff about people disappearing is true and maybe it's not. There's lots of reasons people turn up missing from the worst parts of town."

Deck managed a smile. "So you suspect it may be more rumor and speculation, then?"

Jenny gave him a look. "You'd know more than I would."

"Why is that?"

"Come *on*, Deck. Unless you've completely cut ties with your family..." She gestured to the well-appointed room. "And I really doubt that."

"Fair enough. What if I told you that Banzai Maguire is real? And that the revolution is real?"

"To be honest"—she pulled his handkerchief out of her bag and dumped the bowl of bonbons into it—"I couldn't care less either way."

"Oh?" His eyebrow went up.

Working intently on packaging up the sweets, she shrugged and said, "Nope. The state of the universe, and talk of a better tomorrow, blah, blah, blah, and all that revolutionary crap mean absolutely nothing to me. When you're at the bottom of the food chain, it doesn't matter much who exactly is at the top—it's always somebody who wants you for lunch. History pretty much proves that so-called revolutionaries and 'representatives of the masses' are just as corruptible in the end as natural-born rulers or dictators."

"Perhaps. But this time, I believe it's different."

She looked at him dubiously.

"What if I told you there *is* a revolutionary group called the Shadow Runners? And that I'm part of it, and that I'd like you to work with us?"

Jenny's stomach dropped, and her shock must have been obvious.

Deck leaned forward, his gaze burning into hers. "I'd like you to help me. And, in return, I'd like to help you."

He still had it—whatever annoying pheromone he'd always had that made her absolutely crazy inside. He still had it, and it pissed her off.

She fixed him with a steely glare. "You want to help me?" She laughed bitterly. "I think your opportunity has long since passed."

"I don't think so."

She rolled her eyes. "I thought we were friends, once. I've since come to my senses."

He had a peculiar look about him. One she couldn't read. Maybe he was laughing at the idea of it.

Over a year ago, the day of her father's funeral, was the last time she'd seen Deck. Not to mention the last time she'd been inside the palace gates.

It had been a typical servant's funeral, the service hidden from view outside in the far fields of the palace grounds. She'd made all her good-byes, the attendees cleaned up around her and left. Then it was just her, sitting alone in a chair in the middle of a meadow with her messenger bag at her feet and an envelope in her lap containing a letter of dismissal, a writ of deportation to hell on earth, and some rapidly devaluing currency franked by the palace.

She could still see Deck walking toward her, every inch a prince, a stormy black figure against the white, white palace behind. She'd stood up, wanting to meet him with her chin held high. And she had. He'd walked up to her without a word, a conflicted look in his eye, and just took her in his arms very suddenly, an odd sort of embrace that seemed to surprise them both. A first. And a last. She'd wanted to cry, to beg him not to let them make her go, to beg him not to send her out there alone.

He'd known what she faced and did nothing. He had all the money in the world and he'd let her suffer in desperate poverty. What kind of friend was that? And why would she trust him to help her after all this time?

Deck was staring at her.

"Thanks, but no, thanks," she said casually. "I've got problems of my own, and frankly, any so-called revolution doesn't interest me. Democracy? People here can't afford to have such lofty ideals."

Anger flared in his eyes. "Think! You're turning down a chance of a lifetime! To make a difference. This could be something truly grand we're working at. You're lucky just to get enough odd jobs to afford a few nights outside the flop zone and a decent meal every once in a while. It seems to me like you have nothing to lose and everything to gain."

"How would *you* know what I have to lose?" She pressed her temples with her forefingers. "Deck, how can you think you'll ever understand me? I'll never understand you, that's for sure. I could never figure what you were so anxious to rebel against. You were always like this. Why can't you just be grateful? You were dealt four aces in life and now you want to risk it all by getting mixed up in this insane revolution crap."

She sighed heavily. He didn't really have to explain. Even now, his hand absently crept up to the top button on his high collar and fiddled with the clasp. That was Deck, always as if he never had enough air, as if he could never breathe quite right.

He'd had this brooding restlessness as long as she'd known him, but Jenny began to wonder if he hadn't turned ugly inside in the last few years. Deck had never seemed pliable that way, but if you really wanted something badly enough—like revenge— you might find you'd do just about anything to get it. What had *he* done? "Why are you doing this? Why do you want to get involved?"

Deck studied his hands.

"Okay, let me restate the question. Is this really about the greater good, or do you admit that, somewhere deep inside, part of this is about revenge— your revenge against Kyber?"

He still didn't speak, just looked at her, a faint amused smile playing on his lips.

"Okay, don't answer." Pride prevented her from saying more, from telling him just how hypocritical it was to want to help the masses when he wouldn't even help an individual he knew personally, one he knew must be suffering. "The bottom line is that I've managed. I'm a survivor, and I'm doing just fine as it is."

She didn't need what he was offering. She might be down, but she wasn't out. She was still young, she was strong, and when all of her equipment was working, she was fearless. . . .

Holy hell, who was she kidding? The truth was, she was damn tired of being just a survivor. Bone tired. And he knew it, and he clearly wasn't impressed.

"You're doing just fine, are you?" he asked. "I beg to differ. You can 'take your pride out of your ass,' as you've always liked to put it, and participate, or you can spend the rest of your life here, in squalor."

A long silence stretched out between them. Jenny played with the knot on the bandanna full of bonbons on her lap, and glared at him. "I always did appreciate your directness. So, tell me this. Why me, in particular? There are plenty of people in the slums who know what I know . . . and there are plenty who probably know even more."

"You have something that others don't have," he admitted, almost reluctantly.

"And what's that?"

"A resident card for Newgate."

She stood up so abruptly her chair fell backward. "Conversation over. I'll make my own way out." She walked briskly to the door. "Nice to see you again, Deck. Have a great life." She punched the door open only to find Raidon blocking the way.

She whirled back around. Behind her the heavy cocked his gun. "You rich bastard. This is your idea of entertainment? Forcing desperate people in bad situations into worse ones?"

Deck rose from his chair, eyes flashing. "Listen to what I'm saying. I'm not trying to make things worse for you. I need you to come with me to New-gate. And when we're done with business, in return, you will never be desperate again. There's a better life out there for you. I will make it happen, if you come with me. I need your help."

"I don't care what you need!"

"I'm not asking you to care. I'm asking you to do it."

"Do you have any idea what Newgate is like?"

"Jenny—"

"Don't 'Jenny' me. It's the world's largest penal colony. It's the worst slum in the universe, the biggest wasteland, the worst sort of prison. Aus-tralia is hell on earth, and Newgate City is the devil's headquarters! Every scoundrel, wastrel, blackguard, and all around badass is there." She held out her hands, counting off the variations of scum on her fingers. "You've got your pirates, your renegades, your scammers, your losers, your sickos . . . and the best part is that you don't have any of the good stuff to fend 'em off with. No nanoweapons. No phasers or tazers or second- or third-generation chip-set technology. None of the good stuff."

Deck took his seat again, folded his hands calmly in front of him, and remained totally, infuriatingly silent.

Jenny just about stamped her foot. "There's a reason your family let Australia drift away from their control all those years ago. Who would want to put resources into a place like that? And what kind of business could you possibly have there? I swore up and down I'd never go back. I swore I'd rather die than return. It was that bad. You get it?"

Of course he couldn't get it. Apart from the normal difficulties of the place, he wouldn't know that her face was probably on a big Wanted poster in the basement of the Parliament Club. It would be a ridiculous gamble to go back to that place. Of course, given that she wasn't likely to make it out of Macao anyway, since she was poor and trying to avoid detection, maybe a quick end was better than a slow one.

Apparently Deck got that part. "The very nature of what you want to avoid is what should make my offer so appealing. If you can honestly say that you see things getting better for yourself on your own, if you think that you can pull yourself out of this inertia that has you spending your life here in the slums, then by all means, turn down my offer."

She could feel her determination giving way. "It's easy to get stuck there. That's what makes it so dangerous to go in—it's so hard to get out. You've got value behind you, to grease the necessary palms. What about me? Am I supposed to trust that you'll grease them for me, too?"

"I'm afraid that some level of trust will be necessary," he admitted. He checked his watch. "I'll need an answer from you fairly quickly, Jenny. Are you in or are you out?"

"Damn it!" So much for pride. "What's the job?" she asked wearily. "What are the parameters? How long would I be yours, and when would I get this 'better life'?"

"When the job is done. We have a very specific task to perform. Let's just say that I'm looking for you to help me get around Newgate, to use your connections to get what I need to . . . help the revolution coalesce, if you will. And that's all I can tell you for now."

"Coalesce. I see." She shook her head in disgust. Some deal. With Deck holding all the cards.

Man, how sad. She was his first choice for this type of assistance. How nice that when he thought of all the low-class slummers in the world, he thought of her. How nice that when he thought of Newgate, the world's largest penal colony and toxic waste dump, he thought of her.

She'd sworn to never go back there. It had all the makings of a very suicidal sort of move. And one sorry little promise from Deck was all it had taken to make her break her word to herself. Everyone had a price.

Angry tears welled up in her eyes, and she turned

her face from him, disgusted. She took a deep breath and exhaled.

She'd go with Deck to Newgate. Of course she would. He was right. When your sole possessions consisted of a duffel bag full of skanky clothes and a couple of malfunctioning weapons, you literally and figuratively had nothing left to lose. A slum was a slum was pretty much just a slum. Newgate might be a particularly distasteful one, and a prison, but for God's sake, the bottom of the barrel looked pretty much the same everywhere you went.

And if Deck lived up to his promise, what he was selling her on would set her up for life. Or at least she was sure he'd give her a little square on some isolated patch of land where she could just relax. There were peaceful places out there. There were cities where the residents could just live without worrying about . . . well, anything. If you weren't lucky enough to be born in one and you weren't rich enough to get there on your own, you weren't going to have it . . . and that was that. Unless you had help. This was probably the only help she'd ever get.

She met Deck's gaze and stared into his eyes. In the hazy gray-blue rings of his irises, she looked for lies and she looked for truths. He gave away nothing. At last, she simply sighed and held out her hand.

"You've got yourself a deal. Put 'er there, Deck."

Chapter Four

She could feel the stale air thunder through the tunnel as the transport pulled into Macao Station and reversed its engines for braking. Jenny braced herself for the assault to come and turned to Deck. "Hold your breath when you hear the pop." The huge vehicle shuddered to a stop and was immediately seen to by a ground crew. The swarming crowd of would-be passengers pressed forward against the metal gates, waiting to board like stamping ponies awaiting the starter gun.

"We've got to make this one. Who the hell knows when the next will actually come around? There's no reliable schedule," Jenny yelled to Deck as the engines revved. "Whatever it takes, get on the transport. Got it?"

He looked at her curiously, then comprehension seemed to dawn on him. He'd realized there weren't enough seats for the crowd amassing, despite the fact that they'd purchased passage.

Jenny fastened her hair up tight in her usual faux-hawk and reflexively bent to tighten the straps on her empty thigh holsters. Traveling unarmed made her feel unnerved, naked. Even if this Raidon guy was supposedly back there in the crowd watching their backs.

She hugged her jacket close to her body and zipped it up over the chest strap of her bag. Glancing at Deck to make sure that nothing on him was loose, nothing on him in jeopardy, she put her mouth next to his ear and whispered urgently, "Keep one hand on your bag. Do not let go under any circumstances."

The muscles in Deck's jaw twitched; the tension was getting to him. Well, he hadn't seen nothin' yet, that was for sure.

With a huge bang, the winged doors of the transport yawned open and the cabin depressurized. Jenny quickly sucked in a breath as the departing passengers filed out. Half of the cars were empty. The ones at the very back were septic. The remarkably small number of people arriving from Newgate in comparison to the number waiting to go there made Jenny question for the umpteenth time the wisdom of her decision.

Deck stumbled back in surprise, his hand moving to cover the lower half of his face as the stench of the transport filtered out. Jenny exhaled fast, gulped in a new breath of rotten air, and tried not to smell anything, then shook her head at Deck in alarm and gestured to his bag. He nodded, a pained expression on his face as he moved his hand back to protect it.

The loading bell suddenly rang, and the crowd surged forward from all directions. Jenny and Deck moved, too.

On her left, Jenny saw someone grab Deck around the neck. She tapped the guy on the shoulder and punched him in the face. As he fell away, a hand snaked out from the opposite direction and latched on to her bag, straining the buckles. She struggled backward, then heard Deck swear and grab the guy by the shoulders, shoving him away.

Jenny scrambled forward into the transport and launched herself at a pair of seats, slamming face-first onto the ripped and stained vinyl cushions, and hooking the toes of her boots under the seat edge behind her. The other seats nearby were similarly claimed within seconds.

Over her shoulder, she saw Deck wade through the crowd. He carefully lifted her feet up and slid in past them, then helped Jenny to a sitting position. "No one wants to go there, but God forbid they should miss the bus," he muttered grimly. He craned his neck to have a look behind him, and released an audible sigh of relief. "Raidon's on." Then he fell back against his seat and stared straight ahead.

"Are you okay?"

"I'm fine," he said curtly.

But he seemed uncharacteristically unsettled. He gripped the edge of his seat, slowly passing his steely gaze over the crowd.

"Not a big flyer, eh, Deck? You realize we're still on the ground."

He gritted his teeth. "Yes, thank you. I realize that. For God's sake, what is that smell?"

Jenny smiled. "The cars at the very end carry waste to the dumps. This is nothing. Wait until we get to Newgate."

Deck exhaled loudly and looked away.

Her so-called lucky fellow travelers were still orienting themselves in their seats amidst sudden flare-ups and commotion as a guard, led down the impossibly skinny aisle by an unleashed Doberman, pointed a tazer at anyone without a seat and threw their limp bodies back through the doors to the platform.

Jenny felt almost numb with dread as the doors winged down and slammed shut. She probably wasn't the only one. The inside of the transport had gone near silent, only an eerie murmur threading through the air as a facade of civility set in, a facade that would collapse once more when they arrived in Newgate, if not sooner.

"Welcome to the *real* world," she whispered in a monotone, staring out at the platform as the rejects pounded on the doors. It was all she could do not to cry.

She looked over at Deck. He looked shell-shocked. And all she felt was a horrible, intense resentment. What the hell was he expecting? Missed the comforts of home, did he? Didn't he like the smell? Maybe revolution wasn't quite as much fun as it sounded.

She clenched her teeth and looked down at her hands curled into fists. How could she both hate him so badly and still care about him so much? It wasn't just the physical attraction, although oddly enough, they both seemed comfortable admitting that it still existed, teasing and taunting each other like that in his beautiful marble bathing room. She didn't know why they played that game. Oh, who was she kidding? Admitting to the physical obscured the emotional. Not to mention the power play it represented. At times in the last couple of years, she'd thought about him, alone in her bed at night with the sounds of others taking solace in each other keeping her awake. She'd actually had to remind herself that he'd let her down. Had to remind herself to keep her guard up.

Jenny took a deep breath and exhaled. Obviously, his success in Newgate was in her best interest. But God help her, if he let her down again, she'd find a way to make him and his precious revolution fail. Only two parties she could think of might be interested in making a deal with her: monarchist spies from the Kingdom of Asia, and Newgate's Parliament. Neither of whom she really wanted to get involved with. She didn't want Deck killed, or anything; she just wanted a better life.

And what the hell was wrong with that, anyway? Jenny lolled her head back, trying to ignore the loud argument beginning in the seats behind her. Why was she supposed to feel dirty and selfish for wanting to better her condition? If Deck wanted to traipse around stumping for the collective good, that was his business—but he was already personally set for life; he could afford it! And it wasn't like being one of these Shadow Runners automatically made him a saint. Well, okay, so the ideals of this proposed revolution made him more of a saint than she was, she'd give him that. But that wasn't saying much, now, was it?

"Jenny," Deck whispered, gently placing one hand on her wrist and attempting to unfurl her clenched fingers with his other. The touch drove her slightly mad. "Try not to assume the worst. You're working yourself into a state."

She shot him a look, but his odd solicitousness was rather touching, even under the circumstances. Jenny snatched her hands away, feeling mixed emotions, wondering if he felt them too. She wasn't particularly good at hiding her feelings from him, but his still managed to elude her much of the time. "Don't even," she muttered halfheartedly. "I'm pissed. I'm just very pissed. I think it's best if we don't talk to each other right now. At least for a few minutes."

"I would be pissed too, if I were you," he said simply.

"How touching, Deck." She clutched at her heart in melodramatic fashion. "Really touching, under the circumstances. If I'm not mistaken, I think you just tried to . . . to . . . acknowledge the legitimacy of my feelings or something." Under her breath she added, "I think I might be sick."

Deck grinned, which only infuriated her.

"You're going to get yours, buddy," she said disconsolately.

Deck chuckled, opened his mouth to say something else, then apparently thought better of it. He just nodded and looked away.

Joking aside, Jenny had to force herself to relax back against the seat, erasing from her body any indication that she wanted to scream. Things got so muddled when Deck was around. She wanted to be angry and he made her laugh. She wanted to be immune and he made her feel. She sighed heavily and curled in toward the side of the transport. Bottom line, she needed to get some power back from Deck; she needed more control over their plans.

Nothing got to her more than the feeling of powerlessness over her own fate. Probably because her entire life she'd had no one to rely on but herself. Not her mother, dead in childbirth. Not her father, dragging her behind him on ill-fated double crosses and murderous pursuits, traits she was starting to show signs of having inherited. And certainly not Deck, who could have saved her from Newgate the first time around if he'd so much as had the inclination.

And where self-reliance was all you had, powerlessness and a lack of control were your worst enemies.

Jenny looked over at Deck, still acclimating to the transport. He didn't complain out loud, but his body language indicated his discomfort.

The thing was, he really needed her, and not just because she knew how to get around Newgate. She could see it already. He might be clever and dedi-

43

cated to his cause with the fervor of an evangelist, but that was different from street smart. Deck was going to be totally out of his element in this strange new world they were entering. There were going to be times when everything he represented, everything he was, would be a disadvantage.

He'd be looking to her for true guidance soon enough. And she looked forward to that.

Deck seemed fixated on something in the seats behind them. Jenny followed his gaze past the mass of people, animals, and belongings churning there. The inside of the transport was similar to most third-class travel on Macao, packed with live animals, drunkards and users, interspecies asylum-seekers, and a laundry list of other down-and-outs on the way to their final destination this side of death. The snakes squirming in cardboard boxes, live chickens squawking from burlap sacks, and genetically blended species leashed and peeking out from shirt and jacket pockets weren't the only ones destined for a prison of somebody else's making.

Half a car back, Raidon sat stoically next to a screaming child on its mother's lap in the seat beside him. Jenny looked right at him, but the heavy responded only with a blank stare, showing no recognition—for security reasons, as they'd planned.

Deck turned back, shifting uncomfortably in his seat. "What the hell is going on here? What *is* this?"

It took her a moment for Jenny to realize what he was referring to. She took another look at her traveling companions. She hadn't really noticed it this time around, having spent so much time in Newgate, but there was a costumelike aspect to the assorted dress of a majority of the travelers.

"Is it a masquerade of life . . . or a life of masquerade?" she taunted Deck, with a sweep of her hands meant to encompass the travelers around her wearing top hats with their leather trench coats, cravats with their body armor, and riding breeches with Velcro holsters sewn on to the fabric.

"You tell me," he said, as the strange mockery of nineteenth-century sartorial elegance playing out before him sank in.

"Seriously. The puzzle is the definition," she said, dropping her voice to avoid anyone eavesdropping. "The most powerful group in Newgate is called Parliament. They're an English Regency–era gentlemen's club, opium den, government, power company, God knows what else, all rolled into one. These people are either currying favor from Parliament, or imitating the fantasy that *is* Parliament, or, hell, I don't know . . . maybe they actually took a cheap version of poppers to make the Parliament fantasy their reality, too."

Deck soaked it in, his expression carefully neutral, but he whistled low under his breath.

"Yeah, a complete freak show," Jenny said. "You'll have to see one of the members of Parliament yourself to really understand, though."

And that wasn't going to happen if she had anything to say about it. The last time she'd "seen" a member of Parliament, she'd lived to regret it. No matter where on earth she ran, she was still regretting it.

She sighed heavily, a sense of futility and despair coming over her. Hastily changing the subject, she asked, "Look, no offense or anything, but do you have a plan? You have a plan, right?"

Deck smiled and tapped his temple.

"Great. That either means you don't and you're trying to pretend you do, or you do and you're just not intending on telling me anything."

"I'll give you a little more when we get settled in Newgate," he murmured. His breath tickled her ear.

She snorted. " 'When we get settled in Newgate,' " she mocked. "You make it sound like we're going to a bed-and-breakfast. Look, just tell me what's first."

He dropped his voice more and moved his face even closer. Jenny could feel his lips against her ear now, his fingers gently pulling aside and smoothing her hair back where it'd fallen loose. "We'll need to find a good arms dealer. After that we'll work on getting a little intel together."

"Right." She cleared her throat and turned, nuzzling in close, the stubble on his cheek scraping against her lips as she slid her mouth toward his ear. She whispered, "I've got a hotel I can guarantee and an armorer I'd trust with my life."

"That works for me," Deck answered. His voice was a little clipped, and he shifted away from her. Jenny bit a smile back and looked down. He wasn't totally immune. Two could play at his game.

A gaggle of hawkers appeared from the front thruway and assembled at the front of the car near the guard. Bizarrely uniformed in a mishmash of styles, they pushed their way down the aisle with trays of candy bars, pocket food, drugs, and purified drinks at hugely inflated prices.

Deck pulled out a handkerchief and wiped at the sweat on his face.

"By the way, I can tell we may have issues with you not blending in," Jenny suggested softly. "I suggest you not act like a prima donna. You've got to watch that, you know. Pulling out the fancy stuff."

He looked at the handkerchief and frowned. Then he shrugged. "The closer a lie is to the truth, the better," he said. "I'll make up a believable cover story."

"You don't want to mess with . . ."

She stopped short and looked away as a cigarette girl walked down the aisle. Dressed like the devil's whore in a low-cut scarlet empire-waist gown shortened to expose black fishnet stockings, and a short glossy black bob with a pair of glittering red devil's horns, the girl wore a gun holster affixed to a red satin ammunition strap.

"Hello, handsome. Welcome to hell," she teased. She leaned over Deck to show off her wares, placing her hand on Deck's shoulder and letting one metal fingernail snake up the side of his neck. "Can I tempt you with something, sir?" she purred.

Deck gave the girl the sort of smile that Jenny would have liked to keep for herself, and surveyed the selection of candy bars, hand-rolled cigarettes, and plastic vials of pure water. As he browsed through the products, Jenny saw the girl's eyes narrow and study Deck more closely. Whatever she saw made her lose her bravado. She chewed on her lower lip for a second and then asked hesitantly, "Are you Parliament, sir?"

Jenny held her breath. Deck might not be wearing the Regency-inspired garb of the Australian gangers, but he definitely couldn't hide his aristocratic background. It was something in his bearing, something that just was, like an aura around him.

"Am I Parliament?" Deck repeated and took the girl's hand. Jenny tried to stare straight ahead but noticed the slip of a coin from his hand, the graceful dip of his head, and the way the girl's fingers slid across his wrist as she pulled away. "You never, never know," he said meaningfully.

"I never know," the girl answered with a nod. "I never, never know anything at all." She straightened up, ran one metal fingertip across Deck's lips, and sauntered down the aisle to her next potential customer.

Deck looked at Jenny and grinned. She rolled her eyes. He was good. She'd give him that.

The mood on the transport was becoming more raucous, a sort of panicked energy ricocheting throughout the cramped cabin. Jenny looked at her timepiece and nodded to herself. They'd passed the three-quarter mark and the dread of arrival was sinking in.

"Welcome to hell," Deck said, chuckling softly, echoing the cigarette girl's greeting.

Jenny looked at him with razors in her eyes. "You have no idea."

Chapter Five

Newgate City, Au∫tralia

Stepping off the transport into the immigration hall was like entering a parallel universe, except that everything was somehow upside down.

Deck set his jaw and followed Jenny's lead as she cleared a path, throwing elbows and talking trash. God knew he didn't like playing follower, but Jenny knew the ropes here; that was why he'd recruited her. And if her experience made her the more logical leader of the two at one time or another, then follow her he would.

Frankly, he had to admit that he did feel rather disoriented and out of his element. The stench that filled the air was overwhelming, the crowds pushing and shouting in a panic that was tempting to join. It was neither a pleasant nor a familiar sensation. He kept a firm grip on his belongings, his eyes

49

on Jenny, and the rest of his senses at bay.

As he looked around the place and thought back to Jenny's embittered description, it dawned on him that some things really had to be experienced to be believed. He'd chosen Australia for his depot some time ago, sight unseen. A logical choice, it kept away all but the most dedicated of souls, for as she'd put it, who would ever come here intentionally? One could hide a band of rebels quite nicely in a penal colony, in a vast territory that meant nothing more to the rest of the world than a place to dump their excess garbage, human and otherwise.

But that wasn't the only reason. As Jenny had pointed out, the House of Han had once considered Australia part of its territory. Years of neglect had caused the territory to turn inward for leadership. Now, in this era of upheaval, on the brink of world revolution, the former Asian colony could be used as political leverage. Deck knew Kyber wanted it back. He also knew the UCE was trying for it.

Neither side would know that Australia was already settled by revolutionaries with much different goals. "Beads in the necklace" they'd called it during furtive meetings in Kyber's prison. Each contributor would know only what was needed to accomplish a single goal as part of the larger mission.

Together, the Shadow Runners and the communications depot here were Deck's bead. And until he put the Shadow Voice back online for the world to hear, he hadn't done his part—and the next group of freedom fighters would not be able to do theirs.

Newgate City was the gateway to his mission. He

would not be able to reach the depot, or bring out the necessary equipment and supplies without going through Newgate first. So much was already accomplished. He had the value to pay for resources, he'd found dedicated supporters of the revolution to fashion into a cohesive unit he'd dubbed the Shadow Runners, he'd designed and forwarded the drawings for the depot itself—hell, he'd even finally received an encrypted message with the GPS coordinates. The only thing he didn't have was the know-how to navigate Newgate itself. Jenny was his know-how.

And she was doing her job, leading him through the mouth of the tunnel to a huge open space, a mass of chaos where the crush of people slowed their progress to a halt. Deck's body armor stuck to his skin in the intense, heavy humidity, and for all her self-possession, even Jenny looked like she was only barely holding on to a scream. He felt a wave of sympathy for her. In spite of the keen look in her eye, and the proud confidence of her bearing, he sensed that a lot of the vulnerability she'd once worn on her sleeve was now simply stuffed even deeper inside her.

She'd changed. Well, they both had.

Just remember, you can always leave, he told himself. This was real life—the *only* life—for the rest of these people.

"Weapons registry on your left, line A," a soothing female voice intoned. "Immunization appeals on your right, line B. Miscellany, far corner, line C. Cleared parties, straight ahead, line D. All must declare known contaminants and infections or risk penalty of fine and deletion. Weapons without permit are subject to seizure at will. . . . Weapons registry on your left, line A . . ."

Raidon caught up to them and hovered a few feet behind, still making no attempt at contact. He met Deck's eye briefly, a warning look; it was obvious he wasn't happy with his inability to provide proper security in this kind of environment.

Jenny stuck her duffel bag on the ground between her feet and shook out her arm and shoulder. She kept glancing toward the huge billboard proclaiming the entrance to Newgate proper just beyond the tunnel.

"Immunizations first," she said, her dread obvious.

They stepped up to the back of line B and came to a decided halt even as a man dressed in tight-fitting breeches, a coat of superfine, and a rather outrageous multicolored striped waistcoat strong-armed his way through the crowd, muttering something about "peasants" and "the queue."

Deck raised an eyebrow as a path instantly cleared for the dandy. The man took little time at the front before being ushered through. Jenny shrank into herself and unclipped her hair, letting it fall into her face.

"Parliament," she mumbled, casting wary glances around her. "They don't usually travel."

"How do I join?" Deck joked. He watched the crowd close in and stall out again as the dandy finished his business and left the line.

"Not much point in forsaking one aristocracy for another," she answered.

Deck nodded and stared around him in the large venue. "Why do they bother with all of this if they know for a fact that the vast majority of incoming residents are criminals?"

"Two reasons: disease control and access to fresh currency by way of bribery and fees. This is a major part of Australia's economy. As far as I can tell, there's really no police force in Newgate. The Parliament runs a squad, but it's really just to prosecute people for crimes that interest or personally affect them."

"There's a court system?" Deck asked.

Jenny laughed. "Nah, I should have said execute, not prosecute."

"Have you seen them in action?"

She cleared her throat. "Um . . . well, the only ones I ever saw arrested, per se, were suspected serial killers and contaminators. But I didn't ask questions, if you know what I mean.

"All this," she added as she swept her arm out to indicate the chaos before her. "All this is really to see if they can find something—how should I put this?—unusual."

By all appearances of Newgate's standards, if you could use the term "standards" with a straight face, Jenny had nothing unusual about her save for the fact that she'd returned at all. Raidon, of course, looked like your average heavy. Deck was the exception. He had royal blood running through his veins,

Han blood. But, no. That wasn't unusual, here, now, was it? It sounded like Australia had plenty of blue bloods.

Blue bloods. If Deck were honest, he'd have to admit that a small part of him relished the revenge global revolution would bring. After all, it was once everything he'd wanted. It was once all he thought he had left. But that was before he'd been contacted by the shadowy Voice of Freedom.

What had, in its most nascent stage, been a hastily devised means to wreak revenge on Kyber, had become something very different, something with true purpose and meaning behind it. Well, Deck himself had become something very different.

He'd transformed his few still loyal subjects from a militia ready to strike against the Kingdom of Asia into the Shadow Runners: men and women who would safeguard, or run missions for, the Shadow Voice. His communications depot, set up in Australia, had become ground zero for Shadow Runner operations. And Deck's anger against his half brother became irrelevant once he'd learned of the revolutionary cause and its aims to change the world.

Jenny simply wouldn't understand that thinking. Or she didn't want to understand. Deck looked at her pale, exhausted face. She'd closed her eyes and was working on a series of deep, long breaths.

"Finding Zen?" he asked.

"I only wish. You joke, but in an hour from now when we're still standing in the same spot, you'll be looking for Zen right along with me."

He nodded with resignation. She was right.

An hour later, they finally reached the front of the line.

"Prick, please."

"Excuse me?" Deck asked.

Jenny choked on her own saliva.

The immunization guy sighed impatiently and pointed to the two glass slides on the counter and a small plastic punch gun.

Jenny picked up the gun, tucked the slide into the proper compartment, and punched her forearm near the bend in her elbow. She handed the instrument to the guy, who removed her slide, set it aside with the dot of her blood gleaming on the glass, and passed the gun back to Deck.

Deck followed the procedure as Jenny's slide went through the inoculation scanner.

The inoculator studied her record, cocked his head, and frowned. Jenny shifted her weight from one foot to the other, but didn't say a word.

"Interesting. Your record's screwed up. Got someone with your data with entry several years ago, but no official exit date. Fairly normal criminal record . . ." He peered closer at the screen. "Although, *that's* a bit of a doozy." He looked up at Jenny with what Deck actually thought might be admiration. "Hmmm . . ."

Jenny moistened her lips and seemed to be awaiting a proposal. Deck kept his mouth shut, but if it hadn't been guaranteed to piss Jenny off unnecessarily and hint at his privileged background, he would have simply flipped open his wallet and hur-

ried along this inevitable—and seemingly inter-
minable—entrance interviews.

"There's a couple things we can do here. Chalk it
up to input error and release your inoculation list.
Or I could call a manager to come straighten it out."

The bureaucrat and Jenny went back and forth,
speaking in guarded sentences, insinuations, and as-
sumptions. Deck couldn't help wondering if the
"doozy" was a description of her alleged relationship to his father's murder. Or if she'd managed to
somehow get herself into even more trouble during
her previous stay in Newgate.

That probably wasn't fair. Jenny was as innocent as
he was. Kyber had certainly done a number on them
both. Deck reviewed the sequence of events: Jenny's
father was hired to administer the killing dose,
Deck's true family lineage was made public, and the
monarchy was conveniently turned upside down.
Jenny's father died, Jenny was deported for her sin of
being related to him, and Deck was labeled a bastard
and tossed in prison—accused of masterminding the
attempted patricide in order to prevent the truth of
his birth from coming out. All very neat and tidy.

Prince Kyber, meanwhile, sat atop the Asian
throne drinking cordials, consorting with beautiful
women, and trying to take over the world.

Jenny straightened from where she'd been leaning
on the counter, biting her fingernail. The inoculator
turned away and typed on his keyboard. They
seemed to have come to a satisfactory agreement.

She slipped her hand into her jacket and produced

a tiny amethyst. She held it down to the counter with her finger and locked eyes with the inoculator. A small smile flickered on his lips, but otherwise he proceeded as if nothing unusual or unpleasant had transpired.

"Here we go . . . your munis are outdated. You're missing one, and it's a macro. You may not have contracted anything yet, but you probably will *by the time you leave*." He winked, obviously making reference to her past escape. "I'll do his, now."

He scanned Deck's slide, his eyes going wide for a second as he stared at the screen. He looked between Deck and Jenny more deliberately. "Got a Mr. Fancy Pants here, eh?"

A small sound escaped Jenny's lips.

The inoculator shrugged. "Amazing, huh? I'm guessing 'cause of his diet . . . and he has one of those accents."

"Will I be requiring inoculation?" Deck asked. It was definitely time to move on.

"You've got first-class immunizations," the inoculator said, studying him more carefully. "But as I referenced before, we did just register an outbreak of macrotyphoid in Newgate's western quadrant. They did a sweep and deleted the offenders, but you'd be better off taking a booster." He looked at Deck, waiting.

Deck nodded, and Jenny removed her finger from the amethyst. The inoculator placed two syringe punches on the counter.

Jenny picked hers up in a fist. She tapped the syringe against Deck's as if they were champagne flutes, said, "Cheers," and plunged the needle straight through her pants into her thigh.

"You badass," Deck said, his voice husky.

She rewarded the compliment with the first real smile he'd seen out of her yet, and tossed the spent needle cartridge into a nearby biohazard bin.

She'd definitely grown up. And Deck liked what he was seeing. Jenny was tough, independent—and had a killer smile. Between the two of them they had some pretty significant baggage, but whatever had been blocking the path from his bed to hers didn't seem to be as much of a problem now. The House of Han couldn't dictate who it was proper for Prince D'ekkar Han Valoren to touch, anymore. He swept his gaze up and down Jenny's tight frame. Some days it just felt particularly good to be a commoner.

"Well?" she gave him a jaunty little grin and crossed her arms over her chest.

Deck studied his needle; it looked clean enough. It wasn't exactly what he was used to, but he followed suit.

Behind him, a voice he recognized as Raidon's whispered, "Holy Mother of God."

The inoculator was punching updates into his computer and said, "Never understood how you guys with value throw it away and end up—" Suddenly, he froze as if something had just dawned on him. He slowly brought his eyes up to Deck's face. "Wait a minute. Are you Parliament, sir?" he asked in a shaky voice. "You don't look . . . It's just that

I . . . I . . ." He trailed off nervously and hurried to pushed the amethyst back across the counter.

Jenny's sense of humor vanished as rapidly as it had appeared. She stepped forward and put her hand on the guy's wrist, holding his arm down to lean forward over it. "Not a real smart question," she said.

They remained motionless, eye to eye. Finally, the inoculator swallowed nervously and said, "Hear no evil, speak no evil, see no evil."

"My sentiments exactly." Jenny let go of his wrist and carefully smoothed out his sleeve. "Are we done here?"

"Yes, miss," he said, clearly still confused and wanting to err on the side of safety. He stamped their immigration slips and mumbled, "Please proceed to Clearance."

Jenny nodded to Deck, indicating that he should follow.

They pointedly crossed in front of Raidon, who'd finished up at the counter beside theirs, so he'd know where they were headed. He followed doggedly to the weapons registry. They'd loaded him up with all the weapons he could carry plus a bribe theoretically big enough to get them all through the system.

They waited in the Clearance line for a couple of hours, entertaining their own thoughts, until Deck leaned down and whispered in Jenny's ear, "I think we need to have a serious talk about this Parliament."

"Not here," she said tightly as they handed their slips over the counter.

The woman on the other side had obviously had a run-in with a toxic substance, if the yellow flaky texture of her skin was any indication. She looked up at them serenely. "Do you have anything on your person you'd like to declare? No? There's also an amnesty barrel in front of line A if you're feeling nervous."

"No," Jenny said. "We're good to go."

The woman stared between the two of them speculatively, holding on to a rod projecting a beam of red light. Deck looked up to where several infrared signals crisscrossed the ceiling of the vast immigration thruway. Such beams swung down behind the desks of each of the clearance agents, to be used as pens. "Are you certain, dear? No weapons, inflammatory propaganda, illegal drugs, or any other prohibited items on your persons?"

Jenny leaned over the desk. "We're clean," she said shortly.

The woman shrugged and pointed at the raised bar code on their immigration slips with her pen. She handed the slips back. "Good luck to you." With a wide sweep of her arm, she gestured to the enormous corroded metal archway leading to the outside. Six-foot-high rusted letters spelling NEWGATE were welded to the arch.

Jenny looked at it and froze. A million thoughts were obviously going through her head, all of them terrified. Deck had to take her by the elbow and practically pry her away from the desk toward the exit tunnel.

"Deck," Jenny whispered urgently, her grip on his

arm desperate and pleading. He gently detached her hand and then shoved her through the turnstile.

It was as if she deflated a little. A lack of faith on her part, a disappointment in him.

Deck took her by the shoulders and looked into her wide eyes. "I'm not going to leave you here. I swear it. I will live up to my end of the bargain." He pulled her into an embrace as people streamed around them, and rested his chin on her head, a perfect fit. She didn't pull away; rather she just sort of sagged into him.

He was uneasy himself. It was one thing to talk about revolution, another to be prepared to make the necessary sacrifices. This was more than just sending the value and the blueprints to have a depot built up. He was putting his life on the line. He looked down at Jenny's flaming red hair. *Their* lives on the line.

She pulled away and drew herself together. "Sorry. I'm fine. Are you ready?"

"I'm ready," Deck said, adrenaline leaping in his veins as he walked toward the exit. "Let's do it."

He stepped through and blew his mind.

Metal-modern, wooden-ancient, decrepit, polluted, rats running through the streets with mangy half-breeds hunting after them, the smell of sewage. Manure and straw in the streets. Rickshaws, dune buggies, tricked-out motorcycles and motopods creating chaos on wheels, carts and coaches drawn by broken-down genetically mixed pseudo-horses now banned by many regions of the world. Everything seemed to be patched together, made from disparate parts and pieces, recycled, reinvented, repurposed, reused. Yet it had none of the excitement of new discovery and invention, and all the taint of waste and decay.

Deck turned in a circle, crowds of people streaming every which way. Desperation, aggression, resignation, defiance—part of him felt sickened by this ghoulish sensory overload, part of him heartened by it.

There was no question: Newgate proper was a cross of Kyber's modern-day East Asian Kingdom and a snapshot in time of old historical Europe, the Regency England of picture books. It was the slums of Macao a hundred times worse, a hundred times removed from reality, painted over with the sheen of somebody's crazy idea of what beauty used to be— and still ought to be. But yes, this place was as ripe for revolution as any other.

Unlike with Jenny, the disturbing nature of the place only fueled his purpose that much more.

This. *This* was what revolution was for. These sad people. And the Shadow Voice's communications, recently stopped— undoubtedly filtered and censored by this Parliament Jenny spoke of—would soon again be online, broadcasting its message of freedom to the entire world through every underground source, bypassing all official means of communication.

That was why he was here.

Chapter Six

The narrow cobblestone streets of Newgate were clogged with a teeming mass of men with agendas and missions and business and errands, all mixed in with the stench of the country's rot and the exotic strains of Asian folk tunes. As she and Deck met up with Raidon in the thoroughfare outside the immigration hall, Jenny wondered if the old songs made the former prince feel sad.

She'd never seen him sad; he wasn't prone to overt displays of emotion. She, on the other hand, preferred to express her feelings, loud and clear, whether it be with a punch in the face or a kiss on the mouth. She'd like to give Deck one of each.

They pushed on through the humidity, in and around a maze of back-route alleys and housing complexes toward the armory. On the outside, these structures took their style cues from the Palladian architecture favored by Parliament. Everything about Newgate that could be seen in public, it seemed, took style cues from Parliament.

Yet all of it was just a facade. Which resulted in a city full of dirty gray stucco cornices, columns, and gracefully curved windows covered in grime. The grime hid the contrast—and almost the shoddiness—of the reality.

At last, Jenny stopped at a cavernous warehouse hidden behind a run-down housing project. They entered into a loft space crowded with security monitors and lenses of all shapes and sizes. Jenny disappeared into a small side door and returned with an enormous bulk of a man without a decent neck.

Raidon explained what sort of equipment he was looking for—rifles, a pair of grenade launchers, a few hand pistols, and two high-performance jeeps—and the armorer prepared to return to his vaults. At the last moment, he turned and asked, "How about some smaller items?" He lifted the lid on a large display case to reveal a huge variety of both repurposed vintage and modern inventory. "Tracers, poison darts, shuriken, a few other small tools . . ."

Deck picked out a few pairs of night-vision goggles. Jenny chose a set of forearm gauntlets, grinning as she tried one on. "Look at this. Just leather here, and then this mechanism that lies flat—looks like you just release the safety and . . . here's the digital trigger. This metal bit pops up, pivots, and . . ."

She turned to a dummy impaled on a stake in the practice area and had a go. A metal claw on the end of a thin, tight cable snaked out with a *twang*, jamming directly into the dummy's crotch. "Nice!" she crowed.

Raidon cringed and said, "Try to contain your enthusiasm. We're buying necessities, not . . . accessories."

"You never know," Jenny said, even as she removed the gauntlets and placed them back on the counter.

Deck shook his head. "Just remember that I only have as much value as I arrived here with. It's not as if I can easily pick up a bank deposit without detection." And then he uttered with much amusement: "Women."

Raidon nodded. "She might have a right hook to rival a man's, but she's still a she on the inside."

Ignoring them, Jenny moved to a wall from which hung an enormous collection of swords, sabers, and knives of all shapes and sizes. In the reflection of one of the broadswords, she saw Deck gesture to Raidon. The heavy nodded and placed the gauntlets in the purchase pile. She smiled to herself and turned her attention back to the swords.

Deck came up behind her and gazed into the display case over her shoulder. They looked at each other, then looked at the test floor that took up the bulk of the space in the center of the huge warehouse. Jenny muffled a laugh as they read each other's intent and simultaneously selected two weapons apiece: a long sword and a short dagger.

Raidon slapped his head in surrender. "I guess I'm handling transportation procurement, since you two are busy." He turned back to the armorer. "Can I see the options?"

"It's all garaged out back." The man looked around at their gear. "Say, you planning to store this stuff here awhile?"

"Only a couple of days." Raidon turned, a grin on his face when he saw Deck preparing to fight. "Do try not to kill him, Jenn."

She shrugged innocently and followed Deck to the test floor. It was an impressive piece of work: a round, enormous circular stage with padded walls and hard floor.

Deck removed his jacket, his sleeveless black armored vest exposing taut, muscular arms.

Jenny likewise pulled off her jacket, leaving only a thin shirt—no fabric to grab, but not much protection either.

Deck arched an eyebrow and made a show of shedding his vest for the sake of parity. His bare chest looked lean and powerful; he had a bit of the jungle cat to him. Jenny almost offered to match him skin for skin.

They strolled the perimeter of the fight space, sizing each other up, eyes locked. Jenny dangled her sword at her side with a bit of swagger, a little breathless with anticipation.

Deck went first. Standing tall, balanced, the lines of his body moving slowly, flowing, easing his arms into the space around him as if they simply balanced on air. His legs adopting a slight bend, he saluted her formally, indicating his readiness by touching his sword handle to his heart.

Jenny recognized the stance as the first in a series from the fighting form of martial arts adapted by the Han army, a cross between the aggressive swordplay of kendo and the flowing patterns of tai chi. Jenny could almost still see Deck practicing the rhythmic form in a field on the palace grounds. That practiced grace would always color his fighting style.

Through a fence, she'd watched him and his brother and their security forces practice the katas. She'd learned from watching, imitating the movements and absorbing the patterns if not the mental practices or philosophy needed to create a truly well-rounded fighter.

No, Jenny made no pretenses about being a well-rounded fighter. She couldn't care less about style or the philosophical aspects of warfare. She knew enough to make herself dangerous and unpredictable by combining a mélange of styles, teachings, and observations into something lethal that was all her own.

And she could meet Deck with an equal, if opposite, force.

Her brand of fighting didn't come with a salute. With a quirky smile, she just tossed her sword up in the air, caught it in her fist like a dagger, and pointed it straight at Deck's heart.

"Fire and water, you and me, mmm?" he murmured, his voice husky, his inscrutable gray eyes focused, locked on hers.

He began.

Jenny smiled and found her own stance immediately, crouching low, flexing, and shifting her weight, getting the energy flowing through her body. Jerky movements, kinetic, wired, energy flowing, ready for anything, ready to *fight*.

She lashed out with her long sword, the blade meeting his in a flash of silver. They clashed. Pulled away. Ah yes. He, the epitome of technique and grace; she, the consummate street fighter—quick and dirty.

His eyebrow lifted in surprise—and respect, perhaps.

Jenny smiled indulgently. "Education isn't everything," she said.

They clashed and pulled away once more, and then again, escalating the exercise into something of a true battle. To his credit, Deck didn't hold much back.

Clashing, withdrawing, up close, face-to-face, and away—then, suddenly, Deck ducked under Jenny's blade, reached out, and grabbed her waistband. He reeled her in to him, their two swords crossed just inches from their faces. He held her tight.

And suddenly she understood what this fight was about. She wanted to play power games with him for a reason. She wanted to test him. She wanted to know exactly where she stood. What was he made of? How far would he go for this revolution of his? What was he willing to sacrifice? Would he hurt her? Was he willing to sacrifice her life?

Deck cocked his head, reading her expression. "Okay," he said, smooth menace in his voice. "Now, let's *really* fight."

He pushed his sword off hers and threw it to the mat. He picked up his dagger. Jenny watched him toss it in the air a couple of times, testing the heft and balance. Adrenaline made her shiver as she grabbed her own dagger off the adjoining console and tossed her sword away. The metal clang of the blade echoed through the armory.

She went at Deck, jolting, faking, pressing in, jabbing from the side, thrusting, ducking; he met her every move with one of his own, delivered with perfect, disciplined grace.

They broke apart and put some space between them, eyeing each other as they continuously shifted weight like a couple of boxers just after the bell. Jenny wiped the sweat from her eyes with the back of her free hand and was gratified to see Deck do the same.

"Tired?" he asked with a smile.

"I'm just getting started."

He bowed his head in acquiescence. "A second helping?"

"Please."

They engaged once more, this time with Jenny morphing the fight into something more raw and physical, something more her own.

Deck thrust his dagger forward; she twisted her body and answered with the sole of her boot kicking hard against his chest.

He grunted and threw her off. She lost her balance and hit the floor, completing a shoulder roll and coming back up to fight in one slick move. He began another pattern of his form; she broke it by adding a left hook to one shoulder while jabbing her dagger forward with the right.

He caught all of the blows, met and dispatched all of her attacks, but she could tell she had him off balance. And she could see from the look in his eyes that it excited him.

Raidon undoubtedly had done Deck's dirty work in the past.

"You like fighting me outside of the patterns," she murmured. "How does it feel to be so free of constraint? No rules to be used against you, but then again, no rules to protect you either. Does it make you itch to do something . . . forbidden?" she asked with a sly smile.

He rolled his eyes and stepped back. "I think you know me better than that. I've always done things my way. I just manage to stay under the radar—which is something I suggest you work on. You were way too easy to track down in Macao."

"Well, you found me in one piece. I guess I managed to stay away from the bad guys, didn't I? Until you, anyway."

"You consider me one of the bad guys?"

"You don't give me much choice," she said, lying a little. "Should I think otherwise?"

The question seemed to catch him off guard. The laughter disappeared from his eyes. He lost focus for a fraction of a second. And in that second, Jenny put all of the resentment toward him she'd been storing up into a powerful scissor kick, blasting the dagger from Deck's grasp. The blade whipped haphazardly end over end across the test stage and embedded it-self in the padded wall.

But even the metallic *twang* of the reverberating handle couldn't say it all. She lunged at him.

Her dagger was at Deck's neck for maybe a second before Raidon seemed to materialize out of nowhere. "Stand down," he ordered, pistol out but not aimed, slowly making his way around the perimeter toward her.

"I don't think so," Jenny said calmly. "Deck and I haven't quite finished our conversation yet."

"Stand down, Jenny!"

"I'll handle this," Deck hissed.

He didn't move. And he didn't look down to where her blade pressed flat against his flesh. He stared directly into Jenny's eyes and calmly asked, "What is this about?"

"I'm suddenly not comfortable with my survival potential."

"Go on."

"It's one thing to die in a fight, another to die from . . . say, negligence."

"I'm not sure what you're getting at. Could you be more specific?"

"I'm just a hired gun. I don't work for your revolution. I work for value. I'm not interested in being a personal sacrifice for the greater good, you got that? Do you understand what I'm saying? I'm not your point man."

Deck answered by moving toward her just slightly, oh, so slightly, letting her blade roll up perpendicular to his skin, positioned to cut deep.

It a was power play, even now. Jenny swallowed hard, hating him with all her might. "You trying to prove something here?"

"I think we both are," he growled.

"Why are you taunting her, sir? Let it go," Raidon said.

Deck didn't move, and his heavy gestured to Jenny with the pistol. "I will use this if necessary. I will protect him." The man's voice sounded desperate and pleading, but as he stalked the floor, his body language indicated he was ready to kill.

"Will you? Says who?" Jenny sneered over her shoulder, not taking her eyes off Deck.

Deck was equally keen to stare her down. "What exactly is it that's bothering you? Let's get it out in the open."

She narrowed her eyes, unwilling to let him think he could intimidate her even one little bit. "You say you're just like everybody else, now. You're nobody's prince, and out here, nobody owes you fealty. That means you should be as dispensable as I am. But somehow I don't believe it. I get the impression that our lives just aren't worth the same in all this."

"I'm not afraid to die." Deck moved forward again, the edge of Jenny's blade pressing into his flesh.

She sucked back a gasp, and in the next second Raidon's pistol was jammed against her temple.

"Sorry, Jenny," the heavy said in a steely tone. "It just doesn't work like this. Not for me. Back away from him."

The muscles in Deck's jaw throbbed. "Raidon, I'm

telling you . . . hands off. This is mine. I'm in control here."

"Are you?" Jenny asked.

"I am," he replied. He moved forward again, forcing the tip of her blade to cut into the side of his neck. "I'm not afraid to make a sacrifice, Jenny. Are you?"

She stared at the streak of blood sliding down her blade toward her fingers.

"Damn it!" Raidon cried, cocking the trigger on his gun. "Jenny, stand down. Now!"

She looked into Deck's eyes once more, staring, staring—*Don't break the chain, keep a firm grip on the blade*—but she was sweating so hard, now, the handle felt slippery and unsure. Her entire arm started to shake, the muscles cramping up.

But she didn't give up ground. "I know you're not afraid to die. But that's not quite what I'm getting at." She added, "It's not that I'm afraid, either, if that's what you think. But if someone has to die, and if's someone's planning on it being me, I think it's the sort of thing one ought to have the balls to come out and say," she sneered.

Deck kept his silence. A small smile played at his lips.

"You'd walk into this sword for your revolution—I believe that. But that's not really the question. Would you walk into this sword for Raidon? Or for me? And would you walk *us* into a sword?" She added in a voice almost a whisper, "When push comes to shove, the question is: what's important to you?"

"My first priority is the revolution," Deck admitted calmly. "But I would defend either you or Raidon with my life, if I could."

"Hedging," Jenny said in a singsong voice.

"This isn't funny," Raidon said, digging the cold muzzle of his pistol into the side of her head even harder.

"No, it's not, is it? Answer the question, Deck. If you came here expecting a sacrifice, whose will it be? If somebody has to die, you're going to make it me. Right?"

"Nobody has to die," Raidon said.

"But if they did? If somebody has to die? Deck fights for the revolution. You keep Deck alive to fight for the revolution. That leaves me, fighting for . . . me. Right?"

To his credit, while Deck still didn't answer, he didn't look away.

Raidon mumbled something about hypotheticals. Neither he nor Deck understood what she was getting at. They really didn't get it. Suddenly, Jenny felt incredibly foolish. She opened her hand and let her dagger fall to the floor.

Deck's expression remained impassive as he picked it up and coolly wiped his blood off on his trousers. Without another word, he gathered up the rest of the weapons and headed for the front desk.

Raidon breathed an audible sigh of relief, flipped the safety on his weapon, and let his arm drop to his side. "I don't know you well, but I think you're better than this. Don't put me in that position again."

"It's better that I know where I stand," she said coldly. She looked over her shoulder at Deck.

"Is it?" Raidon asked. He put his hand on her shoulder. "Look—"

"Forget it." She glared at the heavy and shook off his hand. Always the lowest priority, always the most dispensable. For a minute there, leading Deck and Raidon to the armory from immigration, she'd fancied herself critical to their little team. A true part of it. But she wasn't, was she? At least not to Deck. He saw her as a hired hand. A *replaceable* hired hand.

Jenny wheeled around and drove her fist into a hanging practice bag.

Chapter Seven

He might be the one bleeding, but Jenny was obviously still nursing an old injury. Five blocks down the street, Deck was still kicking himself for letting their swordplay escalate.

Arrogance. That was what it was, sheer arrogance that allowed him to goad her on like that when her pride was already battered after being forced to accept his deal. She might have once worn her heart on her sleeve for all to see, but that still didn't mean he understood her. He sighed. At least he was learning.

He barely paid attention to where they were going until Jenny stopped them at the door of a run-down hotel, sign proclaiming: PRINNY'S PLACE. The accommodation was boxlike, save for the incongruous triumphal arch tacked on to the front of the building like an enormous funeral wreath on a coffin.

Through the meshwork of protective bars blocking the entrance wafted the smells of tar and overcooked beef. And from a rigid wire stretching to the highest point of the arch hung a security lens.

Jenny positioned herself in full view and pressed the buzzer. After a moment, the locking mechanism dropped free and the barred door swung slightly open.

The dingy lobby featured a receptionist's counter on one side and a bar hidden back in the recesses of the other. Raidon didn't seem to know which side to be more concerned with. "I'm not sure this is a good idea," he whispered nervously, waving away the smoke, glancing between the front desk and the bar.

"So don't inhale," Jenny answered with a wink.

Deck looked at her in surprise. Her tone was normal, her expression impassive, her sense of humor already showing again. It hardly seemed possible that she could have worked out her frustrations between the armory and the hotel. Her sudden reversal made him terribly uneasy.

"How goes it?" Wearing a too-small sleeveless undershirt and chin scruff of several days' growth, the barkeep left his post and stepped over behind the receptionist counter. "Well, if it isn't Jenny Red."

"Just once it would be nice if someone could sound really pleased when they said my name," she muttered.

Ignoring the comment, the clerk studied Deck and Raidon, then took a long look out the door behind them. "What's all this?" he asked Jenny, gesturing to the men with his chin.

"I can vouch for them."

Deck sighed, and she shot him a death glare. He

was finding it difficult to get used to the pace of this place. The never-ending negotiation for value, the laborious bribery couched as simple business transactions. He wasn't impulsive, like Jenny, but he was used to results. It was all beginning to drive him a little mad. "Two rooms, please, good man," he said politely.

Jenny shot an elbow backward into his gut, nearly taking out his spleen. Raidon stepped forward, but Deck waved him off.

The desk clerk looked at the three of them like a disapproving third-grade teacher and leaned down, eyes level with Jenny's. "Such a itty-bitty li'l thing," he said derisively, "but you gotta lotta tough in you. And I've seen you use it."

Jenny just shrugged.

"Know this. I don't want any trouble, girl."

She leaned over the desk likewise and got in his face. "Me, neither. In fact, we're trying to keep a low profile, if you know what I mean. We'd like that two-bed back corner suite if it's available. Plus water and light. I'm thinking a couple nights or so, I'm not sure yet."

"I'll have to charge a premium. Due to circumstances."

She rolled her eyes. "Come *on*."

"I said I'll have to charge a premium," he said, more sternly this time, and then he leaned over and put his hand out and lifted her chin. "And it ain't just because we're talking water and light for three people. You've got a history of making trouble where trouble just ain't needed."

"Take your hands off her," Deck said. What the hell was this guy thinking?

Jenny shook off the hand before the clerk could even answer. He stuck his hands out front and flipped them over a couple of times to show he was in the clear.

"All's I'm saying is that I got a decent clientele here now."

What was the man blathering about? To be sent here, you already had to be in trouble. For God's sake, what could possibly happen to get a person in worse trouble? Were there places worse than Newgate they sent you to for bad behavior? Hard to imagine. Deck laughed softly, earning a look from Raidon.

"We're decent," Jenny said, obviously taking umbrage at the desk clerk's insinuations. "And I think 'big trouble' is a bit strong," she continued. "Not to mention, I haven't been back in Newgate long enough to qualify for any 'history.'"

The desk clerk didn't relent.

"Oh, fine," she grumbled and pushed forward some coins.

With a quick nod of the head, the desk clerk scraped off the money, leaving just a warped and stained smart-card illustrated with the picture of an ornate skeleton key behind on the counter. "Upstairs, far left, in the back. Just spackled."

"Thank you very much." Deck took the smart-card and slung his bag over his shoulder.

Jenny hoisted her own and pressed Deck toward the stairs. Raidon followed with the extra baggage.

They found the room as directed. The door of the room was spackled all right, with roundish gray blobs about the size of an impact round of the average pistol shell. Raidon ran his fingers over each, but didn't say a word.

Inside the room, Jenny dumped her bag on the ground and immediately began to unlace her boots. "Can we talk a bit more about the plans? I mean, how do I even know when I'm done? Are you eventually going to tell me exactly what the plans are?"

"Are you going to tell me what kind of trouble the hotel clerk was referring to?"

"Nice dodge." She looked woefully at Raidon. "Does he talk to you like this? Answering a question he doesn't want to answer with a question you don't want to answer?" She turned back to Deck. "Look, I'm only asking because if you want me to get some intel about the trip ahead, I've got to know what to ask about."

Deck studied Jenny's face for a long time. Finally, he said, "There's a depot in the outback. We need to figure out the fastest, safest route to get there." He pulled a pen from his pocket and took her hand, then wrote a set of global positioning coordinates on her skin.

Jenny looked at the numbers. She looked closer. "That's definitely the outback. Okay, I'm hitting the spout." She held up her palm. "Consider it duly destroyed."

Without waiting for an answer, she grabbed some clothes from her pack, pulled off her boots and headed for the bathroom, stripping her clothes off on the way.

Deck watched her lithe form disappear into the water closet. Since leaving the armorer, she hadn't ranted, hadn't raved; she had kept her mouth shut. She hadn't been the usual Jenny, loudly stating her case, her point of view, no matter how crazy. That was the Jenny he understood, the girl he knew how to handle.

This Jenny, the one holding her cards close to her chest and keeping her thoughts—especially her pissed-off thoughts—to herself . . . Well, frankly, Deck didn't really know what to do with her. Part of him realized she'd simply grown up and wasn't the same young woman he'd known. Part of him suspected it was simply that she was cleverer than he'd given her credit for.

He felt conflicted about what he'd said during their sword fight, but he firmly believed that the revolution should come before all else. And if Jenny stood in the way of that . . . Deck stared fixedly at the ceiling. It was difficult for him to muster up the rest of that thought. Very difficult.

She returned from the shower with her hair wet and tangled around her face, drowning to her thighs in a huge ratty sweatshirt that apparently doubled as both a towel and a robe. Even Raidon looked up from where he was sprawled on the bed, scrolling through a *Soldier of Fortune* mag-reader attachment on his organizer.

"S'cold enough to make Popsicles out of that water," she grumbled. She found a pair of those little shorts underwear Deck had seen glimpses of and pulled them on under her sweatshirt.

Deck eyed her carefully, trying to gauge her current mood. But she seemed completely over what had transpired at the armorer.

He wasn't. He couldn't quite let it go. "About earlier . . ."

She waved his words away. "Forget it. I thought about it all the way back from the armory. It's done. Let's chalk it up to adrenaline rush. Besides, we're in pretty tight living quarters to be holding a grudge."

"No, I'd like to explain myself a little better."

"What's there to explain? This is all just business, right? I mean, you essentially hired me for a job. I let the past hurt my feelings, I made it personal. But I get it—I really do. We have a business relationship."

"We have more than a business relationship," Deck argued, his voice huskier than he liked. "I think that's our problem. I think—"

"Our problem," she said flippantly, "is that we don't quite know where we need to draw the line between our personal business and this . . . *business* business. What happened at the armory was just . . . reorientation."

Raidon made an indecipherable choking sound, and Deck had the distinct sensation that the conversation was getting away from him. "Reorientation," he repeated, a little numbly.

"Exactly. Obviously, things are different now. You and I used to be an impossibility. You were a prince. I was a nobody. Sure, we were attracted to each other, but we had an excuse, a reason, a justification for not acting on our . . . um—"

"I'm not sure this is appropriate subject matter,"

Raidon interrupted, leaning up on his elbows, his expression solicitous despite the flexing of his enormous muscles.

"Chemical attraction," Jenny said anyway.

"And so . . . what are you saying?" Deck asked.

She cleared her throat. "I'm saying that it's not that you want me, it's that you simply can't have me."

Deck's eyes narrowed, and Raidon exhaled loudly. Deck wasn't entirely sure whether the heavy approved of her cavalier behavior, or whether he found the implied slight amusing. Probably both.

It got worse when Jenny actually reached over and patted him on the cheek. With that, she took back all control. Deck couldn't quite recall anyone treating a prince of the Han dynasty like a toy dog. And she wasn't done yet. "I'm glad we have a business relationship, Deck. And I'm really glad we've clarified all this. I just thought, considering our past . . . I'll make a real effort to keep a lot of clothes on around you. There will be no sex."

Raidon snorted gleefully and dropped his handheld over the side of the bed.

"Why are we talking about sex?" Deck asked, a little exasperated, throwing what he hoped was a silencing glare in his heavy's direction. "I just wanted to clear the air about what happened at the armory. This has nothing to do with sex. It's about—"

"Death?" Jenny supplied helpfully. "Sex and death. Oooh, I think I'm getting hot, Deck. You kill me. Or were you going to say, 'the mission'?"

Deck swore under his breath as she fake-swooned, falling backward on the bed, her shirt billowing up dangerously. Raidon reached over and slapped one huge palm over the edge of the fabric to keep it down.

Deck sighed and shook his head. One minute she had a dagger at his neck, threatening to kill him. The next minute she was flaunting herself half naked around the hotel suite, telling him he couldn't have her—and this attack felt more dangerous than the sword fight.

He stared at Jenny as she lolled on the bed next to Raidon. She was toying with him. Absolutely, positively toying with him. She wasn't really over what had happened in the past and they both knew that.

God, she fascinated him. She was exciting, a firecracker . . . hell, she was a whole cluster bomb. Her fearlessness and total lack of self-consciousness . . . it was one of the things he admired about her: she honestly could survive without anyone or anything. She always had.

Her unpredictability even excited him. Predictability was what you wanted in a plan, not a woman. Jenny put to shame the lacquered palace puppets he'd known. Even when forced into other people's power, she lived by her own code.

And she was entirely correct; they weren't an impossibility anymore. They were different people. And whatever the nature of the flame that still flickered between them, well, maybe getting burned would be worth it. Maybe. If he didn't have a revolution to jump-start. And if deep down Jenny didn't find him so unforgivable for abandoning her to Newgate the first time around and forcing her to come back for more.

She lay on the bed on her stomach next to Raidon, reading over his shoulder with her legs kicked up in the air behind her. Deck devoured them with his gaze, all the way up to her tiny black shorts underwear. Only a few creamy patches of skin remained smooth and untouched, but on the whole, nicked, scarred, bruised— her legs were, in a word, beautiful.

She and Raidon seemed to have overcome their earlier difficulties. The heavy put his hand on Jenny's back and said something that made her laugh. Deck frowned when Raidon's hand slid lower on Jenny's back as he told another joke.

Deck couldn't stop himself from standing up from the armchair, but he managed to avoid making an ass of himself by not telling Raidon to take his hands off Jenny like he'd told the desk clerk. That would be irrational, unreasonable . . . and in his commoner status, beyond his power to command.

He had to laugh at himself, at least a little. He might support the idea of democracy wholeheartedly, but he was still in transition as far as breaking old habits went. Etiquette, rules, regulations, standards—most of all, he had to come to terms with the fact that things didn't happen anymore with just a snap of his fingers.

Perhaps Jenny sensed his mood. She looked over her shoulder at him and flicked her ponytail, sending a spill of red-gold locks across her neck. "Deck? You good?"

"I'm just thinking. I'm fine." *Just behaving like a jealous schoolboy, don't mind me.* Jenny was beside the point. He needed to focus on the revolution.

Raidon threw down his organizer. "I'm going to take my shower now." When he got up, Deck took his place on the bed, and lying next to Jenny made him want to touch her just as Raidon had.

Concentrate on the revolution. Deck cleared his throat. "Tell me more about this Parliament."

Jenny rolled back and looked at him. "Originally, Parliament was nothing more than an energy company. They control the power grid for the entire country, and it's how they first took control of the people. It's not the reason they keep control, however. This world they've created, this society they've encouraged . . . that stuff's more to the point. They've become the de facto rulers here. Everything revolves around them. What else . . . ? Well, they operate out of a compound called the Parliament Club that takes up something like two normal city blocks. I think you can see the backside of it not far from here."

"Who *are* these individuals?"

"Men like you, mostly. Quite a few are the once-privileged sons of countries assimilated by the UCE. The club will welcome any ex-royalty, exiled statesmen, other assorted blue bloods—any upperclassmen, if you will, who are deemed worthy for one reason or another. The reason most likely is an ability to bring value. Of course, most members lost all their privileged status in the rest of the world, so they have aristocratic standing only because they're here."

"Odd. If they've taken over, you'd think they'd be a known government outside of the colony, but they're not recognized as a legitimate power anywhere I've ever been. I'd never heard of them prior to you talking about them. Why do you think that is?"

Jenny sat up. "They want it that way. As I said, it's not about the recognition from outsiders. They don't care about world domination—or world anything, for that matter. The value that flows in and out of this economy from the power grid always stays here, in Newgate. They're not interested in diplomacy, they don't import or export, and all transactions are handled through third parties who work in black markets both here and on Macao. Their hold over Newgate is about one thing and one thing only."

"Which is . . ."

Jenny stared up at the ceiling. "The opiate. The hallucinogen that makes life tolerable for them."

Deck whistled.

"Just as well that they don't have higher aspirations. They don't play well with others. I don't know how to describe this. You'd have to meet one of them to understand, but it's hard to engage in meaningful discourse with the jacked."

Deck quirked an eyebrow. "The insane? You said something about poppers on the trip over. Is this what you meant?"

"Yeah. These guys are literally jacked up on fantasy poppers. Methonetylcetamine. Ever tried FPs?"

"No. My understanding is that they are highly addictive and often deadly."

Jenny shrugged. "Me neither. Could never afford 'em, myself. But I hear they're great," she added calmly, studying the cracks and chips in her fingernails. "That is, until they fry your brain, you completely freak out, and end up killing yourself or someone else." She looked at him and grinned.

"What exactly do they do to you?"

"Well, I can't be more specific other than to say users don't see exactly what we do. The opiate makes them experience a different version of reality. Sorry, I can't really explain it better than that. I mean, obviously, I didn't exactly socialize with the druggies when I was here last. And the Parliament . . ."

"I wonder why their families let them go."

"Why did you let me go?" Jenny blurted.

He stared at her. She'd probably wanted to ask him that question for a long, long time.

She added softly, "You were my only true friend in the world. You knew my father was worthless before anything happened."

Deck didn't answer, and an awkward silence stretched out between them.

Finally, Jenny cleared her throat. "Anyway, people just end up here. Most are criminals sent over from regions with overcrowded penal systems. But many are just—how to put this?—embarrassments, or people somehow in the way. Deportees like myself. A big payment to Parliament might get you out of here, but not many can afford it. So, we're left with a mishmash of people who want to be here and those who can't get out. Addicts, murderers, debtors, outed moles, and spies . . . any and all assorted undesirables. You name it, they're probably here."

"But the sons of—"

"Consider the relationship between you and your brother. From what you've hinted at, the only likely reason he wouldn't let you rot here would be to bring you home and convict you of treason."

"Half brother," Deck growled. "Kyber's my half brother."

Jenny flashed him a snarky little smile. "You know, you're awfully touchy about that. Are you sure you aren't just trying to start a revolution here to get revenge? After all, this colony was once in your family empire."

"No," he said sharply. "The revolution has nothing to do with my personal feelings about Kyber. It's much larger than that. And I'm not trying to start a revolution *in Australia*. This country seems destined to join in eventually, But right now, it serves better as a hiding place for the kinds of operations that will help further the Voice of Freedom's goals—UCE rebels who are close to making a move."

The UCE, or United Colonies of Earth. They included a huge land mass in part composed of the territory once known as the United States of America. In its former incarnation, the country was known for the very brand of revolutionary ideals Deck's Shadow Runners were fighting for, but the UCE had become nothing more than an imperialistic power hammering continuously away at what had once been the inalienable rights of its people: life, liberty, and the pursuit of happiness.

The fact that Deck had grown up quite familiar with the bad blood between the Kingdom of Asia and the UCE only helped to fuel his purpose.

"No, inciting revolution in Newgate right now would call too much attention to the Shadow Runners and their mission," he explained. "But it will come. Look, let's hold off a bit on any more talk of my plans one way or the other." He'd already said more than he was really comfortable with. Even if he was talking to Jenny.

She shrugged. "Fine, but if you ask me, Newgate might not go for revolution. And given what's become of the place, the only real reason to want it is to keep someone else from having it."

"Yeah. I can't really figure out what Kyber wants," Deck muttered sullenly.

"He's not a bad ruler, your half brother. He treats his people pretty well. It's probably hard for you to see—"

"I see very clearly," Deck snapped. "Can you? I don't know how you can give him the benefit of the doubt. When you escaped Newgate, you were living in the slums of Macao, under his jurisdiction. Can you actually say that he treats all his people well with a straight face? He was the one who deported you!"

Raidon came out from the bathroom with a towel wrapped around his waist. He frowned, crossed the room, and peered out the window. "Hey, there's some sort of parade coming. It's real quiet, though. . . ."

Both Deck and Jenny ignored him.

"As far as Macao is concerned, it was the emperor his father who let the place rot. I heard Prince Kyber was working on programs to fix the situation. People were talking about it. There's been progress." Jenny's cheeks flared pink. "And as for the deportation . . . well, I only knew you. I never knew your brother. To him, I was just the daughter of his father's would-be assassin. I wouldn't keep me anywhere near the palace, either." She gave him a disgusted look. "You, on the other hand, were my friend. He owed me nothing. You were my friend."

Deck shook his head. "Monarchy is not in anyone's best interest. This revolution will solve the world's problems at their root cause, by getting rid of those who would seek to control everything based on their own whims. It will go back to ideals that—"

Jenny wrinkled her nose disdainfully. "God, you sound like a recording. Sometimes I think you forget you're talking about actual people, not some theories you can obsess over. Revolution is about individuals. It should be of the people, by the people, for the people. You, of anyone, should get that."

"I get it," he snarled.

"Then you should understand that individuals will always act in their best interest. Monarch, elected ruler—what's the difference?"

"I don't think you're describing most individuals; you're describing *selfish* individuals," Deck snapped. He instantly regretted it. But listening to Jenny talk as if Kyber were the same as a democratically elected leader made his stomach turn. How could she forgive the man for all his evils?

Jenny rolled over and sneered. "So, you think I'm selfish. That's what you just said. Well, you can call it that, but I call it looking out for myself. And I need to. No one else has ever volunteered for the job. Not my father, not the palace, and certainly not you."

And there it was.

"I'm not having this conversation," Deck said to the ceiling. He looked back at Jenny and added, "It's completely destructive to the team attitude we should be developing, and it's—"

"It's stopping here," Raidon called.

"Fine with me," Jenny agreed. "I have nothing more to say on the topic, anyway."

"No. I'm saying the parade, or whatever the hell it is, is stopping here," Raidon clarified.

Deck immediately crossed to the window, Jenny on his heels. In the growing darkness, he could see figures lining the streets with torches crossed above them like an honor guard. To the right, at the far end of the street, more figures began to emerge from the shadowy darkness.

Beside him, Jenny clenched her fists then swore, whirled around and grabbed her jacket. "That's no parade, Raidon. That's Parliament. They've sent an envoy. We've got to get out of here."

Too late. A knock on the door froze them all in their tracks.

Chapter Eight

They shifted into high gear, even as the pounding on the door intensified. Jenny put her hair up in a ponytail and joined the two men in packing for a quick exit: Throwing on clothes, buckling body armor, stuffing belongings into bags . . . Ammunition rolled across the floor, toiletries crashed everywhere and—

"Open the damn door!"

The desk clerk. Jenny actually breathed a little easier.

Raidon killed the lights, then motioned for Jenny and Deck to flatten against the wall behind the door. He got down on his hands and knees and looked through the crack where light was spilling onto the floorboards. Then he stood up, unlocked the door, and opened it, thrusting the muzzle of his gun through the smallest possible sliver of space. "What?"

"I'm alone. Open the damn door."

Deck looked at Jenny. She nodded, and they slowly brought their weapons up, holding them flat against their bodies.

The heavy opened the door and aimed his weapon at the desk clerk's head. But the man hadn't lied; he was alone, tapping his foot on the mangy carpeting. "Nice manners."

Raidon let him in, and everyone took a deep breath.

The desk clerk walked straight over and pointed his finger in Jenny's face. "Trouble. Capital T. You pay me double tonight or you're outta here."

"I'm not sure that's going to be an issue," she said.

He strode past her and flicked out a small, slightly stained, parchment calling card between two fingers. He offered it to Deck. "They'll be waiting."

Deck took the card, and the clerk stormed out without another word. " 'Parliament requests the pleasure of your company.' " he read. "Sounds friendly enough," he added drily.

"They aren't friendly," Jenny warned.

"They certainly have good manners."

"Depends on your point of view." She peered at the card. "It seems they know what you are. They know you're a blue blood of some sort. Hence the invitation. Although I'm a little hazy about what exactly you're being invited to do. They must have gotten a tip from someone on the transport, or through the gates . . . but I'd still be surprised if they know exactly who you are." She nervously tightened her ponytail. "They would have said."

Raidon looked like a cat with its hackles up. "How do you propose we handle this?"

"I think we should run," Jenny said. "The best course of action is to run, and only fight if absolutely necessary. Killing or hurting one of them will make things exponentially worse here."

Deck looked at her strangely. "You think we should run?"

"Well, there's only, gee, a few hundred people outside. Do you think we should fight?"

"That's not what I meant. I think that if they consider me of equal social standing, then perhaps I should act the diplomat and play this thing out as if I were planning to pay them a call all along. It would be unexpected. Running merely makes us look as though we've done something wrong."

Bingo. But this wasn't the time to fess up. Jenny argued, "Don't go to them, Deck. Don't be stupid. Something tells me there will be plenty of other opportunities. I really don't want to have to go to the club and break you out."

Raidon went back to the window. Jenny could hear the clicking sound of him fiddling with the safety on his gun.

A slow thumping rhythm stirred outside, a sort of bass line for the cacophony of barking dogs and humans shouting in the streets.

"Night of the living dead, or what?" he said. "Let's make a decision, already."

"You're not kidding," Jenny muttered. "Let's get out of here."

Deck zipped up his armored vest and covered it

with his jacket. "You stay here. I'm going down to meet them."

"No, you're not," Raidon said, grabbing him by the collar of his coat.

Jenny's eyes went wide.

"I still call the shots," Deck said fiercely. "If you don't want to follow me, you're free to leave anytime."

"Yes, you lead. Regarding everything except jeopardizing your life when there are other options," the heavy said firmly.

The thumping built to a crescendo outside. Jenny peered through the window as a mob congregated at the end of the street, and then suddenly, out of the mass of animals and people, a group of the Parliament rode into view.

They approached the hotel in procession: Five black horse-hybrids nearly blending into the night bearing five gentlemen riders. Prancing and rearing, spooked by the flames and the dogs and the noise of the crowd, the beasts made their way down the boulevard toward the hotel.

As they passed, the crowds on either side cheered loudly, vaguely demonic in their exultation. Jenny could tell the riders were high-ranking members of the club. Top hats, scarlet riding jackets, white breeches, gaudy watch guards, black Hessian boots—all were also accessorized with night vision goggles gleaming translucent neon green. Almost beside the point were the armored plackets strapped to their arms and legs, and the machine guns and swords attached to their horses' rigging.

They were dressed for a hunt.

Jenny cursed under her breath. "Um, guys? We're out of here. Now!"

Deck nodded, but a gleam of aggression sparked in his eyes. "From what you've described, there's nothing a little value won't smooth over here."

Raidon looked at Jenny pleadingly. She nodded. He stepped behind her and opened the door, making sure the hallway was clear.

She said to Deck, "You sound like a man who isn't used to *not* being able to throw value on a problem." He didn't budge. Jenny grabbed him by the collar and got in his face. "Now you listen to me, hotshot. You recruited me for a reason. Because I know what's what out here. When I say going down there is a bad idea, you need to believe me. If you really understood what Parliament was all about, I'd be okay with you calling the shots. But you're paying me to do a job. Let me do it."

Raidon called from the hallway.

Jenny doubled her grip on Deck's collar and held him firm. "We run," she hissed through her teeth. Then she booked out the door. To her relief, Deck followed behind her.

They headed straight for the far window, agreeing with a look and a shout that it made more sense to go up than down to where the Parliament was holding court. Raidon flung open the shutters only to find that the mob had stormed the hotel like marauders, coming up from the streets to hang off the fire escape and jeer at the wishful thinking of the night's prey.

Deck turned and ran back down the hall, Jenny

and Raidon right behind him. Raidon pointed to the staircase at the opposite end; Deck was already there. But no sooner had he opened the door, than a flood of people poured in.

Swept up in the storm, forced down the stairs and thrust through the outer doors onto the road, Jenny thought she might be ripped to shreds. A thousand hands reached out for her, grabbing and scratching and hitting her face and body and bag.

She lashed out with her knife. It dug into flesh and stuck there, disappearing along with the screams of her victim as she was swept down the street.

The sound of a trumpet pierced the air.

A ways away, Jenny could see the members of Parliament surrounded by their hounds, hands in the air, demanding silence. The crowd complied, still bucking at the men holding them back from the street on either side.

The yelling and screaming slowed to a rumble, the rumble to a dead silence, pierced only by a periodic bark from one of the dogs straining at the end of a leash. As silence fell, the mob moved to the curb, away from Jenny, Deck, and Raidon, who remained panting in the middle of the emptying street.

Jenny gathered her wits and slowly looked up. Blood streamed from Raidon's nose. He dabbed at it in reflex as he watched Deck rise from the ground at the feet of the parliamentary quintet, now dismounted.

The five stood in formation, a lieutenant now on either side, and with more Parliament winging out in a pyramid behind them. This second level of the membership were equals in dress with their long sideburns, impossibly high starched collars, and carefully knotted cravats, but these men held back dogs, their fingers twitching on the leash release clips.

Jenny looked at Deck, his knees bent, shifting his weight from side to side, his fingers twitching. He was rumpled, battered, and very, very angry. She sent him a mental message: *Don't attack.*

With a bow and a tip of his hat, the first dandy lifted his arm and very gracefully pointed to the opposite end of the torchbearer-lined street. He uttered one word.

"Run."

Deck looked at Jenny and then at Raidon, but there simply wasn't anything else to be done.

They ran three abreast down the street in a bizarre steeplechase, leaping over empty toxic-waste barrels, dodging buckets of water and random garbage thrown by the spectators lining the streets. Deck tried to dodge a piece of plywood cartwheeling through the air, but they were clearly gunning for him. It tagged the back of his heel and he went sprawling.

"Keep going!" he yelled as he got to his feet. The dogs had almost overtaken him.

Raidon and Jenny kept sprinting as fast as they could. Jenny thought she could actually hear the toenails of the dogs clicking against the pavement, but she forced herself on. Raidon glanced over at her, his expression determined. A huge overturned cart blocked the middle of the street. They leapt over it and just kept moving.

Jenny's throat was on fire. She could feel herself slowing even as the dogs caught up with her, running alongside them. Teeth bared, mouths foaming, overly muscled—it was as if they'd been bred for more than just the chase.

The street curved into a section of town Jenny had seen before. The dogs were snarling at her feet, snatching at the leather of her boots. One good bite and she'd be upturned on the ground. And then what?

Curving around the bend, Jenny lost her footing, dizzy from oxygen deprivation. She slowed down, losing ground, but it didn't matter. Parliament had run them around to the back of the club, defended on one side from the lowest riffraff in town by an impenetrable concrete wall lined along the tops with Roman-inspired statuary. A dead end.

She and Raidon whirled around. Before them was a line of nervous dogs, twitching and barking and licking their chops.

Jenny bent down with her hands on her thighs, trying to catch her breath. Raidon had his hands clasped on top of his head trying to do the same, clearly distressed as he looked back. Deck was held by several men.

"I don't care what they want, they're not getting him without a fight," Raidon cried in rage.

"For God's sake, we're insanely outnumbered. Be smart. They'll kill you. In front of all these people, they'd have to kill you if you made a move. We'll figure something out. . . ."

Raidon looked murderous, the lust for blood filling his eyes. He lunged at one of the guards holding Deck and was descended upon like a pack of hounds around a fresh kill.

Someone rammed Jenny from behind, and she fell into the gutter. A foot on her back held her down, a hand on the back of her head pushed her face into the filthy water and held it until she wrenched loose.

She lifted her head up, choking and spluttering. Her gaze sought Deck, who was shielding his eyes from the torches, soaked to the bone on his hands and knees in stagnant water, encircled by a mob of townsfolk. His jaw worked as he looked around. It was obvious that he was the center of attention.

Slowly but surely, Parliament's practiced formation broke down as they put their people between him and Jenny and Raidon, pointedly ignoring all but the one who "belonged."

Raidon noticed it at the same time. "They only want Deck."

"Enough!" someone cried out. And more Parliament moved in to force back the crowd.

But the crowd wasn't satisfied. They wanted more of a show. As the Parliament guarded their prey, the others turned their attention on the nearest thing they could get their hands on. Through her bleary vision Jenny saw men launch themselves at a utility pole, rocking, pushing, and beating at it until the base came loose.

The pole began to fall, loosening wires and sending a shower of sparks through the air. The crowd roared in approval.

"Get out of the water!" Raidon yelled, himself up to his shins in the stuff.

Jenny couldn't quite make it to her feet in time, and she had to crab-crawl backward as fast as she could to safer ground.

"Pleased to make your acquaintance, sir," she heard the dandy say to Deck in clipped tones, hauling him to his feet. "If you please, show me your empty hands." Deck had lost his weapons a long time ago. He slowly raised his empty hands in the air. Satisfied it was safe, the others descended on him.

Jenny tried to call out, but her words were lost between the din and the filthy water in her lungs. Deck looked so proud, so strong, even dripping with slime and taken against his will. She blinked, her heart in her throat as the common people of Newgate bowed down before the horse-drawn carriage, bearing the crest of Parliament centering on a carefully fashioned "P" of twisted metal, which was taking him away.

All but forgotten as the crowd dispersed, Jenny staggered through the stagnant water to help Raidon to his feet.

Chapter Nine

"This is not good. Not good at all." Raidon hurriedly dumped the contents of his knapsack out on the rooftop, sending pieces of equipment scattering and tinkling across the gravel. Suddenly, he stopped working, jogged to the corner of the rooftop, and vomited again. He'd been ill for the last hour from the parasites in the water he'd ingested. Jenny didn't want to think about what it meant that the parasites didn't affect her anymore.

He returned to their worksite, gargled with antibiotic, and rinsed his mouth out. Without a word of complaint, he got to work once more.

Jenny patted his back and turned to her own task, drilling an anchor clip into the very edge of the rooftop. "Everything's going to be fine."

"Does that mean they won't hurt him?"

"Well, um, no. I don't have the faintest clue what's up their sleeve, but it seems to me there wouldn't be much point in killing him right now. I mean, after capturing him? They could rough him up, but hopefully we'll get to him soon enough to minimize any damage."

"Are you kidding me? 'Minimize the damage?' His Lordship isn't a package."

"Hey, calm down. Really, when you think about it, it's sort of par for the course. I should have expected it."

Raidon froze. "What the hell does that mean? Par for the course? How is His Lordship getting kidnapped by a bunch of crazy people in top hats and breeches par for the course?"

"I'm just saying it's sort of part of the rhythm of this place. The give and take. The ebb and flow. Parliament comes out as a show of strength and sort of reminds everyone that they run things, piss around to mark their territory, and wait for us to give a response so they can see who we are and what we have to offer."

"There must be hundreds of people flowing into Newgate each day. Why are they so interested in us?"

"We should have considered some sort of blood mask for Deck prior to giving his sample at the immigration gates. It would have made him pretty ill for the flight, though. Obviously, they've detected his upper-class lineage."

"They know who he is?"

"No, probably they know *what* he is. And what he is, is one of them."

"He is *not* one of them," Raidon muttered, putting his bulk in front of her to take charge of the anchor.

Jenny elbowed him out of the way. "You're making me nervous. I didn't think you were the panicky type."

"I'm not panicking. I'm just not used to dealing with the unknown."

"Yeah? Well, it's your lucky day, because dealing with the unknown seems to be a specialty of mine."

"Maybe that's just a nice way of saying that you attract trouble. At some point, when we're done with this little operation, you're going to have to fill me in on what went down the last time you were here."

"Stop worrying." But Raidon looked more concerned than she'd ever seen him. She finished testing the buckles on her chest harness and took the heavy by the shoulders, making him look at her. "They were way too interested in Deck to harm him. Really. And we're moving pretty quickly here. By the time I'm inside those walls, maybe half an hour will have lapsed."

"That's enough time to put a bullet through someone's head," Raidon remarked.

"Trust me on this—They don't want to kill him. They want to . . . to . . . to assimilate him or something. I'd go so far as to say that they may want us to come get him. Okay, I've got the anchor in and the harness hooked up. You pull on it and see what you think."

Raidon tugged, his expression showing he was pleasantly surprised with her work. Then he shaded his eyes and looked across the wide boulevard toward the Parliament Club, its massive second story and steeple visible above the vast surrounding stone wall.

"You really think this is a better approach than simply walking through the front door and negotiating his release?" Raidon asked. "I thought I was the muscle and you were the brain."

She gave him a look and finished tying off the rope. "Nice one, but sorry, no dice. First of all, we'd never get past the guards. They're instructed not to allow riffraff from off the street past them. Secondly, for personal reasons I don't want to be recognized or remembered. Basically, I can't voluntarily walk into Parliament Club. It would be suicide, and I have an impossible dream of getting out of this place again."

He gave her a keen look.

She tightened the stay and patted herself down. "Ready to go."

She looked across the boulevard at her target. "I swear to God, that setup Deck's giving me . . . it better be worth a ton."

"You don't have to pretend," Raidon said.

"Excuse me?"

"You don't have to pretend about any of it," he repeated gently. "That you're not worried about him. That you're not scared to go in there. I'm both of those things, but it doesn't make me any less competent. It's obvious you're good at what you do. I won't pretend I didn't have doubts at first. But no more."

Jenny stared at him, frozen, and then cleared her throat. "Thanks. I appreciate that."

"And for what it's worth, His Lordship also has a pretty good idea of how much of you is bark and how much is bite."

She snorted disdainfully, though she couldn't

help feeling it was almost more of a compliment on the part of both men. "Don't think I'm out of surprises. Speaking of which, there's something about you I just can't figure out."

He raised an eyebrow.

"Why you do what you do."

"I beg your pardon?"

"Why do you stay with him? Put your life on the line for him. He's not part of the monarchy anymore."

Raidon gave her a bitter half smile. "No, it's . . ." He swallowed hard. "I swore an oath, Jenny. I swore on my life and the lives of my family that I would defend him above all others."

"That's rich. Given that he doesn't believe in the monarchy anymore, you'd think he'd release all his liegemen."

"He has. I haven't accepted." He shrugged. "I gave my word."

Jenny gave him a dubious look. "You're crazy, you know that?"

He just shook his head, confusion evident for a moment in his eyes. "It's who I am," he said. Then, suddenly, his expression hardened. "And it's also what makes me have to tell you that while I'm very fond of you, there's only so much I'm willing to tolerate."

Jenny narrowed her eyes and stopped working on the harness. "What are we talking about here?"

"You and His Lordship. He has a destiny, Jenny."

"A destiny? Uh-huh." She kicked at some gravel.

"That business back at the hotel . . . the teasing, the innuendo, it's not helpful in the big picture."

Raidon ran his enormous hand through his hair like a harassed mother.

"So, it's working?" Jenny asked with a laugh.

His look was furious. "No matter what Deck says, his blood is still royal, through and through. He's above us. He's *above* us. Please, I beg you. Don't get in his way. If you do . . . I will get in yours."

Jenny's smile disappeared. She gave Raidon a long, hard look, then bent down and returned to testing the anchor. "I'm just about done here," she said curtly. Switching the subject, she said, "Do you remember that trouble we were speaking about earlier? My trouble? Well, it's the sort of trouble that means you really don't want to get yourself in a situation where they start running DNA tests for a profile match. The goal here is to remain anonymous."

"Oh. And crashing through the window will be inconspicuous?"

"It's better than walking in the front door. Remember, we agreed it was going to be a quick smash and grab. I'm going in, tracing Deck, and getting him the hell out of there."

"If he's capable of walking," Raidon grumbled.

"Just stick to the plan. We don't want to risk you getting picked up and . . . say, deleted."

Raidon looked dubious. "It's inevitable, really. If they're interested in 'deleting' His Lordship, I should think at some point they'll take an interest in who His Lordship is with."

She ignored his complaint. "Test this hold." She pulled as hard as she could on the anchor, and it didn't budge. She surveyed her target through a magnifier lens. "Stained-glass hologram. Nice. It shouldn't make a sound."

Raidon nodded, then gestured to her rather unsubstantial hat. "Here, take my helmet. It's adjustable."

She nodded and took off her hat, then donned the helmet he offered. She lowered the visor. "This thing's nice," she said, her voice muffled.

Suddenly, Jenny felt her comm pack at her hip vibrate. The noise instantly generated a bolt of adrenaline. She and Raidon looked at each other, real fear and concern in their eyes. "He triggered the locater!"

Raidon looked sick. "Maybe I should be the one to go in. The rope will hold my weight."

"Raidon, at this trajectory and with this equipment, you'd drop like a lead block and slam into the side of the building ten feet below the window. No offense, but you've got to trust me. Now, go down to the street and hire a getaway vehicle like we agreed. Keep tabs on the signaler and be ready to help me."

He grumbled something about half-assed plans, then said louder, "*No offense*, but this all seems really badly thought up. When we get His Lordship out of there, I want to sit down and do some serious planning."

"How can we make a plan when I don't know what the hell is going on?"

"Well, with all due respect, it's time for His Lordship to come clean. I'm willing to go on trust when required, but if we're going to be effective as a team, Lord D'ekkar is going to have to tell you what's up."

Before Jenny could respond, Raidon suddenly took her by the shoulders and turned her toward him. "I know what I said earlier doesn't sit well with you, but I'm still . . ." The heavy pulled her close to him in a hug made awkward by their combined bulky armor. "I'm still looking out for you. Be careful, kid."

"Don't worry. I live for this stuff." Jenny looked up and tugged a couple more times on the anchor for good measure. Then she jogged back all the way to the far end of the roof, sprinted across the gravel, and jumped over the side into nothingness.

Chapter Ten

Deck lolled against the back of an overstuffed velvet drawing room chair that smelled like cheap women's perfume and mildew. He'd been delivered to the Parliament Club in a horse-drawn carriage still sopping wet, his hands bound, and a dull ache in his head from the "hunt" as they'd termed it.

He had two things on his somewhat muddled mind: Jenny and Raidon's fate, and the best strategy to use to get the hell out of this place.

Of course, there was nothing he could do about the former without nailing the latter. As far as strategy was concerned, the truth happened to be his best option, anyway. Parliament seemed to want him to be an aristocrat, and he could deliver. The big question was whether they knew exactly who he was. Unless they brought it up, he wouldn't provide them with the details of his background.

Several people entered the room; he could see

their colorful jackets meld in front of his blurred vision. Like peacocks, they were. And for them, he could be one too. A lord, yes. In particular, a lord fallen from grace. A condition that undoubtedly paralleled the vast majority of dossiers in this house.

As the room filled, Deck realized he'd have a large audience. He forced himself to sit up straight, blink the water out of his eyes, and concentrate on projecting as dignified an image under his current drowned-rat/bound-wrists circumstances as he could. Image was everything.

Two lackeys unbound his hands, and Deck bowed his head in decorous thanks. "A good hunt," one lackey said to the other, a look of respect in his eyes.

"I think the crowd had quite the evening's entertainment," the second replied.

He'd maintain a gentleman-like demeanor and appeal to them as a brother of sorts. He wouldn't try to fight against them unless absolutely necessary.

Flushed and glassy-eyed; it was difficult to believe these men were the power-brokers of Newgate. They hardly looked capable of getting up in the morning. Deck's lip curled slightly and he looked away. Did he see something of himself here?

This was not the time to show weakness.

Deck sat down and placed his hands on the table-top to give the impression he was harmless. He had to resist the urge to wipe his palms off as a layer of grime glued to his sweaty skin.

"Is this your first visit to Newgate?"

"Yes, it is."

"We hope your stay will be very pleasant."

"Thank you very much. I'm sure it will be." This was surreal. They'd hunted him down like quarry, beaten the crap out of his traveling companions, bound and kidnapped him, and now wanted to treat him like a gentleman? Their idea of hospitality was certainly unusual.

"We make a point to make the acquaintance of all members of the peerage who come this way. My name is Lord James. You are?"

Deck had to think fast.

He certainly wouldn't mention his ties to Kyber. He'd give them the name Valoren, his mother's name. It was the name he'd only recently adopted after learning the truth of his birth. The Han name he'd stopped using anyway—it was a dead giveaway.

"Deck Valoren. Equally pleased to make your acquaintance."

"Ah, Lord Valoren. Excellent.

"Forgive my abruptness," the dandy continued, "but there are generally two reasons one such as yourself travels out this way. Either you are a new resident," he stated delicately, "or you are here on business. May we inquire as to the nature of your stay?"

Deck stalled for time by clearing his throat and readjusting his posture in the uncomfortable chair. Should he play the loose, dissipated aristocrat exiled to debtors prison, or the shady black-marketeer in Newgate on business? Either story could work. Better to admit to having a business purpose. They could probably corroborate any purported criminal judgments that landed inhabitants out here. Again, the truth. Always the truth, when possible.

"Business," he said with a smile.

One Parliamentarian took a pinch of snuff, another poured something that resembled sherry into cracked, filthy cordials.

"I'm looking into an investment," Deck added after a moment's pause. "Something outside of Newgate proper," he added hastily.

The leader put down his glass. "Do you know who we are?"

Deck bowed his head. "I do. I've been looking forward to making your acquaintance."

The man's eyebrow arched upward. "Ah. Indeed? We make a point to remain relatively unknown outside Newgate. Then you know . . . How to put this? There is a—shall we call it a tax?—that we assess on all business conducted."

"Yes, of course. I understand," Deck answered quickly.

The man waved his hand. "If you please to describe the nature of your business."

Deck studied the men's faces. They were glassy, stiff, relatively emotionless. He cleared his throat again. Jenny had told him that at heart, these men were a power company, assessing fees and collecting value. Best to address that directly, make it clear he was expecting to pay the tax, was completely ready to cooperate. Then perhaps it would be as simple as negotiating a fee and they would let him go.

"I am setting up a small factory, to test some telecom ideas. It will require a small amount of power." He took a small sip of wine. "I am prepared, of course, to negotiate a reasonable fee for energy expended."

"Excellent. Your plan is to visit this factory?"

Deck paused, and again chose to tell the truth. "Yes, I'm taking a small team—a few staff members—to have a look at our progress."

"Excellent. Lord Quinn will join you."

Deck sat forward. "I beg your pardon?"

"Lord Quinn will join you in order to assess the appropriate fee for use of our power grid."

"My lord, if I may. It's not a pleasant journey ahead. We'll be traveling to the outback."

"I'm sure Lord Quinn will enjoy the fresh air."

"Why not simply discuss the information and come to a reasonable solution right now? It would save you the trouble of sending a man out on such an arduous journey."

Lord James leaned back in his chair, his bejeweled fingers wrapping around his grimy goblet. "No." His voice was firm, his eyes glittering with a slightly menacing look.

Deck inwardly groaned and opened his mouth to further the argument, but apparently the discussion was officially over. Which was too bad. Frankly, he was a hell of a lot more comfortable with business than with joining them in some sort of ghoulish charade. Attention turned to the door as it opened, and one of the lieutenants entered.

"Lord Quinn has arrived. We can begin."

Lord Quinn was a man concerned with appearances. He bowed in greeting, catching Deck's eye and studying his face. He straightened his clothes and looked as if he'd washed up a bit for the event. He introduced himself by way of a bow, then posed against the mantel of the fireplace in a manner that seemed calculated to show off his best side—although from Deck's point of view, he didn't exactly have one. Then he produced a battered silver cigarette case with a bit too much flourish to be taken absolutely seriously. He offered one of three cigarettes, which appeared to have been previously smoked to varying degrees, and laughed softly when Deck politely declined. With a mannered bow, he took one for himself.

Like several others in the room, Quinn appeared to be one of the lieutenants, a lackey for the triumvirate who seemed to rule the place. In Deck's experience, it was always this second tier, those who could just see true power but couldn't quite reach it, who were the most unpredictable operatives in any management system. And that made them the most dangerous.

The men gathered around, with Deck in his ridiculous, reeking chair as the center of attention, and Deck realized that this unusual meeting, which had begun with him as a rabbit to their proverbial hounds, had nothing to do with business and everything to do with some sort of fraternal initiation process. Why didn't they ask him more questions? Was it because they already knew what they wanted to know?

In the back of his mind, Deck thought again about

Jenny and Raidon. Were they injured? Were they already up to something else?

Lord Quinn opened a satin-lined case, pulled out a tray and placed a syringe on the table. It wasn't the needle itself that brought bile into Deck's mouth; it was the filth all-together. Peculiar tools were all jumbled onto the tray, plastic tubing, random screws and caps, a brownish stain on the grimy towel lining.

And the sickly sweet perfume emanating from the chair was making him that much more nauseated. Or was the nausea from the blows to the head he'd taken when they'd brought him in?

Something about the tools and the crowding, the jostling over and about him triggered the memories. Memories of being beaten like a dog in a filthy prison in Macao. Memories of struggling against ropes tighter than even these. Of tasting his blood in his mouth and struggling to breathe past the panic.

Deck clenched his jaw. He'd been through this before. But Raidon had been there to pick up the pieces, and pick up the pieces was pretty much what the man had done. Shattered bones, some of which still ached. It was one thing to be wrongly imprisoned for a crime you didn't commit. It was another for your own brother—well, half brother, now, wasn't it?—to order your mistreatment in the bowels of a prison he'd never set foot in and probably couldn't conceptualize.

The jailors had been a pack of jackals, almost insanely pleased to be able to wreak terror on someone who'd fallen from grace, someone who'd once occupied such a lofty position in society. Only someone who'd been so oppressed could take such pleasure in hurting one perceived as part of the machine of oppression.

You said you didn't do it. They beat you. You said, of course you didn't do it. They beat you harder. How could they have thought he would try to murder his own father—a man he admired, respected, loved? How could Kyber have thought that even possible?

And you tried to make them understand, and instead merely learned from a kick in the gut and a fist to the face that there are few things worse in this world than being unable to explain yourself when circumstances make you look guilty. Jenny wasn't the only one who worried about betrayal.

A bead of sweat tickled its way down the side of Deck's face. He wiped it away with his shoulder.

The men around him gathered in a solemn circle, a frisson of energy passing through them as they murmured amongst themselves. These men were an odd sight, their graceful movements sluggish but distinctively refined; carefully petting at clothes that looked ratty and stunk of alcohol, antibiotic, sweat, and sickness not really camouflaged by the vast quantities of perfume they seemed to douse themselves with.

They seemed oblivious to their true condition, operating as if through a gauze curtain that separated what they wanted to see from what was reality.

Quinn picked up the syringe and injected a small quantity of watery brown-red fluid from a glass jar. He pressed down a bit, and a small amount of fluid squeezed out of the needle. One of the men caught it in his hands and licked the fluid off his fingers.

The corner of Lord Quinn's left eye twitched and he put two fingers up to his temple. He stared down at the floor for several seconds like this, and when he looked up, his eyes were glassy.

Deck fought a wave of panic as Quinn handed the syringe to Lord James and stepped back. Control. Everything always came down to control. Control your fear, your life, your emotions, your world. . . .

It wasn't that he'd rather die than face torture again, it was more that he didn't want to fail the revolution. And Jenny . . . she would laugh at that. Oh, Jenny, was it all going to be over before it had even begun?

"Please pay attention to what we are doing, Lord Valoren," Lord James said while hovering over him.

Pay attention. Should he think about the pain of the past or the pain of the present? Which would hurt more?

Deck forced himself to keep his eyes open and watch, trying to stave off the memories that flashed through his mind. But when they came at him, holding down his arms, holding him down in the chair, coming at him with the needle, he couldn't accept it without a fight. He roared out a war cry and kicked out with his legs.

There were simply too many of them. They held

him down. Covered his face with their hands. He struggled to remain calm. Felt the prick of the needle in his arm, the peculiar tingle beginning there and in his hand as the liquid distributed itself through his bloodstream.

And then they no longer had to hold him; he was struck with a wave of migraine and nausea so debilitating he could not move.

No longer did he feel quite so calm about the fate of his two companions. Jenny . . . oh, God. Was she even alive? What about Raidon? He'd seen his liegeman take a beating in the thick of it all. It did occur to him that if he himself died, Jenny would probably be stuck in Newgate indefinitely—unless she managed to cut another deal. How she'd escaped the first time was still an unanswered question.

Deck panted, hanging his head on his chest, squeezing his eyes shut against the pain in his temples. Someone lifted his chin, forcing him to pay attention to his surroundings.

The men filled cracked goblets with wine, then used an eyedropper to squirt some of the same fluid from the syringe into each. Deck sat alone in a chair trying to regain his bearings, watching the malevolent aristocrats gathering in a circle, their backs to him. Only . . .

They turned to face him.

"Welcome to the brotherhood," Quinn said, a smarmy smile on his lips.

The circle of Parliament raised their goblets and repeated the toast.

Only they no longer . . . Flashes and breaks in reality showed the cracked and filthy goblet, which contained a murky substance with something oily floating in it, to be wine in perfectly cut, spotless, gold-rimmed crystal.

Blurryness. And then there was a moment when Deck seemed to completely black out. And in the next, there was that pure, pure clarity of vision, with colors and textures more saturated, more sumptuous than he'd ever seen in his life—more so than even at the palace where no expense had been spared.

Where Quinn's clothes had looked ragged and tired, now Deck saw a beautifully sewn garment in the Regency style with boots in supple black leather. Where he'd seen a room with shredded wallpaper and decrepit furnishings, now he saw brocades, toile, rich mahoganies.

Deck's feelings of joy, pleasure, excitement, and relief were interrupted by terror, reality, and bursts of searing pain. His heartbeat accelerated to the point where he thought he might collapse. Deck swallowed, his mouth horribly dry, his head spinning. This was what it felt like to be driven insane.

Quinn offered another goblet. "Drink this. It's . . . neutral."

There was no way he would take more voluntarily. Deck thrust his hand out to push the goblet away, missing entirely, his depth perception shot, his vision still in flux.

"It's pure . . . well, as pure as a water substitute is

around here. You need something to dilute." Quinn sounded almost wistful as he added, "It's so strong when you're new."

"I need to go," Deck said, his words sounding slurred. He stood up unsteadily.

Quinn stood up alongside him. "No need to rush, old boy. You're not a prisoner here, but I suggest you wait it out a bit more."

Deck batted Quinn's hand away. "Jenny," he called uncertainly, although he couldn't quite piece together what he wanted with her.

"Ah. The girl?" Quinn prompted.

"She's my . . . She's my . . . my . . ." He shook his head, too muddled. Deck took a step, and nausea passed through him. He looked at Quinn, almost blinded by the sheer brightness of the colors in the room where once he'd only seen dingy grays and browns. He blinked uncertainly, beginning to feel angry. He slumped.

"Don't be unhappy. The opiate makes everything seem better. Including women," Quinn remarked.

"I don't understand a damn thing you're saying," Deck said angrily—or meant to. His words no longer sounded particularly intelligible, either. He lurched to a more upright position and managed to stumble to the wall, which looked like it was wallpapered in rust-colored silk where it had formerly appeared simply white with rust-colored water stains. "This isn't real," he said thickly. "I'm in the same room, and what I'm seeing isn't real."

"Says whom? If you see it, it must be so."

Deck just shook his head, self-consciously feeling

like a small child about to throw a tantrum. "I'm go. Going. I'm going."

Quinn sighed. "I won't keep you, if you insist on leaving. Until next time. I look forward to our journey." Deck didn't argue; it was all he could do to keep his attention on the notion that he should be looking for the nearest exit.

Quinn took him by the shoulders and rotated him. "Straight ahead, old boy, if you insist."

Deck bowed as steadily as he could, then walked purposefully through the doors, slammed into the door frame in as dignified a manner as he could muster, stumbled out of the building, through the gates, and slipped through the first side alley where he sat down on a trash can that was actually starting to look like a trash can. Most of the time. Except that it was a green satin cushion now. And now a trash can again. . . .

He stood up once more and stared down at the offending seat, then stumbled as far as he could down the alley until the churning colors and confused appearances were simply too much to go on.

He fumbled in his coat for his comm pack, and thought he managed to turn the thing on, only praying that no one out here thought it worth intercepting his signal. And he sat staring down the alley in a daze at the intricate weave of the architecture that was the Parliament Club, wondering how long it would take for this poison to wear off. And if it ever would.

Chapter Eleven

Adrenaline seared through her as she fell, and then the anchor locked in place. Jenny squeezed her legs together, pointing her toes as she made a beautiful sweeping arc in the air straight toward the window . . . only to realize in the last possible second that it was not a stained-glass hologram after all—it was actual stained glass.

She burst through like a ten-ton force, multicolored shards shooting out around her, and just barely remembered in the midst of her surprise to release the harness clip as she overshot her mark. Flying across the dim room, she slammed gracelessly into the opposite wall. She slid in a heap on the floor, slightly stunned. She groaned, poked at a couple of ribs that seemed particularly sore, and self-consciously glanced around to see if anyone had witnessed her dismount.

A scuffling sound came from the room below. She

stood up and cocked her weapon, flattening herself against the wall next to the door. She peeked out and didn't see anybody, although the sweeping cameras were obviously aware of her presence. "They want us to come get you," she murmured. "But why?"

The comm pack at her hip began buzzing. Deck's emergency signal. He was in trouble. Frankly, she was surprised he'd triggered the signal and was a little more than worried that she'd underestimated the severity of Parliament's intent toward him. Of course, it was also possible they'd searched and lifted the comm pack from him and were triggering the signal as a trap.

Very carefully, very quietly, she turned the door-knob and pushed open the door. Leading with her weapon, she took a step forward. The blade of a sword came down from the side and touched her neck.

"Okay! Okay, I'm with you. I'm definitely with you." She held her free palm open to show her surrender and bent down to slowly place her gun at her feet. The sword blade followed, never relenting in its pressure. Once Jenny was down on the ground, her aggressor walked around to the front of her and eased up a little on his weapon.

"Jenny Red," the voice above her said.

Jenny turned her face and found herself staring at two shins clad in tights. For God's sake, the man was wearing tights!

"Oh, for God's sake!" she said aloud.

"Lord Quinn, at your service." He gracefully offered her help up by lowering his open palm to just below her chin. "Do watch the glass."

Lord Quinn. The name meant nothing, but the sight of his face shocked the hell out of her. She'd seen him before. Before she'd run for her life with blood still dripping from her hands. Still, she couldn't place his exact role in that night. No matter; it couldn't be good. She had to get herself away from him, to find Deck, to get the hell out.

"We meet again," he said gallantly.

Jenny sighed heavily, put her hand in his, and stood up. He brushed his lips over the knuckles of her black leather glove, blue, green, and red splinters of glass glistening on his mouth.

She could count on one hand the number of noblemen she'd met personally, and yet they still continued to appear out of nowhere to torment her. Bad karma, or something. Nah, she didn't believe in coincidence anymore.

She angrily brushed the glass shards from her clothes, crunching them beneath her boots. "Damn it!" She threw up her arms in surrender. "Well, don't I feel like the idiot? There's just nothing to make a person feel more foolish than staging a rescue with a really unnecessary dramatic entrance."

"Quite dramatic. We'll have to replay that on the monitors."

Jenny popped the visor on her helmet up since anonymity wasn't an issue anymore, and it was hard to breathe to boot, and took a closer look at the man who knew she'd killed a member of Parliament and still hadn't been paid back for it.

Lord Quinn had most likely been drop-dead gorgeous once, what with his big blue eyes and mop of curly hair. It was the sort of hair a girl might like to run her fingers through, if its owner wasn't borderline psychopathic. And in spite of his carefully selected attire, he was rough around the edges. The vice and misfortune that had landed him in Newgate had killed almost all the natural beauty he'd once had.

Oddly enough, she felt a wave of sympathy. She couldn't figure out why. Something in his eyes. Perhaps something she recognized: that trapped look. But she'd have to find out what they'd done to Deck before making any judgments.

Quinn cocked his head and swept his gaze down the curves closely encased in her leather uniform. "Mmm," he murmured a touch salaciously.

Any sympathy vanished as swiftly as it had come. She was never going to be a whore for Parliament. She'd killed one of the brethren once on that score, and she could see herself doing it again. "Excellent to see you again, Quinn," she lied. "So, where is he?"

"So abrupt," he *tsk*ed.

"What do you want with me?"

"I don't want you to reveal to your companions that we had a past."

"Deck's not stupid, Quinn. I don't know what you told him, but let me be the first to tell you that he'll see through any lies."

Quinn blocked the exit. "Where are you headed? We have business to discuss. Why don't you share with me what all this is about?"

"All what?"

"An aristocrat showing up in Newgate, seemingly

voluntarily. A former inmate who has escaped, returning to Newgate voluntarily in spite of unfinished business with Parliament. Returning for no good reason when—"

"I didn't escape from Newgate. I was just hiding. Unfortunately, at some point hiding becomes worse than dying." It was all a big fat lie.

"Have you come back to pay the price?"

"I don't owe anyone anything. I came to find Deck."

He studied her a bit longer. "Your protectiveness toward Lord Valoren is admirable but curious. Attachment doesn't come without a price. Nor loyalty without compensation. Not here." And then Quinn simply waited, his questions hanging in the air.

Deck's emergency signal still throbbed at Jenny's waist. "I know exactly what you mean," she said. She slowly backed up, assessing the various doorways and hallways for the most likely exit. "The guy's my meal ticket, and I'd like to know what you've done with him. So, if you're not planning to have me arrested or disappeared, I'll just get on with it."

"You don't wish to discuss business?"

"I have no interest in conducting business with you, now or at any other time—but thanks for the offer."

Softly, very softly, he sighed. "You may not wish to, but you will have to. You'll have to pay, Jenny Red. Parliament does not allow outstanding debts for much longer than you have taken. We've already been very generous."

"Oh, please. You didn't even know where I was."

Quinn smiled, and it chilled Jenny to the bone. Had they known where she was? And if so, why hadn't they done anything about it?

"Let me just plant a seed, if I may," Quinn said. "This 'investment' you are going to explore in the outback. I wonder there is not more to it than that."

"Okay. You wonder. And?"

Quinn looked at her.

"I'm not sure I understand what you're asking," she said innocently.

"Oh, bloody hell, girl," Quinn said, obviously much annoyed. "Let's not beat around the bush. I'm suggesting that you might wish to part with the information."

"Are you threatening me?"

"If I were, I hardly think you should be surprised. But I'm merely suggesting that if you're amenable, perhaps the two of us could enter into an arrangement."

She preferred not. While it was generally accepted that if one had to live in Newgate, living under the protection of Parliament was the best way to do it, Jenny hadn't even seen it that way—and that was the point of view that had gotten her into trouble with them in the first place. Accepting their patronage now—if patronage was really what they were offering, as opposed to the sort of servitude they'd wanted from her the first time around—would be a last resort. And Jenny had to believe it wouldn't come to that. If she allowed herself to believe it would, there would have been no good reason for her to sign on to this project with Deck in the first place.

"I'm not interested," she said. "But again, thanks." She turned toward the door, just itching to get out of the place.

Quinn shrugged languorously. "We have a long journey ahead of us. There's plenty of time for you to consider your options. Or perhaps I should say reconsider."

She slowly turned to face him. "We?" she asked. A sense of dread filled her.

"Yes, of course. The journey to the outback. I'll be joining you. As I indicated previously, we're very curious about His Lordship's investment out there."

Jenny's heart sank. "I really don't recommend it. It'll be much more ... primitive than what you're used to."

He smirked. "We all have to make sacrifices for the cause."

The cause? Did he mean Parliament's cause ... or Deck's revolution? Either way, Jenny was beginning to think Deck had told more than he should have. Had they hurt him? The possibility sank in. "So, um, where is he?"

Quinn didn't move. "I believe you just missed him."

Jenny squinted over her shoulder. "How so? He was just in here." She bit her lip. "He's ... outside all of a sudden?" Then why was his emergency signal still on? Suddenly, she felt true terror. "What did you do to him?"

Quinn smiled with some amusement. "*For* him."

"Great. You know that's crap."

Something in Quinn's eyes flickered, as if the man behind the posturing dandy was uncomfortable with the truth. The fear and uncertainty in him made her much more uneasy.

"Well, gotta run," she managed to say. She opened the first door, which happened to be a closet. "I haven't packed for the, er, journey yet." She ignored Quinn as he watched her open and close several more doors in the octagonal room. A sense of panic began to flood her senses.

Quinn came up next to her and said in a kindly, gentle manner, "The third door. Go to the end of the hallway, then take the grand staircase straight down to the front entrance."

Jenny nodded. "Oh. Right. Sorry again about the window. I thought it was a hologram."

Quinn's lips twisted into a knowing smile. "We'll simply add it to your tab." And then he bowed in farewell.

Chapter Twelve

Jenny hit the outside air with a huge sense of relief, and looked around. Raidon was nowhere in sight, and her heart sank. She stared wildly again in each direction, shocked to see what appeared to be Deck's boot peeking out from a side alley across the street. He was obviously lying on the ground.

She sprinted across the street.

Deck lay slumped on the ground, his back against the dank alley wall. He was still breathing. In fact, he was breathing rather heavily, laboriously, and his eyes were opening, shifting in some sort of constant delirium.

"Deck? Oh my God." She took a deep breath and exhaled, refusing to panic.

She checked his pulse. It was racing. His pupils were dilating in and out. And then she noticed his sleeve, carefully rolled up. She looked closely at his arm, and then ran her finger gently over the slight bruise at the bend in his elbow. The tiny evidence of a pinprick was revealed. She licked her fingers and smoothed away the faint smear of blood.

Deck's hand lashed out, and he grabbed her wrist in an ironclad grip, squeezing her fingers together painfully. He was looking straight into her eyes now, but was still totally out of it—totally out of control, which was not a state in which she could ever remember seeing him. She'd wished a time or two to wipe the arrogant look off his face . . . but not like *this*. Not like this.

"It's me," she said. "Jenny. Everything's going to be okay now. I'm going to get you home."

He eased up the pressure on her hand but didn't let go.

She put her other hand to his forehead. Through the fine sheen of sweat and moisture from the humidity glossing his skin, he was burning up. "Say my name, Deck. Just so I know you're okay."

Deck's eyes searched her face. "Jenny Red. You look more beautiful than I have ever seen you look in my lifetime."

She swore under her breath. "Now I know you're not okay. Let's get you a little more comfortable. Raidon should be here soon." She twisted her body and tried to put Deck's arm around her shoulder to move him, but he was too focused on her to care about his situation. He let his arm slide off her shoulder and snaked it around her waist. Jenny just looked at him a little helplessly. Such intensity from the man unnerved her. Excited her.

He moved his free hand up to her face and caressed her cheek, letting the arm around her waist slide away. Jenny swore under her breath and put her arms around his torso. She hoisted him to his knees with some success, propping him up against the brick wall. When she went to release him, he covered her arms with his own, turning their positions into a rather intimate embrace.

The humidity in the city seemed to have reached some sort of milestone. Deck was clearly overheated, and both he and Jenny were sweating in the hot dank mist of the alley.

She freed one hand and took him by the chin, forcing him to look her in the eye. "It's just me, okay? It's just an ordinary day, and we're the same as we've ever been. I don't think you really want . . . this." Her throat felt oddly clogged as she looked at his lips.

A strange glassiness clouded his eyes, and with his body against hers, she felt his heart skip a beat. Her own surged.

He looked lost. Hell, he *was* lost. Somewhere between Parliament and here, they'd screwed him up royally.

His arms suddenly fell away from her, and Deck lost his balance, crashing forward into the opposite alley wall. With Jenny underneath him. It was a mockery of an embrace, but only as far as she was concerned. Deck seemed serious. For once in his life, he seemed to have something other than the revolution on his mind.

He dug his teeth into the side of her neck, an electric shock Jenny wasn't prepared for, then kissed, nuzzled, and nipped his way toward her ear.

"Your eyes . . . so blue. Bluer than I remembered."

Jenny groaned deliriously. "Deck. You don't know what you're about. You'll regret this." She knew he would. And she would.

He didn't seem to notice. He was in flames, his mouth suddenly tasting hers in a kiss that caught her completely off guard. She felt incredibly alive, and his fingers madly tangled in her hair and stroked her skin. It seemed as if his entire being entered their kiss, was embodied in the luscious warmth of his tongue meeting hers. It was everything she could have imagined; everything she *had* imagined a hundred times or more.

He had absolutely no inhibitions, and apparently was operating under the assumption that neither of them did. And for a moment, it was true.

Jenny lost herself in him for a moment, in the idea of the two of them finally together, in the memory of how she'd once wanted him, in the fantasy of it all. There was no sense in refusing to admit that she loved the feel of his mouth on hers, the way his body seemed to reach for hers, his strong fingers so openly roaming her body, impossibly, impossibly . . . impossibly.

Impossible. And yet such a carnal response from him must be grounded in some small kernel of truth and reality.

He held her to him, biting delicately at her lower lip, the damp of his tongue caressing her lips. She could feel the power of his body holding back though, as if being so careful, so deliberate took great effort on his part—as if he might bury his sex in her with the slightest signal of acquiescence.

Torn, Jenny couldn't quite handle the intensity of his gaze. She twisted her body, trying halfheartedly to put space between them, but only managed to face the wall, with Deck pressing up behind her.

He was a man out of his head with desire. What had happened? How much of this was real? She couldn't imagine that he could feel so passionately about her, not having abandoned her all those years ago. If she wanted any reciprocation of her feelings, this was her chance. However delicious the moment, however she might store away this memory and suck in a quick hot breath in the dark quiet of future nights, the fact of it was that it surely wouldn't happen again. So Jenny gave in to him, gave herself up to sensation. Wherever he wanted to go, wherever he would take her, she would follow.

His hands wrapped around her torso, his fingers finding their way through her clothing to caress her breasts. His mouth was wet on the back of her neck, his groin pressed against her backside. He was hard and greedy, and if Jenny had ever had cause to wonder about his ability to desire her, he was answering that question now and forever.

"Ah, Jenny," he breathed into her ear on a sigh.

Jenny closed her eyes as a coil of pleasure built inside her. Deck's hands worked over her skin, and with her name on his lips, he slowly rocked himself against her.

"I want to see you," he whispered. "Look at me. *Look* at me."

Jenny glanced over her shoulder and stared into his eyes, aware of every nerve in her body. *How can the one man I can never really have be my destiny? But you're the one. I always knew it. I've been waiting for you all this time.*

"Get a room," someone said sarcastically, pushing by in the alley.

Deck lost his footing, Jenny her grip on the wall, and they stumbled apart. It was like being ripped from a beautiful dream.

And there was no going back. Raidon appeared at the mouth of the alley and came swiftly over, kneeling down between them, his eyes quickly taking in their thrashed and wild appearance with a frown.

"I can't control him," Jenny blurted.

"Try to get a hold on him for just one second." Raidon walked around to examine the bruises and the red streaks staining Deck's arm. Jenny moved forward and steadied Deck with a hand on each shoulder.

It was hard to tell who was shaking more. Deck stared back at her, but the spell was broken. She could see he was coming out of his altered state by the rapid dilating of his pupils, and Jenny could feel the moment slowly seep away.

Deck's pupils suddenly shrank and his expression hardened. "Get away from me," he said to Jenny, throwing her hands off him and looking wildly about. "It's not safe."

She slumped against the alley wall and stared at him. *You were never meant to really be mine,* she admitted to herself.

"My God, is he all right?" Raidon bent down and checked Deck's pulse.

"He will be," she said, her voice hoarse.

"He'd better be," Raidon snapped.

Jenny recoiled, and he immediately softened. "Sorry. You're not to blame. He *will* take chances. And there's nothing anyone can do about it. Not even me."

The drug in his bloodstream must have surged once more, because Deck very suddenly opened his eyes wide and began thrashing and flailing in Raidon's grip. "God, he's all over the place," the heavy complained.

"It seems like they jacked him up on FPs," Jenny said.

Raidon looked at her askance.

"He'll recover," she said numbly.

He'd recover and not remember a look or a touch or a word about any of this. She forced herself to focus on Raidon. "Do you know what's strange? They basically let us have him back free of charge. I went in there and they'd already let him go."

Raidon paused, mulling that over. "You're surprised it all wasn't bloodier, is that it? Because this whole experience has been pretty strange if you ask me."

"All I'm saying is that . . . is that . . . What am I saying?" Jenny trailed off as she remembered Quinn's

141

words. She'd been about to tell Raidon of their conversation, but suddenly opted to keep the exchange to herself.

Raidon was busy trying to make Deck a little more comfortable, and he made nothing of her hesitation. She watched him give Deck a cursory examination for broken bones, which she could have told him wasn't likely, and had to smile a little at Deck's belligerent reaction to the heavy's concern. Some habits were just real hard to break. Like her feelings for Deck. Or giving up a solid backup plan in the event things went hideously wrong. Even if it would require selling out to Parliament, and was fundamentally from her point of view a really bad idea, it was always good to have options. For a moment she struggled with the ethics of keeping the conversation secret, wondering for the millionth time if a lie of omission was really still a full-fledged, class-A, really-bad-idea lie.

Jenny decided it probably was. But she decided to keep it to herself, anyway.

Remembering Deck staring at her with lust in his eyes and desire on his lips . . . even so, she was very much alone. A backup plan was just good policy, insurance.

"I, uh . . . I dunno. I guess I'm just wondering if they suspect we're up to something more than whatever story Deck gave them." She bent down and smoothed a rakish lock of hair from his forehead. "Seems like he's coming down from the high."

Raidon looked at her and did a double take. "Say, are *you* okay? You look like you've seen a ghost. And you've got a cut on your jaw there. Probably from that glass."

Jenny swiped at her face. "I'm fine. We should move. You got that transport around here somewhere?"

"I told him I'd wave him over. I just wasn't sure where things stood."

She nodded and wondered for a moment how they might drag a raving, thrashing madman through the streets most inconspicuously. Of course, her next thought was that two people dragging a lunatic between them wasn't especially out of the ordinary.

She glanced down at Deck. His pupils still pulsed as the drug leeched from his bloodstream. He seemed to be in some sort of transition period, finding it difficult to reconcile what he was seeing in front of him from moment to moment—recoiling with horror for a time, then delirious with delight, and then half asleep.

Raidon waved the transport over, and as he lifted Deck into the backseat, Jenny had the unsettling sensation of being watched.

She looked across the street. Quinn leaned against the heavy gates of the Parliament Club, watching from under hooded lids as he exhaled a set of near-perfect smoke rings. As she got in the taxi and it drove away, through the window Jenny watched him toss his cigarette to the ground with a flourish and crush it with his boot.

Chapter Thirteen

Muffled whispers.

A shriek of laughter.

Deck rolled over in bed and winced from the pounding ache still in his head. He wasn't entirely recovered from the previous day's rather bizarre events. He flopped his arm off the side of the bed and searched the floor blindly for his canteen, finally making contact, then guzzling the brackish water inside as if it were the purified version he used to drink at home.

From the adjoining room, Raidon said in a voice choked with laughter, "What you did back there, setting up that rope swing, it was really impressive. So, I'm waiting there just long enough to make sure the anchor holds and you hit the target, and I'm watching, and you make this sweeping arc in the air like ballet or something and come up just perfect for the target . . . and it's a real window! You smash straight through a six-foot-high stained-glass window. A real window!"

"What's so funny? My dismount may have been a bit hinky, but like you said, the takeoff and in-flight technique were brilliant." Jenny's voice was filled with mock outrage, but obviously she was finding Raidon's amusement somewhat contagious.

"Your technique!? Your technique was . . ." The heavy choked on his laughter again. "You're so . . ." He couldn't even finish his sentence.

"Well, I work with what I've got, you know what I'm saying? No fancy academy training for me. Look, I would have sworn on anything you wanted that window was a hologram. I mean, who would pay for a real one here? And you didn't say any different." She started to laugh again. "Surprised the hell out of me, though."

"I can't believe no one caught you. It sounded so *loud* from the outside."

Jenny stopped laughing and cleared her throat. "I know. Lucky, huh? By the time I got inside, Deck was already out. And so I just followed the signal. . . ."

Deck closed his eyes and tried to block out the conversation. He felt an odd tugging sensation deep within him.

He was jonesing for those FPs, as Jenny had called them. Desperately jonesing for whatever the hell his "brothers" in Parliament had stuck him with yesterday. And yet he was quite certain he never wanted to experience them again.

That business with Jenny had him unsettled and

confused. Well, "business" wasn't exactly the word for it. She probably assumed he'd forgotten about it due to the drugs. But the FPs didn't seem to work that way.

No, he hadn't forgotten a thing, and in fact he had woken several times in the middle of the night, aroused beyond belief and unable to do a damn thing about it. Once it had something to focus on, his mind had fastened on to the memory of kissing her. Fastened on with full force. The FPs had projected his secret desires about Jenny, magnified them, and then ripped them away as he'd come down from the high. As he'd stared at her face in that alley, everything that he'd ever felt about her, every thought, every tiny speck of a moment, condensed into one powerful sensation.

The trill of her laugh filtered through the paper-thin wall once again. No, he hadn't forgotten a thing. He remembered the sense of being able to have anything he wanted, exactly what he wanted right then and there. He'd wanted Jenny. All at once he'd been blindsided by a collection of moments from the past—mere seconds, even—in which he'd wondered what it would be like to hold her, kiss her . . . Hell, he would have tried for as much as she was willing to give.

And so now he wanted more. Temptation. This was how it worked.

Deck ignored the wave of nausea that rolled through him as he sat up in bed, but he couldn't help wincing from the aches and pains all over his body. Jenny had been right about Parliament: Its members

147

were more dangerous than they looked. And the source of their control, the end-all and be all of their existence, was temptation.

He got up and found his clothes from yesterday draped over a chair, and suddenly a faint memory of his captors searching through his pockets jabbed at his brain. Quick to open the zippers, the hidden compartments of his clothing one after the other, he found . . . everything was still there, in the proper places.

Sighing with relief, Deck moved to the mirror hanging lopsided on the wall to study his bruises. He ended up simply staring into the eyes of someone who'd seen so clearly that he'd managed to muddle everything up. *Temptation.* For him, to tempt him, they'd used the drug. For others outside of the aristocracy, it would be something else. The promise of a better life, perhaps? The same sort of promise he had used to gain control over Jenny.

The only definitive thing separating Deck from the men of Parliament, self-styled aristocrats of another time, was self-discipline, self-control. It was the only defense against temptation, was its flip side. Many of those men, he suspected, had blood as exalted as his, perhaps even more so. And yet he could almost feel the traces of drug in his bloodstream tug at him, call to him.

Deck turned away from the mirror and let Jenny and Raidon's chatter once again meld into white noise. He was strong, but he couldn't ignore the demons that rose up before him. Why was he here? Was Jenny right? Was this about revenge? Or was it simply about desperately needing something to hold on to? He was a black prince, a bastard son. He was royal without a country, after all. He had no one to command, no imminent leadership role to play. Were those men at Parliament people with similar stories? Had the twin fates of overindulgence and deprivation been their ultimate downfall? Was this to be his fate, too?

For the first time since he'd begun work on plans for the communications depot, Deck began to wonder about his motives. It had seemed so simple, felt so clear. He'd thought he'd found his calling. Lying on the cold floor of Kyber's stinking, rat-infested prison, he'd carved out his given name, in all its pompous royal glory. D'ekkar Han Valoren. He'd scratched the letters into the stone walls, rejecting the idea that his new status as a royal bastard, a half brother, made him less of a prince.

And then, within a week, he'd tried to obliterate the words, his given name entirely, digging at the wall with a small rock until his fingers bled. He'd replaced it with his nickname, the name used by the only commoner he'd ever really known. *Deck.* Jenny's nickname for him.

He'd met a group of men in prison, rebels who spoke of revolution with the fervor of saints. They stood for something. Something important. Something that would help people. He'd listened eagerly, hanging on their words. He'd decided he could make a difference. He didn't have to stay mired in petty plans to overthrow the Han dynasty when he could help replace the world's monarchies with a better system on a much larger scale. He could back a system that treated everyone fairly.

He'd come to believe that everyone should have a choice, and that the only way to do that was via acquiring information. He'd had the know-how, the resources, and the drive to make anything happen—he'd sworn that if he ever got out of prison, he would take his early plans for revenge and dedicate himself to the fight. Everyone everywhere, in every coffee shop, library, store, bar, or whatever, would have access to freedom. That's what the Shadow Voice seemed to be about, which was why he'd been trying to help it.

But now, now he just wasn't so sure what this was all for. What did he truly believe? What did he want to believe? And what had he convinced himself to believe?

A squeal of laughter broke his focus. He turned and stared at the wall.

"You know, Raidon, you're sorta like the brother I never had," he heard Jenny say.

Great. They'd bonded over his sickbed. Why this should annoy him, he'd rather not analyze. It would come down to jealousy, and that was a small-minded sentiment. Yet he still felt irrationally annoyed that the two of them had already developed such an easy companionship. He should be pleased; it would ease the trip ahead.

He went into the washroom, freshened up at the basin, and then pulled some clean clothes from his bag to dress. The crash of what sounded like a box of ammunition scattering across the floor startled him, followed by a loud "Ssh!"

Deck opened the swing door and found Raidon on the floor, locked in a wrestling hold with Jenny sitting on top of him, bedsheets rumpled, pillows in disarray, bullets everywhere.

Jenny released Raidon, and the heavy scrambled away from her. "I beg your pardon, sir. We were just . . ."

"Bonding," Jenny finished, apparently trying not to laugh for Raidon's sake, who was struggling to regain his professional appearance by demonstrating excessively good posture. "Just letting off some tension."

Deck sat down on the side of the bed and tried to smile pleasantly, not at all confident that pleasantness was the impression he was projecting.

He stared at Jenny. She arched an eyebrow at him, then got up and went to her bag. Deck watched her rummage around for something, spritelike in a skimpy tank bra, shorts underwear, and, somehow adorably, heavy socks.

God, he'd been so very in the now with her in that alley. The moment played like a movie in his mind, only it was flat gray where it had previously been so much more vivid. He would love to see her one more time the way he'd seen her yesterday: senses amplified, magnified, saturated—her eyes supernaturally blue, her hair otherworldly in the radiance of its redness, the curves of her flesh pale, perfect, and without the bruises or scars that suggested she'd ever been done harm.

But even as intense as the magnificence he'd seen and felt had been, the emptiness he was experiencing now that the FPs had worn off was almost double. "I'd kill myself before I'd live like that," he muttered between gritted teeth.

"What's that?" Jenny asked, handing him her canteen and a couple of aspirins.

Deck washed down the pills, then looked at her squarely. "I said I'd kill myself before I'd live like those men in Parliament. Whatever crap they are on, it's just not worth it."

Raidon and Jenny looked at each other. "I think you'd only kill yourself if you *allowed yourself* to *realize* you lived like that," she said. "The minute those guys start coming down, they take more . . . and the minute they start running out, they go find more. I don't think many even realize the difference between reality and fantasy any longer. Being cognizant of that split is what makes it so undesirable." She looked at Deck more closely. "The split fades if you can keep up steady use. It's why those who are assimilated into Parliament never leave. Who the hell wants to see the reality of Newgate after you've lived for years on end in a glamorous world made to your own specifications? Who wants to remember that their lives have sunk so low? The dreamworld wins as long as you can keep it going, I should think."

Deck shook his head in disgust. "What a way to live."

"It's a coping mechanism. Imagine how important

that would be for someone who once had a lot of value. Hell, it still takes value to purchase the opiate. Which is why Parliament's monopoly over Australia's central power grid is so important to them."

"You'd think their families would buy them out of this place," Deck repeated. "Someone who loved them." He was immediately sorry he'd done so.

"Sometimes it's just not convenient," Jenny said pointedly. An awkward silence fell over them.

She shrugged and added, "Not everyone wants a dissipated, drug-using criminal back in the family, even if they are a firstborn son or a member of the aristocracy."

"Especially not if you're the second-born," Deck said bitterly, thinking of Kyber.

"True enough."

"Jenny?" Deck knelt down beside her. "Do I owe you an apology?" He could have meant anything, any part of the days' past activities; he was purposely leaving it open to interpretation. She flushed, and Raidon, ever the sensitive type, made himself busy on the other side of the room.

"Nope," she said after a moment, her attention turned toward folding some of the clothing in her bag. He'd noticed she was normally a practitioner of the roll-and-stuff school of packing, so he tried again. "Are you quite certain?"

She glanced over her shoulder and gave him a queer little look, a hint of slyness. "Do you *want* to give me an apology for something?"

Deck ran his thumb over his lower lip, seeing

flashes of their mouths clashing, licking, tasting. . . .
"Not particularly," he answered. He couldn't help a
bit of a smile.

"Well, then, I think we're squared away." She
looked somewhat pleased. For Raidon's benefit, she
asked loudly, "When do we want to get going?"

Deck stood. "I'm sure I'll be ready first thing tomorrow morning. There is one thing I wanted to mention,
though. We have a member of Parliament joining us
on the trip. His name is Quinn. Lord Quinn." He
braced himself for the inevitable dissention.

"What?" Raidon wheeled to stare at him. "You
said there were already people at the depot, that we
just needed enough of a crew to get us safely out
there. I thought we were going lean and mean. Just
the three of us."

Jenny frowned and chewed on her lower lip.

"It's not up for discussion," Deck said.

"There's no way we're taking a wildcard with us,"
Raidon complained. "It's a horrible idea. A huge
mistake."

Jenny nodded in agreement. "He'll be an opiate
addict, a negative in every possible way."

Deck laughed. "Wasn't it you who always said
that consistent negative behavior is better than inconsistent positive behavior—because you know exactly what you're getting?"

"I think you're paraphrasing," Jenny grumbled.
She shrugged. "On the other hand, maybe it won't
really make a difference. He'll be half off his rocker,
souped up on that fantasy cocktail anyway."

"I think it's a terrible idea." Raidon repeated. He

sat back resignedly with his arms crossed over his chest.

Deck sat down next to him. "I know it's not ideal. I realize that. But here's the situation: Parliament didn't really give me a choice. They bought my story about this being some sort of telecom investment—or pretended to—and they claim they just want to make sure my activities out there are appropriately taxed. This is the path of least resistance. It will get us what we need."

"But what if they learn the truth? Do you think Parliament will possibly be in support of your revolution," Jenny said. "How can they be of support in anything except their own power?"

Deck shrugged. "It's something I'm struggling with. It's hard to guess their motives one way or another. But maybe we can deal. If they still get the opiate, maybe they won't care who's really in charge. Obviously, they'll control whatever they can at the least risk to themselves.

"They're probably neutral at this stage. And if they know anything about the state of the rest of the world, given their unique one-sided interest in the opiate, perhaps they'll play both sides of the fence."

Raidon spoke up. "The reason they hold power is that the regimes around the world don't know them or haven't figured out how to depose them. What if a new regime takes over, a regime that is diametrically opposed to their claims of royalty and knows about them?"

"And they have to know about the Shadow Runners," Jenny said. "Or at least have heard enough rumors to become curious if not uneasy. Personally, I'd like to stay as far away as possible from anything having to do with Parliament."

Raidon nodded in agreement. "We bring a member of Parliament into an operation center for the Shadow Runners, we're basically guaranteeing everything going on there will be compromised."

"Not if we're clever," Deck argued. "First of all, none of us will be mentioning the revolution or the Shadow Runners in Quinn's presence." He paused and let that sink in. "As far as he and the Parliament are concerned, I really am developing a telecom base that wants to pay for use of the power grid—until he learns otherwise. We show him what he wants to see and tell him what he wants to hear. And we negotiate a reasonable fee, which we will actually pay out."

He added, "And if Lord Quinn is 'souped up enough,' as you put it, he will be lacking a certain clarity as to the events going on around him. It's more suspicious to try and prevent him from coming when we know we don't have a choice than to bring him in and control his experience."

Jenny shook her head. "Just by involving yourself with the Shadow Runners, you probably set yourself up to be arrested and executed for treason by your own family," she said matter-of-factly. "And now you're getting involved with Parliament. You're risking a lot."

"Some risks I'm willing to take," Deck said.

"Sometimes we must make small sacrifices for the good of the whole."

The conversation had reminded Deck of what was important, and that Lord Quinn's presence and Deck's own safety were two of those sacrifices.

Chapter Fourteen

To Jenny, Lord Quinn seemed like a hell of a sacrifice for them to make. He'd shown up at the hotel in a horse-drawn carriage packed to the gills with wardrobe trunks, hat boxes, and other assorted accoutrements that made Raidon throw up his hands in disgust.

Jenny shrank away from the ruckus, settling on the ground against the wheel of her jeep, and tried to focus on plugging coordinates into her GPS handheld. The last thing she wanted was to draw attention to herself in front of any Parliamentarians as Deck negotiated a tough deal with the dandy for the amount of luggage he would be able to bring. There was no question that Quinn could easily manage putting a bullet in her head if he was able to hold a gun steady, and if the others were reminded of her presence . . .

No, she was not pleased to have Quinn along. She

might not have much reason to support the revolution, but she was losing any enthusiasm for the idea of making any deals against the cause or Deck. And having Quinn around bothered her more for the reminder that she hadn't quite fessed up to Deck about their conversation than it reassured her that she had a plan B in the event Deck didn't pay up as promised.

However, kissing boys didn't deplete brains cells—or at least not too many all at once. So while she desperately wanted to trust Deck, their quality time in the alley still hadn't convinced her to give up that ace.

Jenny sighed. They hadn't even left Newgate and she was already wishing the whole mission was over and done with. Well, she'd been wishing that since the day Deck and Raidon had picked her up.

The trip out would last somewhere between three and five days. Going into the outback on a blind route for the first time took some care. After getting Deck to bed last night, she'd picked up terrain-based intel from a couple of old acquaintances regarding known minefields, particularly nasty toxic waste dumps, and a couple of other things she was willing to take a little longer to avoid—like some aboriginal sacred land that was probably booby-trapped up the wazoo.

Not to mention that they were caravanning in jeeps Raidon had purchased from the armorer, rather than traveling individually on the horse hybrids bred for speed and staying-power in the ultradry climate they were heading for. Once they made it beyond the Kimberley range that blocked Newgate in, there was a stretch of desert that would seem to last forever. Nothing like a good microclimate change to keep a person from falling asleep at the wheel.

Raised voices drew her attention, and Jenny peeked over the top of the jeep to watch Deck and Raidon continue an animated discussion about sleeping arrangements. Raidon was making it clear he didn't want Deck bunking with her. And Deck was arguing that Quinn was a bigger security risk than Jenny was. Good point.

She nearly dropped the handheld when she heard Deck actually lose composure and say, "If you really believe I am still your liege and your loyalty is to me, then what I say goes! I'm bunking with her. There's no security argument to be made. Quinn is more dangerous to me and the cause than Jenny!"

"I wish I could believe that," Raidon responded tightly.

She peeked out. The two men stared at each other in uncomfortable silence. Deck seemed shocked at himself for playing the "royal dictate" card he'd been pushing away for so long. Raidon seemed equally stunned, as it seemed to dawn on him that he'd just argued against his liege's wishes.

Well, it was none of her business, and far be it from Jenny to complain about the situation.

Okay, well, she'd have to call herself on that one. She might act cocky about it now, but she was guaranteed to melt into a puddle any time Deck made her think the two of them were actually going to spend time together. Alone. No question; she was definitely like a moth to a flame as far as the man was concerned—she'd fly straight into his arms the minute he turned on the heat. At least she was honest about that. And he'd been honest enough to admit that he remembered turning on the heat. How about that!

She watched him now—his lean body, his taut muscles as he turned away from Raidon to gather his wits. She shook her head and blew out a breath, then stood up. The last thing she wanted was an apology for that kiss in the alley. It almost made up for the way she still felt about him. Everyone knew that unrequited love was bad for one's health; a singed heart was a more than reasonable price to pay for moments like that one.

All set now, it seemed. Raidon hopped up and jammed his bulky frame into the driver's seat of one of the jeeps, while Quinn approached the vehicle as he might mount a horse, using the hand of a Parliament servant to help him swing one leg and then the other up and over the top of the jeep door.

Deck took a last look at how they'd loaded Quinn's belongings.

"Please note that, as of this moment," the Parliament man said, "I will try to stay out of your way entirely. This is merely a fact-collecting mission for me—a recon assignment, if you will."

"You realize the risks involved?" Deck asked.

"Always did enjoy playing hazard," Quinn answered with a queer smile.

Deck shook his head and walked back to where Jenny was leaning on the second jeep. He tossed his bag into the back. "Are you sure you have sufficient intel about the terrain?" he asked. "You've plugged in the coordinates? Taken external information into consideration? Do you feel confident—"

"Deck," she interrupted.

He shut his trap.

"This is why I'm here," she said firmly. "You're driving. I'm navigating. I know what I'm doing. We can discuss the details at the first camp, but let's get the hell out of here. This city makes my skin crawl."

He chucked her gently on the chin and paid her the respect of not pressing the issue further.

Hopping in the jeep, he kicked in the ignition, and they headed off—for the Shadow Runners, for the mysterious team at the mysterious depot, doing mysterious things that Deck hadn't really told her a damn thing about, in the middle of a toxic-waste filled desert.

It was like a nice, big, dysfunctional family vacation. Except with guns and ammo.

The tropical humidity of Newgate City had already dissipated considerably by the time they made their first stop. Pavement had become muck and dirt hours earlier, the muck was now gone, and dirt was already turning into sand and red-streaked sandstone. Newgate was just a sheen of lights faintly winking through the smog layer clogging the airspace around it.

They'd pitched tents, lit a fire, and Raidon had even condescended to patch in some low music from an outback satellite in spite of his concern over at-

Liz Maverick

tracting undue attention. He was still unhappy about Quinn's presence, although the dandy seemed primarily interested in accidentally blowing smoke in everyone's face and lying in the back of a jeep with his Hessian boots jacked up on the door frame and his hat tipped at a practiced angle—jaunty and clever, approximately twenty degrees over his eyes to keep off the sun.

He seemed more than happy to spend his time staring out at the stark landscape, although from his drugged point of view he was probably enjoying some sort of tropical beach scene complete with coconut-bra girls and parasol drinks.

At least it was easy to keep track of his whereabouts. Wherever he was, a curlicue of red-brown smoke drifted upward like a smoke signal. Deck found the scent most annoying, which probably accounted for the seemingly exponential number of times Quinn lit up around him.

And there he went again.

"Quinn, look," Deck said, keeping his tone even-keeled in spite of the harrassment he obviously felt.

"*Lord* Quinn, if you please," the dandy said with a polite bow, trying to force a little life into the droopy gray cuffs at his wrists. "Although I'm only a second son," he admitted in a rather sudden, chatty manner.

All three of his traveling companions looked up warily.

"No responsibility, but only half the money," the man continued. "Though it really wouldn't have made much difference if I'd had twice the amount. It just would have taken a bit longer to get here."

164

Jenny sat down on a supply box next to him. Deck poured himself a cup of coffee and hovered within earshot, although when Quinn lit another cigarette Jenny knew he wouldn't sit down. "What happened?" she asked.

"I spent it all. Wine, women, gaming." He shrugged. "And when I was done spending, I borrowed. And, of course, I couldn't pay it back."

"Your family didn't step up?"

"Wouldn't. And why should they? I was really of very little use to anyone. Not especially marriageable, and what's left of the world's monarchies are crumbling, you know. Not too many alliances requiring a marriage seal. Really, I can't say I blame them. I was a bit of an embarrassment. I killed a man, you see." He took a long drag, as if he were sucking in pure oxygen, and it was a little while before he spoke again, becoming rather preoccupied with looking at everything around him through the rose-colored glasses of the smoke.

"I like to believe it was a mistake. After all, I'm not really the sort of chap who goes about starting arguments, much less fighting them. I'm neither a particularly good pugilist nor a decent shot."

"Mistakes happen," Jenny said. Quinn gave her a long look but didn't comment directly.

"Unfortunately, I haven't the foggiest idea either way whether that was the case," he continued after a moment, a faraway look on his face. "I have absolutely no recollection of the event whatsoever. But I suppose I must have done the crime." He heaved a sigh. "For I am certainly doing the time."

165

Deck had had enough. "Jenny, I'd like to go over the routes through the outback if you don't mind." He turned on his heel and headed for his tent without waiting for a response.

"Jenny," Raidon called.

She ignored the heavy and stood up, following Deck into the tent. He was already lying down.

"What's going on, Deck?" she asked. "Since leaving Newgate you haven't said much. You just look like you want to kill somebody."

He put his arms behind his neck, his expression softening. "I'm just a little on edge."

Summoning all her courage, she lay down on her sleep sack next to him and rested her head on his shoulder. She'd wanted to do it since the encounter in the alley. She felt him flinch in surprise, but a few seconds later he put his arm up and around her, and pulled her closer.

There was a long pause. Finally he said, "I know this may sound strange, but Quinn's smoke . . . The smoke from his cigarettes—I feel like it gets under my skin. And occasionally, I'll have flashes of . . . scenes of . . ." He covered his forehead. "I don't know what . . . I just can't stand being around that stuff. I think I'm still coming down from that injection they gave me."

Jenny rolled over on her stomach and looked at him with a frown.

"About the trip," he said firmly, before she could say anything on the subject of FPs.

She showed him the handheld onto which she'd programmed a primitive map. "We want to stay along this road. Well, 'road' is a bit of an exaggeration. But I would expect we'll find several sets of tracks along the same trajectory, and we'll want to follow these. According to the information you gave me, the depot should be just here." She pointed to a large X.

She continued, "But this sort of empty area around it, as we come out of the city center—well, it's anyone's guess. People and things that go out there don't want to be found, and we'll want to stay with given tracks, snaking the route if we have to and watching for anything that looks suspicious.

"Obviously, I can't tell you precisely how we're going to navigate until we get out there. We'll work as we go. We'll be taking it a bit slow on any hinky areas, but I've marked the passages that are known trading routes, and we'll be able to pick up the pace on those—and we'll want to, to avoid any pirates and highwaymen. How does that sound to you?"

Without waiting for an answer, she pointed to a different spot. "See this squiggle I've drawn here? Well, that's the part we can have the most confidence about. It's cut into a mountain, pretty winding, pretty steep. It's got the cliffs on the left, and the rock face on the right. As long as we hug the wall, we'll be fine."

Deck took his time considering the map. She figured he'd find something to contradict in her suggestions, but after some moments, he nodded and looked up at her. "It's a good plan. It really helps to have you here—I want you to know that."

"Thanks. I appreciate it." She paused. "Um, I want

to talk to you about something." She poked at a lump in the mat. "What happened in the blank years?"

He looked surprised, obviously having expected her to ask about something else. The kiss, perhaps. "The blank years?"

She nodded. "Yeah, those years I was here. What were you doing, what were you thinking? I never even heard what happened in the end of that big mess at the palace. I was already being deported when you came under suspicion."

Deck cleared his throat. "I suppose you know Kyber threw me in prison for several months."

She hadn't been entirely sure.

"Let's just say it wasn't pleasant," he said after a moment.

Jenny chewed on her lip. "Funny. I never knew him like I knew you, but . . ."

"But what?"

"From everything I've read or seen, he's a kind man. He wouldn't specifically have requested anyone mistreat you." At least, she didn't think he would. Or was that just part of the empire publicity machine, making its monarch seem kind and good? It hadn't worked with the emperor, though. "Are you sure Kyber knew the extent of what happened to you in prison?"

"It doesn't matter—I shouldn't have been imprisoned. I should have received the benefit of the doubt."

"Yes. You always said you two found it difficult to get along, but he is your brother of sorts."

"I suppose that depends on whether you view family as a state of mind or a fact of birth." Deck looked at her coldly. "Like you said, you never knew him. Let's get one thing straight. Daily beatings, some foul-smelling miscreant screaming obscenities in your face . . ."

He struggled to remain calm, and Jenny couldn't remember him ever sounding so bitter.

"Well, let's just say I don't care whether he specifically ordered it or not. The jailors did what they did, and what they did was in Kyber's name." He bowed his head over his hand and rubbed his temples. "Sorry, Jenny. I just get a little worked up about it."

She didn't argue the point. Who the hell was she to judge what was or wasn't possible? After all, Kyber had deported her to Newgate, the daughter of a criminal but with no other crime. He was capable of callousness. He was capable of a certain kind of tyranny. Even if many of his people loved him.

"How long have you been involved with the Shadow Runners, Deck? And how did you meet them?"

"Well, after getting roughed up by my brother's people and tossed in prison for a crime I didn't commit, all my prior thoughts and feelings kind of gelled about the unrighteousness of a monarchy as a political system." He gave a sardonic laugh.

"So, it's revenge."

"No. The men I met in prison, they spoke of the end of monarchy as a form of government. They talked of the old days, of ancient history. They spoke of change, of a new revolution, of a better world."

169

He rolled over on his stomach and moved closer to her. "It might sound ridiculous, but I wanted to be a part of something like that. I wanted to be a part of something that had meaning, something that could change the world and make it a better place. I resent Kyber for what happened to me, but that's not why I'm doing what I'm doing."

"Have you seen the queen?" Jenny asked.

"My mother?" Deck gave the ghost of a smile. "Not since she pardoned me, exiled me, then paid me off to stay away."

Jenny shrugged. "I'd rather have value than an apology any day."

"Really?" Deck asked. He looked surprised. "I found it rather galling. One has to be considered guilty in order to be pardoned. I didn't harm a hair on the emperor's head. They all just blamed me." After a pause, he looked curiously at her. "Now, can I ask *you* a personal question?"

She nodded.

"Do you believe your father had anything to do with what happened?"

Jenny chewed on her lower lip. What could she say? She decided to go with the truth. "Yes. Yes, I do. I think he tried to kill the emperor."

Deck stared at her. "That's not what I expected you to say."

"You know there's no love lost between us. Why should I pretend otherwise when I believe he's guilty?" She looked around and changed the subject. "So where is she or he—where's the Shadow Voice?"

Deck grinned. "Not here."

"Not *here*? Are you kidding me? We came all this way and the Voice of Freedom skipped town?"

"It's not like that. Where we're going is the primary transmitting station. The Shadow Voice sends us the signal from a different place—we're its conduit."

Jenny laughed. "You're signal-laundering? That's funny. I guess I kind of assumed the Voice of Freedom would be broadcasting from out here. Where is he, then?"

"I don't know. That's the point. This communications depot is a hub to disseminate information and make it difficult to track. Broadcasts are untraceable when the security systems and scramblers are online and going back from here to the Shadow Voice is just as tough."

"How do you know so much about all this if you've never even been here?" Jenny asked. She was amazed.

"I designed the technology, the system. What you're going to see are my plans, my designs, my people."

She whistled. "All that work really paid off. Kinda had you pegged to invent the next generation virtual realitor, not use it for politics," she teased.

"Who needs VR when you've got FPs?" he shot back.

"Funny. Ha, ha." Jenny couldn't contain her curiosity. "So, who do you think is the Shadow Voice? Seriously, do you know?"

Deck shook his head.

"So how do you know that you're not being played? That you're not a pawn in something that's not actually as righteous as you think?"

"I won't say it hasn't crossed my mind. But it's a chance I'm willing to take. What the Voice talks about . . ."

Jenny stared at him. "You believe in the idea of revolution, of democracy, that much?"

"Yes. I do. If I die and it's revealed to be a trick, at least I'll die in the name of something meaningful."

"Although you'll still be dying in vain," Jenny pointed out.

"No. Because it may inspire others to stand up for what they believe in."

Jenny was silent a moment. "I don't think I've ever believed in anything that much."

"In all fairness, Jenny, I don't think you've been given enough reason."

"Thanks, Deck," she said almost shyly. "That's just about the nicest thing you've ever said to me."

He looked a little surprised, and lifted his hand to her cheek. "You know, I do care about what happens to you," he said softly.

Raidon called Deck's name from outside, and Deck let his hand fall. He turned away.

Jenny smiled. "I know," she whispered. And though she would have preferred to stay in that moment, a little voice in her head accused him: *You just care about your revolution more.*

She watched Deck walk away, then lay down on her sleep sack in their tent. She stared at the place where his body would lie later that night and reached out, placing her palm on the thin fabric.

"They say what doesn't kill you makes you stronger," she muttered, unsure whether she was referring to the attraction between them they kept thwarting or the tug of her conscience for not meeting Deck's show of trust with one of her own. She should have told Deck about Quinn's earlier insinuations, about her own background with Parliament. She couldn't imagine using any of it against him anymore.

Yet his damn fanaticism scared her. His dedication to the revolution gave her pause. Their feelings for one another had nothing to do with anything so self-righteous, and that worried her. Would he be as fanatic in caring for her?

She pulled her hand away and closed her eyes. "Just give me one more sign, Deck, and I swear to God I'll believe in you more than I've ever believed in anyone in this godforsaken world. Give me one really good reason to trust you."

Chapter Fifteen

"Come on, Raidon, you must be good for something . . . dance with me!"

He grinned from his chair, but didn't get up.

"Come on!"

Raidon glanced over at Deck, who shrugged lackadaisically. The heavy stood up, walked over to Jenny, and then managed to plaster her to his body for the next five minutes in a rip-roaring tango that had Deck's attention as much as it seemed to have hers.

"Raidon, I'm shocked," Jenny teased. "You're not supposed to be so cavalier with the ladies. It's not fitting of a royal bodyguard."

Raidon winked and dipped her, then pulled her close again and tangoed her back a few steps.

"I think he's jealous," Deck heard Jenny say.

Raidon frowned, abruptly missing a step. He twirled her in what was clearly to be a final pirouette and said, "I believe that's everything I know about dancing."

Even so, Deck felt like he was going to explode. So, Jenny was off-limits to him but fair game for his heavy? No, with this business, Raidon was close to overstepping his boundaries. It was . . . it was . . .

Deck suddenly realized that he'd given up his right to complain about such things. He almost had to laugh; one had to admit that being a prince had its advantages when one wanted another man to take his paws off a woman. And now all that was gone.

He remembered the earlier argument with Raidon, when he'd pulled rank like a royal and said Jenny would be bunking with him, no further discussion. It nagged at him, how the vestiges of his former life seemed to be seeping back into his actions, his behaviors, his speech. Did he believe in the revolution or not? Did he believe in equality for all . . . or not? Did he really believe? Was time enough to change his upbringing and make him the man he wanted to be?

Do you believe in the revolution, Deck? Or are you here for revenge? "Of course I do," he muttered aloud. "I believe."

"Is something wrong, sir?" Raidon asked.

Deck managed a half smile. "Just thinking."

Quinn sauntered up to the fire, placed two handkerchiefs on the ground—one for each knee—and knelt down in front of the flat piece of rock Deck had designated as the cooking stone. He pulled out a rusty yet dainty filigree penknife and sliced lacy strips off his brown opiate stick, which he then rolled in thin papers squired from his cigarette case. After refilling the case, he politely offered one to Deck and ignored everybody else.

Deck rubbed one hand over the stubble on his chin. "Lord Quinn, with all due respect, this is my expedition, and therefore I must ask you in the spirit of . . . brotherhood . . ."

Jenny rolled her eyes.

". . . to respect my rules. I've asked you once already to please smoke that crap downwind of me. Now, stop offering it to me."

Jenny raised an eyebrow.

"Of course," Quinn said with a bow.

A howl pierced the air. Everyone froze.

Quinn paled considerably. "What in God's name was that?"

"It sounded like a dingo," she said. "But they usually travel in packs, so it's not a dingo, per se. Oh, shit. It's a bingie, I think."

"A what?" Raidon asked.

"A bingie. Sounds cute, huh. It's not. It's slang for any uncategorizable mutt animal in the outback. In general, part dingo, maybe part bimbie or whatever the hell else might have grafted together somehow and then eaten a shit load of toxic waste. Just think of it as a pissed-off animal mutation. Short life expectancy, but pretty nasty while alive."

The animal howled once more, an old-fashioned fingernails-across-blackboard sort of sound that made everyone shudder.

177

"Perhaps it's attracted to the fire," Quinn said helpfully, barely able to lift his fag to his mouth his hand was shaking so badly.

Jenny pulled her pistol from her thigh holster and flicked off the safety. She checked the barrel for rounds.

Raidon dragged his equipment bag toward him, then pulled out the night-vision goggles, and tossed Jenny and Deck each a pair. Deck put them on. Quinn cowered closer to the fire, in spite of the heat, his composure evaporating by the second.

Through the lenses, Deck saw out in the distance a neon-green animal pacing unsteadily one way and then the next. He whistled in awe. The bingie was about the size of a child's pony, its movements inconsistent, awkward, as if something weren't quite right with it. Just like Quinn. Maybe the two could make friends. They were probably on the same page.

Deck edged backward to one of the parked jeeps, and grabbed a grenade launcher. "It's coming closer," Jenny murmured as he sidled up beside her.

It howled again, much louder. Deck focused his goggles in time to catch a nice, zoomed image of pointed bared teeth, dripping with saliva.

"Damn," Jenny muttered beside him. Deck was doubly glad Quinn didn't have night goggles on; the dandy would have completely lost it if he'd seen more of the animal.

Quinn lost it, anyway, when he saw the huge animal emerge from the night, snarling and prancing. He ran screaming out across the sand with Raidon running after him, then doubled back, stumbling toward camp in some sort of slapstick routine that might actually have been amusing under less dangerous circumstances. Of course, his panic likewise scared the beast. Foam dripping from its mouth, the creature erupted in a shower of spiked quills that rained down within a two-foot radius around its body, and prepared to attack.

Deck aimed the grenade launcher. "Quinn's coming in dead ahead; there's not enough surface area to get a decent shot with him in the way."

The Parliamentarian tripped and nearly fell to the sand, his expression more extreme than anything they'd seen since he'd joined the group. The opiate was surely intensifying everything, so he must be scared to death.

There wasn't time to plan. "I'll be the bait!" Jenny yelled, and took off running.

Deck swore furiously.

The startled bingie turned his attention to the shouting Jenny, sending another shower of quills out from its body even as it presented its broad side as a target for the launcher. Jenny cried out in pain, her hand at up to her chest. Deck took aim and blasted away. As the grenade rocket shot forward toward the bingie, she dove to the side with her hands covering her face. Sand sprayed everywhere. Deck dropped his weapon and ran to cover her motionless body as the grenade hit.

With a hideous squeal, the bingie just about disintegrated in an explosion of flesh and gore. Raidon ran to deal with the rest.

Jenny didn't move underneath Deck. She was facedown in the sand, groaning. He could feel the pulse in her neck under his lips, though, and her heart hammered wildly.

Deck knelt in the sand beside her, and carefully rolled her over. She winced, her hand moving up to her collarbone. A third of a broken quill still stuck out of her. And then she suddenly seemed to collect herself and got to her feet. "It's not that bad," she said.

"You're not going anywhere." Deck backed her up against the sandstone wall behind them and quickly pushed apart her jacket. A small bloodstain dampened the black fabric of her T-shirt. The quill had gone in at an angle in the fleshy area just above her right armpit. "Hold still. It's not in that far, but it will hurt a little."

She nodded. He held down her T-shirt and pulled the quill out as fast as he could; she made only a slight sound when he pressed his fingers to the tiny wound to stanch the blood flow and fished his med card from one of his pockets.

Deck took a deep breath and exhaled his relief. The injury was minor. He swiped a dab of nanomeds off the card and spread it over Jenny's wound.

"A bingie quill. Well, that's a first," Jenny said weakly, cracking a smile.

He took her by the shoulders and slammed her against the rock wall. "Don't you ever pull that kind of stunt again," he said in a violent whisper. "Don't you *ever*."

Jenny's breath came out in gasps, and she stared back at Deck without a word.

Raidon appeared from the darkness, an uncertain look on his face. Deck looked over his shoulder at Quinn, who was retching on his hands and knees in the sand. A moment later, the Parliamentarian rose and ran off into the night.

"Go deal with him," Deck said to his heavy, who immediately did as commanded.

A tremor rippled through Jenny's body, and she sagged back a little. Deck didn't let go of her, just held her up against the wall by her collar. Her face was still streaked with grime and sweat. She looked a bit out of her head, and he figured he looked much the same.

Jenny reached up and roughly brushed sand off her mouth, then moistened her lips with her tongue. She just stared into his eyes, and even as he was still trying to play it smart, analyze all the angles, she simply reached out, clawed into the ridges of his body armor, and brought her mouth within a whisper of his. Pure adrenaline lit the blue of her irises.

The girl had almost no impulse control. Ah, God, he wasn't doing too well, either.

He answered the challenge by forcing her body back against the rock wall with his own, running his thumbs across her cheeks.

He put his lips against hers, so slowly that his intent could not be questioned. It couldn't be passed off in a drugged-up moment. The charge between them ignited in an instant, and it was as if he were

181

Liz Maverick

drawn to her beyond everything that he could control. Perhaps beyond anything that he wanted to
control.

The hands that clutched at his armor relaxed, fists
uncurling against his body, now unhooking his armor and crawling under his very defenses. She lay
her palms against his shirt, their damp warmth pen-
etrating the thin fabric until it seemed as though he
and she could not be any closer. But they could.

He wanted to be part of her, to break down the old
barriers for good—in this moment, there wasn't
anything is the world that was a good enough reason to keep them apart. Not class distinction, not
trust, not the mission.

Deck simply didn't see the point in fighting it anymore, not when it was obvious she felt the same
way. And in addition to understanding him, Jenny
was unique; he had no illusions of any promises or
expectations that making love to her might call up.
Which was how it had to be.

Didn't it?

He pulled back from her, studying her face, trying
to read her, and under his searching gaze a slow
smile crept over her lips. "Don't break the spell," she
said softly. "And don't overanalyze or explain. I already know it's not meant to be forever."

He nodded, not entirely sure he agreed with the
absolute in her statement, but entirely sure he didn't
want to debate anything at this moment. One thing
they had in common was a life of risk. And you accepted that risk and you made sure you took your
opportunities when they came along while you still

had the chance. If this trip was their opportunity, it seemed foolish to spend time thinking about the details of the future.

She moved her hands up to cradle his face, and slowly, slowly brought her mouth to his. It was searing hot, liquid heat.

And still it wasn't enough. There was still too much between them.

As she first bit down on his lower lip and then entered his mouth with her tongue, Deck reached under her shirt, ran his fingertips down her back, and roughly pulled her closer. They couldn't get enough, their mouths wet and hot and their lips and tongue and teeth drawing blood as they nearly clawed at each other in abandon. Their embrace was an attack, almost, with pleasure and pain mingling into one.

He just wanted to get at her . . . couldn't get close enough, it seemed. He pulled her jacket away, tossed it on the ground. He could feel her heart pounding against his body from some heady mix of adrenaline and lust, and her excitement fueled his own.

Her fingernails dug into his back while his hands strayed all over her body, touching everything he could reach, any skin he could find.

He put his hands under her thighs and lifted her up, leaning her against the wall; she wrapped her legs around him, her thighs squeezing back.

Her eyes glittering, her lips parted, she arched back as he pressed against her, hard and wanting. He could feel her, wet and swollen against him.

She ripped her T-shirt off over her head and threw it to the ground, then worked on his and stripped it off likewise. Her ponytail fell loose in the motion, sending a cascade of red-gold hair over her pale, delicate shoulders. It was too much. It wasn't enough. He wanted to get at her. Get inside her.

Deck buried his face in her body, sucking roughly on her hard nipples. Just like he liked it. Like she clearly liked it, too.

She exhaled, rough and shaky, then reached down and undid the catches on his trousers. Her hands moved between their bodies, caressing and tantalizing between his legs, stroking, pulling, kneading.

He wanted desperately to be inside her. He wanted to end the cycle of teasing, of wanting but never having, of pretending and hiding, then calling each other on it, but never, ever doing anything to make themselves happy.

"I want you, Jenn," he whispered into her ear as his fingers nimbly set about unbuckling the catch and shoving down her trousers.

She nodded, too breathless to speak, her body tensing as he snaked his fingers down over her thigh and inside her panties. Wet, wanting, ready. Jenny's smile, her body, everything seemed to him to indicate every fiber of her being wanted this.

"I've always wanted you," he whispered in her ear.

He moved his hand away and freed his member, then pressed himself into her. She leaned forward with a joyous gasp, pushing off the rock wall at his penetration, pressing his face between her breasts.

After a moment, Deck moved inside her. With one arm holding her up, one hand down against her, his fingers played against her sensitive flesh, bringing gasps, moans, delicious dirty little murmurs to life with each stroke, each pet. It shocked him, what she said as he thrust furiously inside her.

"You nasty little thing," he said against her ear, loving every second of it.

Jenny laughed, a sound colored by pure ecstasy. She tossed her head as he worked her toward climax, and she was a glorious sight to see. Panting, a smile of abandon on her face, hair flying, half naked, getting done against a rock wall with a streak of blood running down from her collarbone over her breast, goading him on, flexing her body, no inhibitions whatsoever, not caring about anything or anyone except the two of them right here . . .

He seriously thought he'd died and gone to heaven, and when he came, the reality of it was better than the brightest moment he'd felt from the opiate.

He leaned her gently back, spent, and Jenny unfurled her legs. They clung to each other, sweating, forehead to forehead, her eyes closed as if she were trying to commit their union to memory.

And he realized it couldn't have been further from being just a screw against a wall, a release of tension. It was something more than that; and rather than frightening him, Deck felt tremendous joy—as if she were helping him put the pieces of his life together and suddenly everything was forming a complete picture.

"I can see you in the picture," he murmured.

"Mmm?" She opened her eyes, still smiling.

"Nothing." He put the back of his hand on her neck and gently pressed her head to rest on his shoulder.

I can see you in the picture.

NAME:_____

ADDRESS:_____
_____
_____

TELEPHONE: _____

E-MAIL: _____

_____ I want to pay by credit card.

__ Visa _____ MasterCard _____ __ Discover

Account Number: _____

Expiration date: _____.

SIGNATURE: _____

*Send this form, along with $2.00 shipping
and handling for your FREE books, to:*

Love Spell Romance Book Club
20 Academy Street
Norwalk, CT 06850-4032

*Or fax (must include credit card
information!) to:* 610.995.9274.
*You can also sign up on the Web
at* www.dorchesterpub.com.

Offer open to residents of the U.S. and
Canada only. Canadian residents, please
call 1.800.481.9191 for pricing information.

If under 18, a parent or guardian must sign. Terms, prices and conditions
subject to change. Subscription subject to acceptance. Dorchester
Publishing reserves the right to reject any order or cancel any subscription.

Chapter Sixteen

Jenny woke up in the tent alone, Deck's pillow cold beside her. She wasn't surprised. The closer they got to the depot, the more restless he seemed to become, manifesting in earlier and earlier wake-up times that she wasn't in a hurry to match.

She could hear voices outside, and hurried to dress and check her wound—a mere nothing, under the circumstances. It was already healing.

She pulled Deck's makeshift pillow—some of his clothes stuffed in a bag—over to her side. It smelled of leather, sweat, dirt, and the faintest whiff of opiate, courtesy of Quinn's indulgence. Plus it held that indescribable something all Deck's own that was making her insane. No, it wasn't making her insane. Everything already was insane. Insane: lying in a tent in the middle of the Australian outback in Deck Valoren's arms. Insane: Jenny Red sniffing his pillow like a silly schoolgirl and allowing herself a grin. It was as if she'd asked for the world and was getting it.

"Jenny! Get your ass out of bed!" Well, Raidon was clearly not feeling the same way. From the sound of it, he wasn't even in a pleasant mood. She rolled up her belongings, pressed the bedding down into a compact heap, and dragged it all with the tent back to the jeeps.

The heavy was working on obliterating the evidence of their campsite, stealing sidelong glances at Quinn, who had fallen asleep on his back in the sand, and muttering to himself.

Deck seemed to be humming an old empire folk tune, for God's sake, as he checked the oil in the jeep engines. Given that he wasn't normally a humming sort of person, Jenny felt pretty confident that there wouldn't be one of those tiresome "morning-after mistake" conversations. Which could only mean that he wasn't sorry he'd made love to her.

Perhaps she'd overreacted during their joust in the armory about her status on this mission, her dispensability. Perhaps she'd become overly cynical, suspicious after all this time. It sure as hell seemed like she finally had someone on her side besides herself.

"We should have let the bingie get him," Raidon blurted when he saw her.

Jenny patted him on the back. He'd probably been babysitting Quinn all night. "Trouble sleeping?"

"You'd think the damn animal was a hundred times bigger . . . and some sort of alien species for all his babbling. It's embarrassing. Embarrassing! I can't do my job. The best I can do is to watch this guy, try to keep him out of trouble and out of the way. We really should have brought a few more of our men over with us. Meaningful security is impossible."

"I'm with you. Deck is out of his mind," she said, knowing he was within earshot.

Deck walked over. "Being out of one's mind is a relative thing," he said with a smile.

"I won't comment on His Lordship's state of mind," Raidon said uncomfortably, then muttered, "Ragtag team of imbeciles." A little louder he added, "I include myself in that statement."

"And Deck?" Jenny asked with amusement.

"And His Lordship," Raidon agreed. He wheeled around to Deck. "What were we all thinking, allowing along this drug-crazed blue blood? We can't trust him, and I end up having to watch him. Do you know how long I chased him last night?"

Deck seemed to realize that his heavy needed to rant. He gave Jenny a wink, pointedly keeping his mouth shut even as he picked up the other end of a supply trunk and helped her hoist it into the jeep.

Raidon continued throwing camping equipment around with more-than-necessary force. "He's a damn liability and nothing else! Forgive me if I seem a little sour, but when you told me you wanted to add a few members to the team . . . well, what we've ended up with is a pint-sized ex-con, a prince who puts idealism over personal safety, a bodyguard who clearly has no common sense or he wouldn't have to be moaning about this now, and a drug-using fop likely to hallucinate he's at a party right in the mid-

dle of battle and then run around like a madman
when he should be sleeping!"

"Pint-sized!" Jenny protested. "Now, *that's* a relative thing. I just happen to be smaller than *you*."

Raidon stopped what he was doing and crossed
his arms over his chest. "Since we're on the subject,
I'm not trying to lecture here, but you've seriously
got to think things through before you act, kid."

"Sometimes you don't have time to think about
things, you just gotta do them. I mean, it turned out
okay, right? Everybody's fine, the bingie is dead."
She shrugged dramatically.

And besides, there was nothing like an injury to
jump-start a love affair.

Raidon looked at Deck and pointed at her. "She
could have been killed and the girl can't stop smiling. I think she's got a head injury we missed."

"Come on. It was a tiny little puncture wound. I
can barely even feel it."

Deck looked at the ground, then knocked a little
sand off the top of his boot. "Well, she must have
something else to smile about." He put his hand on
Jenny's back in a deliciously possessive sort of way
and looked her in the eye. "Raidon's right about one
thing, though. Be careful. As you noted not so long
ago, you're not my point man."

Jenny leaned sideways into him and patted his
chest in amusement. "I'm used to handling myself."

"Well, handle this," he replied, tucking the GPS in
her hand and her hair behind her ear.

Raidon eyed the two of them, a muscle working in
his jaw. He'd obviously worried about what had

happened between them last night, and now his fears were confirmed. "I'll wake up Quinn and shove him in the jeep. We can have breakfast en route." He turned and headed off, cursing softly.

Deck wheeled around and grabbed Jenny by the waist. "Good morning, gorgeous."

"Good morning . . . sir." She grinned.

"You want to help me bolt these things up?" he asked, gesturing to the space between the back of the first jeep and the front of the second. "We're using gas up like it's free. We've got to start conserving."

"How do they fit together?" Jenny lifted the connector latch on the first jeep and held it up for him to see.

Deck pushed the insert from the second jeep into that of the first and let the bolt fall into place, effectively locking the two vehicles together as one. "Tab A, slot B," he whispered into her ear.

She leaned away from him, still caught in his embrace. "You are most definitely flirting with me."

"Why so surprised?"

"We're on a very serious mission, mister," she teased. "We don't have time for frivolous, lustful behavior."

"There's always time for lustful behavior. And there's nothing frivolous about it," he said.

"I'd think you would have to remain focused on the goal," she challenged.

"I'm an excellent multitasker. I can focus on two things at once," he responded, nuzzling her neck in a very focused manner.

"Mmm . . ."

"Indeed." He bent her backward, leaning her against the hood of the second jeep, then stepped between her knees. "There's something about a beautiful girl, an important cause, and a quest that just gets my blood boiling."

"Any beautiful girl?" she asked, nuzzling him back.

He pulled away and cradled her face in his hands, his fingers caressing her skin. "Oh, Jenny, I've wanted you so. The redheaded spitfire I simply couldn't get out of my mind since . . . way back when. You had no idea. And it seemed absolutely impossible. Unthinkable. And now . . ."

Jenny flushed with pleasure, tracing her finger from his throat down to the catch of his trousers. "I wish we had time to bring you to a boil," she said wickedly.

The sound of a throat being cleared preempted Deck's answer. He slowly helped her up and coolly turned around.

Quinn stared curiously between the two of them. Raidon appeared and raised and lowered an eyebrow.

"I'll be driving with *him*, I suppose," Quinn drawled, rather rudely, with a gesture at Raidon.

Jenny stifled a laugh as the heavy rolled his eyes. Then they all piled into the jeeps.

The next hour reminded Jenny of one of those old road-trip cinema clips, even the parts where she could hear Raidon yelling at Quinn from behind them in the second jeep, telling him to get the hell out of his personal space. She was having the time of her life—thighs squashed against Deck's, practically bouncing into his lap every time he steered over a bump and laughing hysterically about it all. But most of all, she loved seeing Deck relax next to her, enjoying it all as much as she was, and knowing that she was the cause of it.

Well, with that on her mind—and with all the carnal pleasures of the night to come, too—it wasn't at all surprising that she wasn't paying attention when the dune pirates appeared. She wasn't surprised they came to play; she was surprised they hadn't come sooner. And paying attention wouldn't have done much good, anyway, because such pirates always seemed to materialize out of nowhere. It was a pair of them, driving a ramped-up buggy—nothing more than a recycled pipe framework supporting an engine, a gas tank, a bucket seat, and a large trunk to hold loot.

They came up fast and were well camouflaged. All Jenny could see of the occupants was long matted hair flying out behind them, dun-colored clothing, and a fine layer of red-beige sandstone dust kicked up all over everything.

One drove, the other stood up on the trunk where they'd mounted artillery on the roll bar. Without delay, the pirate angled his gun toward their tires. A burst showered the base of their jeep as Deck hit the accelerator. It sounded like the bullets only nicked the back corner.

Jenny reached into the backseat to grab her pistol and the grenade launcher, and looked behind her.

With the bolt engaged, Deck controlled the steering for both cars; all Raidon had to do was fight. One hand on the roll bar to steady himself, the heavy used his remaining hand to load an explosive into his autorifle chamber with a single violent thrust. Quinn seemed to be flailing about wildly in terror next to him in a distinctly unhelpful manner. Raidon grabbed Quinn by the cravat and yelled something in his face. Apparently dissatisfied with the response, he threw the dandy back to the seat, put his foot on his back, and shoved him down into the footwell.

Crouched low in her own seat, Jenny was only able to get off a few quick, untargeted shots with her pistol. A couple of return-fire bullets ricocheted near her and away. This wasn't going to work. Jenny stood up as Raidon was doing and aimed the grenade launcher at the pirates.

Deck grabbed the back of her jacket, perhaps thinking to steady her or perhaps to get her down and covered. She didn't look back, just shook him off and concentrated on aiming the launcher.

The jeep hit a rock and swerved as she fired. The grenade went wide, exploding in the sand behind the speeding dune buggy.

Mocking her with whooping Indian calls, the pirates prepared to fire once again. Jenny showered them with her best trash talk as she reloaded.

Raidon got off another shot and managed to strike near gas tank. Not bad aim under the circumstances, which had Deck purposely swerving both jeeps back and forth to avoid a well-placed bullet, but again, it was not a critical hit.

She finished reloading as the dune pirates fired back. Again a shower of bullets; no direct hit. In part, maybe it was because the dune buggy seemed to be losing ground. Or perhaps it was purposely decelerating.

Jenny didn't want to lose them now only to have them come back around at some point on the journey and strike again. "Drive absolutely straight on the count of three. I'll get 'em, and we can peel away to the left."

Deck nodded and she counted down. On three, Deck stopped swerving and she took her shot, past Raidon to the back where the buggy continued to decelerate. The driver saw it coming and managed to swerve enough to catch the blast on only one side of the grill. But it was enough. It hit the gas tank, which exploded. The driver tried to keep control as the flames licked toward him. He lost control, the buggy hit a rock and flipped.

The impact broke several of the welds on the vehicle's huge cage, which flew apart. The flaming engine shot out the front, breaking up in flight. Globs of burning metal fell into the sand just ahead of Deck and Jenny like tiny meteorites, followed by heavier pieces of metal. Propelled by inertia, the largest piece of the engine never stopped; it flew over their heads and just disappeared into space.

As Deck slowed the jeep, Jenny watched the sand in front of them for the fallen engine to appear, listened for the sound of the impact. It was several moments of silence as she stared through the windshield, trying to figure out how metal could evaporate into thin air, before the odd sensations of soft heat and the acrid smell of burning rubber came to her attention. And then it came, the strange delay, the sound of something smashing against something much harder than sand.

Jenny looked over her shoulder and saw Raidon working on the hitch on the back of the second jeep. It was snagged on a piece of the heavy metal buggy frame, showering sparks into the air.

Deck was saying something to her, his foot heavy on the brake, and she turned back around—and suddenly it was like being on the front car on a roller coaster ride.

The jeep she was in rolled across the edge of a sandstone cliff that she would have sworn wasn't there a moment ago, hesitated for a fraction of a second . . . and then tipped forward and went down.

Jenny flew over the windshield from her seat with a startled yell, grabbing at anything she could to stop herself. Windshield wipers! They broke off in her hand. Windshield! No grip. Hands scrabbling for traction against the sleek hood of the jeep, there was nothing to hold on to. Last chance, last chance—the grill!

The grill. Jenny's fingers closed around the grill and a horrendous screeching noise seared the air as the second jeep, still attached and perched atop the cliff, protested the shift in weight. Someone must have thrown the emergency brake.

Jenny swung freely off the front of the jeep, her legs dangling beneath her. Looking down, there was nothing but a sheer sandstone crevasse. The buggy engine lay in pieces somewhere far below.

Looking up, she saw Deck was still strapped in by his seat belt, almost in a standing position as the jeep hung vertically over the side of the cliff. Quinn was nowhere in sight, but Raidon remained on relatively safe ground, atop the cliff's edge with the second jeep, looking down on them in horror and disbelief.

The entire lot of them were still anchored to solid ground only by the second jeep and the remnants of the dune buggy.

Jenny adjusted her grip on the grill, aware of her breath puffing out in jerky fits and starts. She closed her eyes and forced herself to exhale slowly, to conquer the fear that would breed panic only to lead inevitably to death.

The violent screech of metal against metal rang out again, and the entire vehicle lurched forward. From the trunk space behind Deck, boxes of food and weapons rained down into the crevasse; Jenny had to twist her body to avoid being hit, even as she held on to the grill for dear life.

The jeep jerked forward again. Jenny cried out as the entire bolting mechanism appeared at the top of the cliff. They were all being slowly dragged toward the abyss.

"Nobody move," Raidon hissed.

Jenny suppressed a cry of dismay as her arm muscles protested. She was strong, but she couldn't hold on like this too much longer. She looked into Deck's eyes. She saw the prince there, strong in the face of powerlessness, determined in the face of terrible odds. The wheels were turning, and yet ... she knew he didn't have the answers. Not on this one. Not yet. Her heart sank.

The sweat on her hands made it so hard to hold

on. Willpower wasn't going to be enough. Not for this one.

"Help me, Deck."

He looked tortured, immobilized in his cage of seat belt straps, staring both into her eyes and into the chasm below. Moistening his lips, he stuck his arm through the webbing across his body and held it out to her, around the windshield, desperately trying to reach.

Jenny gasped. It made things worse, seeing that the distance between them was so very far.

"Hold on, Jenn. Just hold on . . . Oh, God."

"I'm losing it," she said hoarsely.

He wrenched his body closer, pressing against the straps, his hand still held out in the air. The shift in his position caused another ominous lurch. Jenny could see more of the second jeep peeking over the side of the cliff.

"Nobody move," Raidon said quickly. "Or we'll all go down." He straddled the bolt and held his arm out to Deck. "Sir, grab my arm and then release your seat belt, and I'll pull you over."

"Get Jenny," Deck said. "I can't reach her like this."

"No, sir. We'll get her after."

But the way he said it, Jenny understood the subtext. There might not be an after.

The jeeps lurched again. One of Jenny's hands slipped off and she nearly fell. She held on with the one hand while she wiped the sweat off her free palm and grabbed a better hold on the grill.

"I'll have him grab me, and then I'll grab you," Deck said.

She looked up at him as he reached one arm up to Raidon, grabbed a hold of the heavy's arm, and released his seat belt.

As the straps fell away, her heart leaped. "Please. I can't hold on like this much longer," she whispered, beginning to go dizzy. "Don't let me fall."

"I've got you," Raidon said to Deck as he grabbed his master around the collar. "I'm going to pull you up."

"Wait! I can reach her now. Help me reach her." Swinging in midair from Raidon's grasp, he reached out to Jenny. "Grab my hand."

She reached up to him. Their hands would not meet.

"Let her go, sir. You have to let her go."

Deck's fingers splayed as if he thought he could will their hands to reach.

The jeeps jolted forward more, the wheels of the second vehicle digging into the cliff's edge. A spray of sand scattered downward.

Raidon swore. "This car is going down."

Jenny adjusted her grip, her body swinging as she tried to lift her weight up and reach Deck's hand. Another jolt, another slip.

"I can't get both of you at once," Raidon said in desperation. "Sir, it's one or the other. I'm pulling you up."

"Let me reach out to her," Deck bellowed.

"Don't let him pull you up without me," Jenny pleaded. "We can reach."

"Sir, the revolution needs you!"

And with those words ringing in the air, Jenny

sensed Deck's hesitation. It was there in the details. His shoulder rotating back just slightly. The tips of his fingers reflexively curling away from her into his palm. And his eyes, stormy and for the tiniest fraction of a second . . . unsure.

Raidon made a pained noise, a tortured sound. Then he said rather desperately, "I'm pulling the bolt, Jenn. I'm sorry. You have to know I'm sorry."

How, oh, how could you be unsure?

"No," she whispered breathlessly to Deck. "Don't let me down."

Deck's lack of clarity, his split second of indecision had already vanished. He reached out to her once again with his prior intensity and fire, saying her name, telling her to reach farther, try harder, try *harder* . . .

Above him Raidon pulled the bolt clip with one hand and yanked his liegeman upward with a yell.

Still staring up at them as she plummeted downward in a chaos of flying metal parts and supplies, she watched the world playing out above her in slow motion: the jeep slowly flipping end over end in the air, Deck shoving Raidon away and scrambling to the edge of the cliff, Deck again roaring out her name in anguish and then disappearing from her sight.

And at the last, Jenny just saw herself falling, wrapped in a blanket of swirling sand and her fear from the armory ringing in her ears.

Somebody has to die and it's going to be me.

200

Chapter Seventeen

She fell onto a narrow lip jutting out from the cliff below, scraping her cheek, slamming her tender shoulder. A huge portion of the ledge crumbled away as she scrambled to regain her balance; all she could do was hug the sandstone wall, poised awkwardly on the remaining shelf that was just barely wide enough to hold her on tiptoes.

Then she closed her eyes and concentrated on bracing herself for the rest.

It came only seconds later, the jeep making contact with the rocks below, totally obliterated in a cacophony of smashing metal. A cloud of dust, heat, and fire shot upward, clogging the air around her.

There was nothing then, nothing but an eerie silence and the sound of her hyperventilating, still plastered to the wall on her toes.

Jenny didn't move as the dust cloud dissipated.

She just stared blankly at the red, gold, and cream streaks in the sandstone.

Deck called out to her. They'd seen her down there, still holding on. He shouted her name, over and over.

She didn't answer. She didn't want their help now, late and short. But more of the lip crumbled away, and she knew she had to make something happen.

You get yourself out of this mess, Jenny Red. You figure it out.

She inhaled a huge, halting breath of air, but it still didn't seem like enough. She could hear Deck and Raidon more clearly now, shouting something down to her, instructions maybe, promises, whatever. Her mouth tasted salt, her cheeks were damp, and she leaned her forehead against the wall in front of her, giving in to the tears.

She wasn't wearing the gauntlets; the only tools she had were the knives in the toes of her boots. They would have to be enough. She took deep gulping breaths and focused on the task ahead. Her body trembled as she slowly bent her knees, still facing forward, trying not to disturb the lip any further. She gently lifted one palm away from the wall, and, balancing her weight against the rock with her forehead, she reached behind her boot to the flick-switch on her heel. The knife shot out, digging straight into a soft spot in the wall. She lost her balance for a minute, her heart in her mouth, and then recovered.

Right palm back on the wall, left palm off, down to

the heel, she reached for the flick-switch. The knife shot out of the toe of her left boot but struck a harder area of the rock face. It snapped off and fell away, a shard of glitter tumbling into the crevasse.

Sobbing uncontrollably now, Jenny finally found the courage to look up. It seemed so much warmer and lighter up there, where Deck and Raidon stood silhouetted against the sky. But she was glad she couldn't see their faces. See their sorrow or pity or guilt or whatever they were feeling. She wanted to be angry.

She reached up with one hand, every muscle in her body protesting and trembling, and dragged her palm across the cliff surface until she found a divot. She pulled herself up a bit using the makeshift hold, jammed the knife of her right boot into a higher spot on the cliff like a crampon, and propelled her body upward with every ounce of strength she could muster.

She copied the pattern, fiercely yelling out each time she powered herself a little farther up, just to keep the momentum.

Raidon and Deck threw down a rope. It snaked down along the rock to her left. She ignored it, still powering up on her own.

Raidon begged her to take the rope. Deck leaned over the edge of the cliff, pointing to the rope, his arm outstretched, hand reaching toward her, almost a perfect twin of that moment earlier just as his fingers curled away.

Nose running, tears streaming unchecked down

her cheeks, dripping from her lips, she still refused them, unwilling to give them a second chance. Foolish, maybe. She could easily fall; her remaining boot knife could snap.

But she persisted on her own, free-climbing her way up: two steps good, then one falling away as she lost her footing. Pebbles, sand, and clumps of the petrified dirt showered down around her as she went, clawing at the soil, her fingernails ripping and her skin cut by a thousand jagged pieces of sandstone.

Her heart nearly pounding out of her chest, every muscle protesting, she caught herself and continued her ascent.

Almost at the top, she looked up to see Deck's face. An indescribable look of torment filled the gray depths of his eyes. He was talking, pleading . . . She felt the meaning in his words, but blocked out the sound. She *wouldn't* listen. He had no words left she wanted to hear.

The edge was just above her head now; she'd slowed down considerably, her strength tested beyond its limit, nearly giving out. With a grunt of rage she began to pull herself up and over.

Deck's hands locked around her wrists and dragged her toward him. "Let go of me!" she shrieked in fury. Raidon grabbed her torso and helped as she screamed over and over for them to let go, still fighting and kicking and yelling even as they pulled her to safety.

When her knees hit solid ground, she flung them off and stood up, using all her remaining strength to lash out with a kick, cutting a neat gash in Deck's thigh with the crampon.

The look of shock on his face both frightened and pleased her.

She wanted to hurt him. To show him what it was like to have someone you loved turn on you, to betray you when it really mattered. Just like he'd done years ago, and then again, not ten minutes before. Another data point, another piece of proof.

The heavy wasn't having it. He forced himself between them and tried to shove Deck away. But Deck wouldn't run. It was as if he wanted her to cut him. She struck out again, much weaker this time, still trying to make him bleed, all the rage in her heart boiling over.

Raidon finally tackled her to the ground, deactivated the boot. She stopped struggling, gasping for breath, and just let the tears flow freely, not caring that they all watched her cry.

Raidon reared back, and he and Deck stood frozen in place. Deck took a step forward as if to help her up, but Jenny managed to stop crying and get to her feet on her own.

She ran her sleeve across her face to wipe off the paste of grime and sorrow and looked directly into Deck's eyes. "You make it impossible for me to believe in you."

Then she turned her back on them and limped toward the surviving jeep, which had been moved away from the ledge, and where Quinn now sat atop the remaining supplies. The Parliament man leaned over, opened the back door for her, and moved his feet. Wincing, Jenny heaved herself into the back and lay down.

She understood better than they all did about self-preservation, and while she couldn't exactly fault Deck and Raidon for their choices, she could hate them for them. And she could still wish . . . Well, this was really about Deck, now, wasn't it? She could still wish that Deck prized her more highly than that.

The anguish in his voice as she'd fallen and in his eyes even now didn't make a difference. She'd already known they'd had something drawing them to each other, binding them together all these years.

Because of it, she'd misinterpreted his actions in the alley by the Parliament Club. But the opiate wasn't the truth serum she'd thought it to be. It didn't reveal what was true, it revealed what you wished could be true. And that wasn't the same thing at all.

In the end, Deck believed in and cared for his revolution above all things. Raidon believed in his word to protect Deck. Quinn believed in his opiate.

And what did she believe in when all was said and done? Nothing at all.

No, that wasn't true. She believed in herself. She could count on herself.

Several minutes rolled by in silence, Quinn still perched above her. She could hear him rolling his evening cigarette. Finally, when Jenny sat up and brushed the hair out of her face, he took it as a signal and spoke.

"Are you ready to talk?" he asked, as casually as if he were asking for the time.

She turned her head and looked up at him as he struck a match, the flame flaring noisily between them. He quirked an eyebrow, inviting her to a game he'd probably been waiting to play for days.

Jenny shook her head in the negative with the maximum possible display of disdain, but inside, she was more than tempted. Betray Deck? Put herself and her own safety before his?

She glanced back toward the campfire. Deck and Raidon huddled together, probably discussing how to make it up to her. Biting her lower lip, she turned away once more and curled into the back of the seat.

Suddenly, Raidon appeared above her, hovering. The heavy's face was twisted with unhappiness. "Why don't we boil some water to sterilize those cuts and scrapes? You're sure nothing needs to be set?" he asked.

Jenny sat up. She couldn't quite think rationally, couldn't control her anger, and she sure as hell didn't want to be around anyone. "I'm going to take the jeep and check to make sure those pirates are dead," she muttered. She knew they were, but she had to get away.

Without being asked, Quinn gracefully dismounted from the vehicle, and she climbed into the driver seat.

Raidon put his hand on her shoulder, but she shrugged it off. The heavy rubbed the back of his neck looking like he wished he were anywhere else. "Jenny, I'm sorry. I'm so, so sorry. I know that's not enough, but—"

She gripped the steering wheel. "It's all about him

207

and that stupid title, that stupid oath. You make me sick. If he told you to walk back there and jump off that cliff, I think you'd do it. *He released you.* Accept it. He's not a prince anymore. Go home. Pick your own wars, fight your own battles. You're helping him with a revolution you don't even—"

"I know it's hard for you to understand."

"Yeah. Real hard. Deck gave up his claims and obligations to the monarchy. When they gave up on him. And let me tell you something else: We made love last night. Get used to it. Whether he was born a prince or a low-life scum like me, I'm good enough for him—no matter what you think. I'm just not good enough for what you want for him. But frankly, I don't give a damn."

Raidon looked furious. "You don't understand. I look out for you. What it is, is that—"

"Shut up. Just shut up. I know what it is. I know what's what. You're the one who has everything all mixed up." She laughed bitterly. "You looking out for me? What a joke. You can't even look after yourself. If you really believed in the revolution the way he does, it might make sense. But you just believe that his life is worth more than mine because of some dumb oath. Okay, by all means, next time let me die. But maybe you should think things over. Maybe you should think about what's really important. Maybe you should see that a team works together and doesn't prize anyone more highly than another. Then, next time, you'll think twice before you sentence a person to death. Now leave me the hell alone."

Raidon turned to walk away, but then he suddenly whirled back to face her, his finger almost in her face. "I'm sorry about what happened. I told you so. But don't you dare judge me. Think about your own life. Nothing's more important than *you*. You live under the control of whoever can blackmail you or tempt you. I may be forced to do horrible things because of moral duty, but it's better than being moved by selfishness."

She paused. "I'm not entirely sure there's a difference."

Raidon sighed and walked away.

Jenny kicked the ignition and looked over at the passenger side of the jeep. Quinn was leaning on the door frame. He inhaled deeply, then exhaled a series of fine rings in the shape of a bull's-eye. A small smile played on his lips. He stepped away from the vehicle and bowed.

As she put the jeep in reverse and hit the accelerator, all Jenny could think about was how easy it would be to change sides and work with Quinn. Then she would be doing exactly what Raidon accused her of. How easy it would be on the side of power instead of with Deck on the side of futility. If she wasn't worth Deck fighting for, maybe he wasn't worth her fighting for, either.

Chapter Eighteen

"That didn't go well." Deck moved the pot of boiling water to the sand at Raidon's feet and stood up to stamp out the campfire embers.

"No, I didn't make it any better," the heavy admitted. "Maybe I *should* have let you go, but . . . Look, she doesn't want the water. She pretty much doesn't want to have anything to do with us at the moment. I think we should just keep moving."

"Her injuries?"

"From the way she was holding her sides, I'd say bruised ribs. But I think that's the worst of it. Otherwise, she has your basic cuts, scrapes, knocks. She'll pour some antiseptic on then and we can leave it at that. If she wants to mix up some antibiotic, she'll do it on her own. What about that cut on your leg?"

Deck waved him off. "Already handled it." He finished dismantling the makeshift firepit by tossing the stones in different directions, while Raidon

kicked everything around to give things a more natural appearance. Deck brushed off his hands and
looked at his heavy. "She's a wild card, now. She's
definitely a wild card."

Raidon kept his focus on his work. "She's always
been a wild card." Suddenly, he blurted, "And I
don't blame her!"

"I don't either. From bad to worse," Deck muttered.

This emotional fallout from the accident wasn't
even the whole story. Things seemed to have rapidly
degenerated on all fronts. They'd lost a massive
amount of supplies along with the ill-fated jeep, and
while theoretically they were within twenty miles of
the depot, there was no telling what could happen.
Nobody felt particularly hopeful.

Even Quinn was in an unusually foul mood. He'd
realized a large portion of his opiate stash had gone
off the cliff along with the first jeep.

The food and purified water they'd brought were
perilously close to running out, assuming Jenny
came back with them; the temperature was climbing
and it would be difficult to stay hydrated enough.
This wouldn't necessarily be as critical if it weren't
for the kicker: They'd come close to where the first
depot marker was supposed to be located and there
didn't seem to be anything there.

For the hundredth time, Deck looked across the
dunes. There simply didn't seem to be anything but
outback.

It was sand as far as the eye could see, and the
only thing Deck could hope for was that when they

finally traversed the final leg of the journey and stood at the correct spot, they would benefit from a miracle.

He sighed and turned away.

How had everything become so muddled? For the last hour, it seemed that he'd heard Jenny calling out for him in every sound that was made. His mind was playing tricks on him, and no wonder; he'd been slowly making himself insane by replaying the accident over and over in his head, trying to figure out how things had come to this.

Raidon was apparently thinking along the same lines. "It was impossible see that cliff coming," he said, shaking his head.

Deck ran his index finger across the red blurry line soaking through the bandage on the gash in his leg. "The sand dune camouflaged it."

"I just didn't see it coming." Raidon paused, then opened his mouth again to speak, but ultimately closed it without a word.

Deck often got the impression his liegeman wanted to unburden himself of his thoughts, but the man simply couldn't allow himself to treat Deck as a friend. At least, not as an equal. Deck sat down and looked at the heavy. "If you were calling the shots—if you weren't once my liegeman, I mean—what would you have done?"

Raidon gave him a small, uncertain smile. "I've been unable to reconcile my word with the recent events. When I thought she'd gone down . . ." His voice turned rusty. "Things that once seemed black

213

and white are suddenly turning gray." He slowly met Deck's gaze, and added obliquely, "You let me out of my responsibilities long ago."

"Yes, I did," Deck said softly. "You know that you are always free to go your own way. So, tell me what you would have done."

Raidon stared out into the darkness. "The way I saw it, I had a one hundred percent chance of saving you if I grabbed you first. If I'd gone for her, the chance of saving you would have decreased. Obviously, that was not acceptable. However, if I had gone for her first, I probably would have got her. It's also likely I could have gotten both of you up alive." He spoke matter-of-factly, as if it all were a mere question of strategy.

Then he sighed. "Who knows? When and how the car fell was the question mark in all this. If I'd gone for her first, the car could have flipped and taken everything down. It's impossible to say."

"What would you do next time?"

The heavy stared at his feet and then suddenly swung up his head and looked Deck straight in the eye, as if he had to force himself to do so. "To be honest, my lord," he said, his voice becoming so quiet Deck had to strain to hear it, "if something similar were to happen again, I'm not entirely certain I would play it the same. It's just that I'm not entirely clear my choice was the right one."

It seemed to Deck that somewhere along the line, Raidon had begun to form his own opinions, his own beliefs, but was constrained from using them because of something very old-fashioned—he'd given his word. Unthinking loyalty was prized in royal bodyguards, and Raidon was one of the best that had ever been. Which meant he'd given his word to do what he should do, not what he wanted. But could Deck still demand that of him? "What do you mean?" he asked his heavy.

"I don't know. There was very little time. Did I choose to save you because of my oath of loyalty? Do I still believe in that oath? If I do, Jenny is a commoner and you are a nobleman—the nobleman ranks higher in any choice of life and death." The look in Raidon's eyes was a mixture of confusion, shame, hope, and also the look of a man who'd come into his own somewhere along the line. It was a surprising look for someone who'd been a servant at the royal palace almost all his life. "Or perhaps it was because you are fighting for a cause, a cause big enough to trump, say, even an oath of loyalty.

"Or maybe I was just selfishly holding on to the way I've always known."

Deck realized it was the first time in the ten years or so that he'd known the man at his side who was protecting him, that Raidon had verbalized any doubts or displeasure with an act made to protect Deck's life. That he was questioning his oath, comparing its relative value to the revolutionary cause or another person's life, was telling, indeed.

He himself was having a similar attack of conscience. For the first time since he'd reshaped himself as a Shadow Runner, since he'd committed his resources, his skills—his entire life, really—to the revolution, staring into Jenny's wide frightened eyes

215

he'd felt his conviction weaken. It now manifested itself in the most profound sense of shame he'd ever experienced. It was a shame so intense, there was no justification that could make it go away.

He rubbed his eyes, sore from the swirling sand since he'd lost his goggles in the accident. Perhaps in his other lifetime, as a prince, he could justify anything he'd ever needed or wanted with just his title. Well, he'd surrendered that privilege, and with his new life came a completely different set of responsibilities as a man.

He nodded and stood up, shaking out his cramped limbs.

He put his hand on Raidon's shoulder and said, "Consider whether you gave your word to the man or the title. I'm a man, just like you. Prince D'ekkar Han Valoren is a phantom. I have no surviving allegiance to the House of Han. I am a prince no longer. I will never be king, and the monarchy is destined to fall. Any debt of honor you once owed me has been paid many times. My name is D'ekkar Valoren, and as you know, my friends just call me Deck. As I've said before, your life must be your own."

The heavy looked relieved he didn't have to reply, for Jenny came roaring back into camp in the jeep. She rolled to a stop, jumped over the door, wiped the sweat off her forehead, pulled her comm headset off, and tossed it on the seat next to her GPS.

Raidon handed her the water they'd boiled and she took a swig.

"The pirates are dead. I didn't go too far after that, but for the next couple of miles it looks like a bona fide trade route. Seems safe enough." She looked away, toward the horizon. "It's pretty bleak, though," she added dully.

The three of them just sort of stood there awkwardly, probably all wanting to say something, yet not wanting to all speak at the same time. Saying thanks seemed inappropriate. "Thanks for checking that out." With the subtext being, "Sorry I would have let you die back there." Deck shook his head, wondering how all those years of practicing diplomacy at the palace couldn't help him with this situation.

Jenny broke the silence. "Well, I'll get Quinn."

Deck just nodded. She was doing her job, but it was as if a light had gone off inside her. She was cold, distant, and horribly efficient. She was blank.

Deck already missed her, that wildcat with one hundred different kinds of attitude, fighting back, taking names, not afraid of confrontation. Not afraid of him. They'd touched briefly, intimately, the way he'd always wanted. But now she'd built up an impregnable wall around her, worse than ever, and if he even made a step toward her, she seemed to sense it and recoil. Maybe he should do it anyway: muster up some sort of apology that would sound reasonable under the circumstances—but he knew her well enough to know that she would take it as a hollow, token excuse. A weakness. Any such attempt would only make her respect him less.

In a way, he struggled with the same issues as Raidon. Had his hesitation in that moment been a reflex, or had letting her go been the decision he thought he should make? Did it reflect his true feelings about the revolution and about Jenny—or had it been a stupid blunder, his mind warring with his heart?

There was nothing he could do to make this right. Nothing right now, that was for certain. He turned on his heel and helped Raidon ready the jeep for departure.

On the road again, Jenny sat in the back. Deck watched her hang over the front seats with the GPS device directing Raidon as they turned in and out of nowhere and nothing until a road of sorts seemed to emerge. They followed it for miles.

Then, "I think this is right," she said. "Slower . . . slower . . ."

Raidon downshifted. Deck's heart beat faster.

"Slower . . . a little more, just a hair . . ." Jenny raised her hand in the air, then with a quick downward slicing motion yelped, "Stop!" She snapped the lid of the positioning device closed and, without a touch of humor, said, "We're here. We made it."

The vehicle rolled to a stop. Nobody dared look at Deck. He could feel them purposely avoiding his gaze. They didn't have to; the tension in the air said it all. There was no structure towering out from the sand, no busy communications depot manned by the Shadow Runners. There was nothing in the sand at their feet indicating an underground facility. There was nothing around but miles and miles of sand and a hot sun beating down on them.

Raidon's hand reflexively crept to the canteen hanging off his utility belt. He shook it and let it drop; it sounded near empty.

Deck shaded his face and looked up at the sky that wasn't going to provide any relief any time soon. He sighed.

"What were you expecting exactly?" Jenny asked roughly.

He looked at her. Well, snideness was better than blankness, anyway.

He jumped out of the jeep and began to walk away from it. Raidon called out, something about land mines or some such crap. He kept walking. He had to get away.

Suddenly, a ripple pierced the atmosphere. It wasn't something Deck heard, so much as a thickness he felt. "What the hell was that?" he called.

From the jeep, the three looked at him as if he were insane. He walked forward another few steps and the ripple was all around him. "What the hell *is* that?"

Raidon looked at Jenny, then jumped out of the vehicle and walked toward Deck with his pistol cocked.

"Where have I smelled this before?" Deck murmured, unable to put his finger on the odor suddenly assailing him. It wasn't a bad smell, but a . . . a burning smell, perhaps?

"It's familiar," Raidon agreed. He obviously smelled it, too. Jenny jumped out of the jeep, grabbing the grenade launcher, and joining them; Quinn climbed out to stretch his legs.

Deck just shook his head and continued to walk the dunes. In certain directions, the thickness and the smell were more pronounced. He followed the strongest areas of the sensation.

Out of nowhere—what literally seemed like nowhere—a shot rang out.

"Son of a bitch! Everyone on the ground. Get down and make sure your armor's in place." Deck hit the dirt next to Jenny, throwing a protective arm over her back. She shook it off.

Raidon army-crawled toward them.

Deck looked for Quinn who had ducked behind the jeep. He almost smiled at the grimy grayish-stockinged ankles visible in the gap between the ground and the vehicle; the Parliament man was bent over at the waist, unwilling to get the knees of his stockings or his pantaloons dirty. The idiot was going to get himself killed one of these days.

"Do you see where it came from?" Jenny asked.

"The bullet struck about there," Deck said, pointing at a faraway hole in the crusty sand.

Jenny crawled on her stomach to the mark, then extended her handheld to register the location and angle of entry. She pulled the box back and read the result. "Thirty-two degrees south." She tucked the handheld into her jacket, then programmed the trajectory into her grenade launcher, staying low to the ground.

"Don't shoot. Do *not* shoot," Deck warned her.

"I won't shoot until I'm sure," she said and kept moving, scrambling across the sand to a large rock, which she used to brace her weapon. She bent her head to the sights, then pressed the automatic aim button. The launcher muzzle pivoted slightly, locking in on the spot from which the bullet had fired. She looked there, then looked behind her. "There's nothing to be seen for miles," she called. "It's completely desolate."

Deck moved up behind her.

Another shot rang out; both he and Jenny flinched. Her index finger bounced on the trigger but didn't fire. She adjusted her weapon. "Is anybody hit? If anybody's hit, I'm pulling the trigger," she announced grimly.

Deck leaned up on his arm and looked behind him. "Who's hit?" he called out. Raidon shook his head in the negative, perplexed and gestured outward as if to say that no bullet had connected.

"What the hell is going on here? If I didn't know any better, I'd say that these were just warning shots into the air."

Jenny wiped the sweat from her forehead, and her palm on the front of her shirt, then moved her finger back to the grenade launcher trigger. A moment later, she lowered its muzzle. "Deck, there's really nobody to be seen for miles."

He figured it out. "Hologram technology," he explained. "That smell; it's a hologram, a mirage. We're here!"

Come to think of it, he'd encountered the same smell and feel just before the jeep had gone off the cliff. Had that been why they hadn't seen anything?

"You've gotta be right," Jenny said. "And it doesn't explain the target practice."

"The depot's here," Deck said. "I know it's here." He jumped up and began to walk briskly forward, with his hand out slowly, groping through the air like a blind man. An odd ripple filled the atmosphere around him. Like a warm breeze, but thicker, he felt the strange substance touching his skin. He stumbled, feeling almost as if he were being pushed slightly by the thickness.

He kept going, and behind him heard Jenny swear and say, "Deck, just . . . I wouldn't, Deck. Don't!" From the corner of his eye, he saw Raidon leap up from his duck-and-cover position and race across the dunes toward him, once again ignoring concern for his own protection.

And suddenly Deck's hand disappeared into a shimmering blur of a wall before him. The landscape that stretched out ahead like an endless desert, rippled like a warped painting.

"Get back from there," Raidon yelled, his rifle raised.

Deck turned back and waved the others on. "It's okay! You can bring the jeep."

Jenny was still for a moment, then she ran to the vehicle, pretty much pulled Quinn in, and started the engine.

Raidon yelled all the way across the dunes and, never slowing down, dove headfirst through the hologram.

Deck calmly stepped through to the depot he'd built long ago but never seen.

Chapter Nineteen

A hive of activity buzzed behind the hologram. Deck's arrival, oddly enough, sparked something that reminded Jenny of the sort of jubilant royal reception Kyber had received when visiting one of his territories last month. She'd seen it on one of the holoscreens in a bar in Macao. Deck wouldn't like that comparison—or the implication that Kyber was beloved, but there it was.

She narrowed her eyes and slumped against the wall with her arms crossed, watching the scene play out. The depot was much smaller than she had imagined, but not in a bad way. It was compact, sleek in construction, and even surprisingly clean, without feeling overtly sterile. The only decorations Jenny could see from the lobby were huge, brightly colored and framed photovids and holoscreens of cities throughout the world.

The so-called Shadow Runners came out of

nowhere to shake Deck's hand and greet him, taking his bags, handing him bottles of purified water, even snapping scrapbook vids. They welcomed him like a damn messiah or something, and when a call went out for an emergency meeting, it was like watching the emperor himself being led to the conference room.

Deck's joy was truly something to behold. Though Jenny still wanted to believe the mission was built on Deck's hubris or desire for revenge, watching him now, she simply didn't think so. He did not act regal, simply greeted each of his revolutionaries with a hug and encouraged them to stay focused. They obviously all shared a common cause. And the sad thing about it was, after all they'd been through, she and Deck, this success still wasn't Jenny's to share.

As the crowd trickled away, it became obvious that he'd completely forgotten about her.

Curious in spite of herself, Jenny grabbed her bag and followed behind. As she tried to pass through the conference room door, an arm came down, blocking her passage. "Sorry, but do you have some ID?"

She looked up at the guard. "Are you kidding me? I just came here with Deck."

The guy looked sympathetic, but not sympathetic enough. "Did he give you a security card, by any chance?"

"No, but—"

"I'm really sorry," the guard repeated, and literally closed the door in her face.

Jenny stared at the gray paint and tried to listen through the metal. The muffled sounds of cheering and some laughter escaped—something clever Deck had said, undoubtedly, she thought bitterly. But she couldn't hear what was said.

She listlessly walked around the conference room. She didn't belong. She never belonged, to anyone, anywhere. Deck had called her selfish once. So had Raidon. Well, maybe so. Always the outsider, she was always looking out for number one—because no one else would. If that was selfish, she'd be happy to wear it on a badge.

She looked up at the bright photovids on the wall. They were probably supposed to remind everyone what they were working toward—freedom around the world. Jenny was simply reminded that she'd likely never see any of those places.

The look on Deck's face as he'd disappeared into that room, in the last moment turning to look at someone behind him—he'd been smiling, happy. Overjoyed. This place perfectly embodied him. It was off-limits, his secrets were off-limits, his trust was off-limits, and the one thing he cared about most was off-limits. Bastard.

Standing outside the conference room door with her hands clenched into fists, Jenny felt a rage unlike anything she'd ever experienced in her life.

She reeled around and started running—through the corridors, haphazardly trying to open the doors lining both sides. She couldn't open any of them; they all required a key card. Lost in the maze of hallways, she looked around for the exit, stumbling and suddenly desperate. This was what he would have let her die for, just this: steel and stucco. Her shoulder and ribs ached as she careened around a corner, picking up speed, running as fast as she could, wanting to have a shout, leaping up to tag the ceiling with her hand. She ran in circles, it seemed, head pounding, ribs throbbing, but nothing was more painful than the ache in her heart.

And just when she thought she'd go mad if she didn't get out of the place, there stood Quinn, striking a pose in the center of the hall, his intentions as transparent as a punch in the gut. He had one hand's palm against his hip, finger curled slightly for effect, and one hand up to the brim of his hat. His eyes glittered like the fake diamond in his cravat.

Jenny slowed to a jog and finally to a walk until she stood in front of him.

It was just the two of them, on the outside looking in.

"Come with me," he said. His gloved hand reached out and grabbed her upper arm in an iron grip, the most deliberate act from him she'd ever witnessed.

She let him drag her back down the corridor to the unisex bathroom, shuttling her hastily into one of the stalls and checking beneath the divider to make sure no one else was around. She let him back her up between the toilet paper and the tampon slot, not even fighting, feeling a certain inevitability to all this. When he realized she wasn't struggling, he actually seemed surprised and simply let go of her.

"I do apologize for manhandling you, my dear girl. For some reason, I expected this to be a bit of a harder sell."

His gentlemanly manner under the circumstances seemed ridiculous. Jenny laughed, her ribs protesting once again, reminding her that her world had turned upside down. Enemies were friends, friends enemies. She was working for one side . . .

. . . she was working for the other?

She sucked in a quick breath of air. "You haven't sold me anything yet." But of course, that was what he wanted, the hideous, crazy, whacked-out little bastard. He had no worthwhile future of his own, and he was just another of the spokes in the same wheel that had her trapped like behind prison bars.

"Yet."

She closed her eyes, hands curling into fists.

"It's quite all right, my dear," he said, incongruously, gently tucking stray wisps of hair behind her ears.

His touch sent a sick little shiver down her spine, and she opened her eyes again. She surveyed him coldly, as if from afar, and calculated the distance between her fingers and her gun, her fingers and her knife—a simple matter to delete him with a bullet through the head or a blade into the gut.

But murder and Parliament didn't mix well, and it was what had ultimately landed her in this unfortunate mess in the first place. And now that she might or might not escape Newgate again . . .

Parliament had come for her at last. In its own time, with its own agenda.

"I think this is as good a moment as ever," Quinn said.

"For what?" And so the dance would begin. The

negotiation. The conflict. The weighing of the options. The inevitable sacrifices. The wrong choices. The revenge. The necessary bottom line that required her to look out for her own interests because she knew no one else would.

"For settling your debt with Parliament," he said. He gave a flourish of his hand.

Jenny chewed nervously on her lower lip. "It was self-defense."

"A member of Parliament died at your hands. Somebody has to be held accountable. You know how that is."

"I didn't mean to kill him, believe me."

"It doesn't matter what you meant. It matters what you did. I'm sure you know that."

"It was self-defense," she insisted.

"Call it what you will. The outcome is the same."

"You'd better believe I'll call it what it is," she said, infuriated. "You don't just grab people off the streets and expect them to be your personal whores like it's some kind of honor."

"Most ladies are delighted to receive an invitation into the Parliament family."

"Invitation? Your buddy tried to force me, and when I fought back, when I pushed him away, he hit his head. It was that simple. I'm not saying I didn't fight, but I never tried to kill him. And—"

"You've killed men before, no? Why should we believe this was any different?"

"It was self-defense. I've never killed anyone with my bare hands. Or point-blank, for that matter. And

I've never shot at anyone without a good reason. I don't initiate conflict. I run from it and—"

"And it just finds you," he finished. "This conversation is making me very tired. I'm frankly not particularly interested in the hows and whys of your life. You killed a member of Parliament. Nobody cares why you did it. They care that you did it at all. We have to act. That's how it works. You obviously know this, or you wouldn't have run in the first place. I'm telling you, this is the end of the line. You work with me now, do what I ask, or there will be a clip notice out as soon as I return. Or if I don't."

She folded her arms across her chest. "There's already one out on me."

"Not with a bounty offering and a K.O.S."

Kill On Sight. Jenny licked her lips. "So that's how it is."

"That's how it is." He waved his hand languidly in the air. "You can dye that lovely red hair of yours, but we'll find you. You'll be looking over your shoulder for the rest of your life. And don't believe those who say Parliament's reach extends only to the shores of Australia. We have eyes all over the world. After you left Newgate, I believe you made unauthorized visits in New Seoul and Hong Kong prior to your longer stint in Macao. I'm sure it was rather difficult to find employment." He clucked sympathetically. "Am I correct?"

There was no way he could possibly know that she'd been to those places, hiding there, unless Parliament's reach really was a lot farther than she'd thought. A shiver ran down her spine. Quinn gave her a most demure look while waiting for some kind of answer.

His cavalier behavior infuriated Jenny all the more. Why was she always at someone else's mercy? If you don't do this, yadda yadda. Why didn't she have the right to control her own life? Of course, that wasn't entirely fair, now, was it? She *had* been given choices. Difficult choices, impossible choices, granted, but choices nonetheless.

She slammed her head back against the stall, the metal sheet rippling from the impact. No, it simply wasn't fair to call a choice between the greater of two evils having true control over one's life.

"It's time for you to decide, Jenny Red, what your future will bring." Quinn rubbed his lower lip with his thumb and studied her. "This is very simple. You work with me now, your debt to Parliament is paid. All your running, hiding . . . it will all be over."

She laughed hollowly. "Is that so?"

"You'll live at the highest echelon in Newgate, with free reign of all of Parliament's resources. Just imagine. Never again will you be asked to do something you don't want to do. By anyone," he added meaningfully.

"That's not what I want."

Quinn looked extremely bored. "Please. Use your head. Whatever Lord Valoren offered you outside of Newgate, consider this: He will never pay up on the deal you have struck, and you will never get what he promised."

Jenny swallowed, hard, suddenly feeling a new

terror. Did Quinn know something? Would eventually Deck's alliance with the revolution lead to his death? Was he doomed already? Or did Quinn mean that Parliament itself would kill him? "You don't know that," she snarled.

Quinn tipped his head to one side and studied her. "You never did tell Lord Valoren why there is no love lost between you and Parliament, did you? Tsk, tsk, my dear. That's not a very strong show of trust, is it?"

Jenny felt her face flame. She looked away.

"Funny how your ties to Parliament just get stronger and stronger while that with Valoren becomes weaker and weaker. Best take advantage of my offer. You will find that it will not be so easy to escape Newgate as it was the first time. Even if you fled now, or killed me . . ." Quinn lifted her chin and forced her to look him square in the eyes. "If you don't look out for yourself, no one will. His Lordship has proven that he can't be trusted with your life. Something greater holds his attention."

She just stared at him. For a guy who seemed on another planet most of the time, Quinn sure had figured out just where to hit her to make it hurt.

"He would have let you die, Jenny. He would just as soon have let you die—had he not needed you to bring him here."

His words shocked her. They shocked her because she knew in her heart that they weren't true. She'd wanted to indulge in her anger enough to justify turning on him, but Deck cared about her. He might still choose the revolution first, but whether she lived or died was of no small consequence to him. It was in his touch and in his eyes. She couldn't betray him.

"No," she said as she shoved Quinn away from her. "That's not how it went. I don't care what you thought you saw or think you know. You weren't the one looking into his eyes." She shoved him away and barreled out of the bathroom stall.

Quinn was on her heels. He reached out and grabbed her fauxhawk, yanking her backward. "This is turning out to be a bit of a hard sell, after all," he said with a frown. He casually reached into the breast pocket of his jacket, but instead of pulling out his cigarette case, he pulled out an illegal neuron fryer. It probably had a kill attachment. Portable, painful, and eventually deadly.

He pointed the weapon at her temple and then wrapped his arm around her neck, shoving her toward the door. As they passed the mirror over the sink, Jenny saw a white-faced, redheaded girl with dark circles under her eyes and a crumbling dandy not quite far enough along the road to decay and self-destruction to save her.

Chapter Twenty

Quinn hustled her out the door and down through the back halls of the depot. Jenny stumbled, hardly seeing where she was going.

Glancing up, she couldn't see any inside cameras. There weren't going to be a lot of security systems, here. And why would there be? It was tough to smuggle in parts. The Shadow Runners' depot was small, their operation was small, and their team was small. Everybody knew everybody else. And everybody who'd otherwise be keeping an eye on things would be in Deck's impromptu meeting. Had Deck trusted Jenny to keep an eye on Quinn? The thought made her cringe.

They stopped in front of an unmarked door, and Quinn kept his eyes focused on hers as he reached into his coat and pulled out his cigarette case. He opened a false bottom and flourished a blank card—obviously a keycard, though his looked slightly different than the ones she'd seen brandished around the depot thus far.

"Look familiar?" he asked.

Jenny arched an eyebrow. "Where did you get that?"

"Lord Valoren visited us at the Parliament Club, if you recall."

They must have gone through his pockets and copied the code after drugging him. How gentleman-like.

Quinn seemed ragged. His quirky arrogance was dulled, and he was paying little attention to his appearance. His hands shook. It was obvious he was running low on opiate. Jenny wondered how she might use that fact to her advantage, but everything was happening so fast.

Parliament must have known about the Shadow Runners before she and Deck ever set foot in Newgate. They probably just hadn't known a safe way to get at them until Deck willingly entered the country. They'd known exactly what they were doing when they sent Quinn along, and it had had nothing to do with electricity costs. It was about power, yes, but a different kind.

Perhaps the Newgate aristocrats saw the Shadow Voice's revolution as a direct threat to their own power, as Raidon and Jenny had warned Deck before Quinn came. Well, it was probably what Deck had in mind eventually, challenging them, although fighting even just the UCE would keep the world's revolutionaries busy for a long, long time.

Quinn finished wiping the card off on his cravat,

which he left mussed and half hanging out of his waistcoat. He handed it over to Jenny, pointed at the card reader, and waited, brandishing the neuron fryer menacingly.

Two options, here: Actually play the game with Quinn, or just pretend to play the game with Quinn. She could do whatever he asked her to do, then get away from him as soon as possible, double back around, and fix the damage before anyone was the wiser. Or, she could do whatever he asked her to do, but under the intent of actually taking Parliament's offer, thereby never again having to worry about their bounty hunters coming up behind her in a market square. Meaning, she could play the ace. After all, time and again it seemed that when the chips were down, Deck chose his revolution over her. He could hardly fault her for doing the reverse. That was what she could tell herself, anyway, in the middle of the night with her heart pounding and her eyes filling with tears.

"Could we please get on with it?" Quinn hissed. He pushed her up against the door.

Whichever option she chose, this part was going to work out the same. She slid the key card into the reader and—*click*—bumped the door open.

They stepped into what was clearly a small but well-organized data center, filled with a couple of enormous servers, data storage systems, and then a maze of wires and whatnot that were clearly related to the telecom matrix.

Oddly enough in this sterile place, Jenny thought of making love to Deck, passionate in the crazy aftermath of that animal attack. She'd thought they'd reached a new level in their relationship. She'd allowed herself to dream that maybe they could be together in this new world order that he believed so strongly in—that there was a place for them together in the heart of the revolution. And then . . .

She shook her head, trying to clear her mind of the memories, but they came around to the back of the facility and Jenny could actually hear the hum and cadence of Deck's voice through the wall as he talked with his Shadow Runners. She could not make out his words.

"What do you want me to do?" she asked, making a mental note to remember as much as possible about what was to happen here, in case she wanted or needed to undo the damage.

"You're going to get me the scrambler chip," he murmured. "The one that keeps the whereabouts of the Shadow Voice hidden."

"What does it look like?"

Quinn slapped her hard across the face.

Jenny sucked in a quick breath. She hadn't expected that. It was a strange movement, outside of Quinn's normal code of conduct, and a much faster reflex than what she'd seen from him before. He was going into withdrawal; she was sure of it.

"I'll tell you exactly what you need to do. Keep your voice down."

She ignored her stinging cheeks, wishing he was holding just about any weapon but a neuron fryer. He'd more than just proved that his mental state and reflexes weren't reliable, and she wouldn't take the chance of jumping him, however much she was tempted.

In a low voice, Quinn began to rattle off a litany of instructions. He recited the procedure robotically. It was obvious he'd studied the order of things carefully, and obvious that Parliament had a lot of information about the Shadow Voice probably no one knew they had. But then again, it wasn't too surprising. Parliament's trafficking of information was probably as big a covert business for them as the providing of Australia's power supply.

She unscrewed the back panel from one of the machines per Quinn's explanations, fiddled around with a couple of wires, pried off the lock holding it in place, then carefully extracted a green, wafer-thin chip plate, committing to memory everything he said to her—and the order in which he said it.

Once the chip plate was free, Jenny paused, half expecting some sort of alarm to go off, and for the room to be stormed by a huge security detail.

Nothing happened.

Naïve revolutionaries. They didn't see the depot as a fighting outpost. Just communications. They probably believed that if an attack ever came, they'd be able to catch it with the hologram, that they'd have time for a defense. They didn't suspect sabotage by someone whom their leader had brought in himself. Even if there was a security tape, no one would be reviewing it for a while.

Quinn peered at the tiny chip.

Jenny sighed. It was done. From what Deck had told her, with the scrambler chip out of play everything would be exponentially more open to trace when the Shadow Voice came back online. The location of this depot could be traced, and likely other devices abetting transmission from the Shadow Voice—meaning that many of those revolutionary transmitters could be located and arrested.

She held up the chip between her forefinger and thumb, wondering at the notion that world freedom was somehow connected to the tiny piece of hardware.

"Screw the panel back," Quinn ordered.

She laid the chip on one of the machines and began to work on putting the panel back. "If you already know exactly what to do, what do you need me for? Why didn't you just do it?"

"What? Don't you want to help?" He smiled at his joke and cleared his throat. "I think you'll be glad to benefit from our little offer. You can trust us."

He meant to remind her of the Parliament's deal, which was apparently still good, and that Deck wasn't someone she could rely on; he meant to make her feel justified in what he was forcing her to do.

Jenny stared at him. "You don't want to touch anything, do you?"

He gave her an indulgent smile. "It's much better if it's your prints, your presence, and"—he reached up to the side of her face and, when Jenny tried to turn away, yanked a strand of hair from her head—"your lovely, unique hair." He levered his arm toward the wall and dropped the strand behind the machines. "Don't bother trying to convince Lord

Valoren you were forced into all this. There will be no evidence I was ever here."

"I could theoretically just tell him what happened. You know, like the truth?"

Quinn laughed rather hoarsely. "Do you really think he'll believe you? He let you fall off that cliff to protect his interests, girl. Your revenge now is a natural reaction. And Lord Valoren is a man who should know." He stood there, looking as though she were the one who'd gone insane.

Maybe Deck would believe her. Maybe he wouldn't. Jenny wasn't certain of anything at this point.

Quinn suddenly coughed, choking on his own saliva. Jenny smiled, inexplicably triumphant as the man retrieved a stump of his opiate stick and sucked almost desperately on it. She could see the moment the drug passed into his system. He reminded her of a shorted robot that had just been plugged back into its power supply. When he turned to look at her, the raggedness was gone, the swaggering, decadent hero of his own vidclip was back.

"Put the chip in here," he said, handing her a thin plastic case.

She took the case and opened it. "What's the point of all this?" she asked casually. "Why do you care if they're broadcasting a voice about revolution from out here? You have an ironclad hold over Newgate. And the criminals here? They don't want democracy. Nobody will dare try to rise up against you."

Quinn just smiled and gestured for her to finish.

"Whatever," she snapped, and then with a quick

flick of her wrist pitched the cased chip neatly into the sliver of space between the floor and one of the standing servers.

Quinn's jaw clenched. To Jenny's surprise, he flung himself to the ground and tried to squeeze his hand into the narrow slot, to no avail. "I should shoot you for that! Do you have any idea how much that chip is worth?"

She shrugged. "Whatever," she repeated, with as much attitude as she dared, suddenly noticing that she wasn't the only one sweating. Quinn wiped his forehead and looked wildly around the room, probably for something with which to fish out the chip.

The rumble of applause shook the back wall, and Jenny knew Deck must be finished talking. She looked at Quinn, and grinned. "Do you want to keep trying to get it out from under there?" she asked.

The Parliament man looked nervously from the wall to the crack beneath the server. "It doesn't matter," he said under his breath. "Though it would have been nice to have the proof."

How odd. He seemed wistful for a moment, as though bringing the chip back to show his Parliament peers would have been more of a triumph to him than the idea of thwarting the revolution. But he said no more, simply turned to the door. "Let's go."

Fine with her. All she wanted to do right now was to get out of this room and put some distance between them.

They sprinted through the doors and back down the hall. Jenny tried to veer off to the bathroom to get away from Quinn, but he snatched the back of her jacket and held her fast. "Why in such a hurry?" he hissed. "You don't want to make us look guilty, do you?"

They stood there at the wall in the main lobby, pretending to admire a photovid of the Tri-Canadian border as if they'd been closely examining the framed vid for the last twenty minutes. Jenny's heart pounded in her chest as a crowd of Runners began to empty out of the meeting.

A guy stepped up next to her. "Sorry about the warning shot. We didn't recognize you at first." He peeled off before she could answer.

Jenny looked around, unsure where to go or what to do. She tried to head back into the bathroom to hide, but Deck arrested her with a shout over the growing chatter.

"Jenny! Over here." Jenny's eyes met his and she pushed through the crowd toward him.

"The Shadow Runners, Jenny. We made it!"

She looked up and gave him a brilliant smile, and then they both suddenly seemed to realize at the same moment that they were on the outs.

Raidon appeared and cut through the awkward silence. "The inner circle is gathering to plan the logistics of tonight, sir. We've been contacted by the Voice. It's ready to go."

Deck nodded. "Look, could you get Jenny a security pass? I think she should be here for it." He turned to Jenny. "If you're so inclined. Sorry about the meeting, but—"

"We can take care of it right now," Raidon interrupted.

"Quinn needs to be watched," Jenny blurted.

"Yeah. Like I said, sorry to keep you on babysitting duty so long. We've got it covered now," Deck said. "It's time for his tour."

Jenny turned and saw a small woman with neatly tied black hair approach the dandy. She recognized the woman as a scullery maid from the old palace in Han City.

Quinn said something to her, then turned and caught Jenny's eye. "My dear girl!" he called. "A lovely chat. I enjoyed it very much." He removed his top hat and executed a beautiful, sweeping bow, then gave the tour guide his arm.

"Go to hell," she answered under her breath, ignoring the surprised looks around her. She had to wonder if she only just hallucinated his mocking response:

"Already there, Jenny. Already there."

Chapter Twenty-one

Deck watched Quinn stare at the holovid of Hong Kong Harbor through the glass above the console. The man looked like hell. He remembered the hangover he'd had after just one exposure to the opiate; it was not pleasant, and undoubtedly whatever Quinn was experiencing after using so heavily for so long had to be much, much worse.

Deck excused himself from the control room and walked out to join the man, who seemed about to wander off aimlessly. "I'd like to talk to you, Lord Quinn."

"Of course. I was hoping to run into you. I wanted to thank you for arranging the tour. My guide was most helpful with respect to explaining the rather complicated design of your station. I confess, some of the details elude me, but I'm impressed with your operation, nonetheless. I think Parliament will be quite pleased with the settlement. Did you wish to discuss the terms?"

Deck smiled. "Your guide has approval to negotiate the settlement with you directly. She'll fill me in later. It was about something else I wished to speak with you."

"Tell me what's on your mind." Quinn's voice was hoarse, his eyes bloodshot.

"To put it bluntly, you don't look well."

Quinn pulled out his cigarette case and displayed his sorry remnants of opiate. "A bit low, my friend. A bit low." He pulled out the shortest stub and relit it with his lighter, while Deck watched in disgust.

"Well, if you plan to stay at this depot awhile, I suggest you report to the medic immediately. See what they can do for you, or catch the supply transport. There's one going to Newgate tonight. It's your call."

Quinn perked right up. "Oh, I think it's definitely time to head back. I've seen what I came for."

Deck nodded. "I'll see if Jenny wants to get on it, too."

Quinn got a queer look in his eye. "Best not, old chap. I think the poor girl needs more rest before another trip. She'd never admit it, though. I suggest you keep my departure quiet."

Deck considered. "You're probably right. I can send her back separately in the next couple of days. You'd both be more comfortable with a little more personal space in the transport, anyway." Not to mention, he wasn't quite sure he was ready to part with her yet. Perhaps there was a way to fix things.

Quinn cracked his neck and inhaled the tinted

smoke floating in the air. Then he blew a cloud of it directly into Deck's face.

Deck waved it away impatiently and gave the man a steely stare. How many times did he have to ask Quinn to stop? He moistened his dry lips, feeling nervous and unsettled, feeling the pull.

"Do you want some?" Quinn asked.

Something dawned on Deck. Something that had been nagging at him for some time. "Why are you constantly offering me that crap? Nobody else, just me."

"My dear man, I'm not about to waste it on the hired help. You know, I rather think . . ." the dandy began, taking a long drag on his short cigarette as if it were some sort of life preserver, his hands steadier now, "I rather think I both fascinate and repel you."

"How so?" Deck asked, unwilling to keep the loathing from his tone.

"I'm just like you."

"You're nothing like me."

Quinn looked much amused. "I am. Well, with one minor difference. I'm you without a shred of hope."

"I think you've got it right. And it's because of one other really big difference I can think of. It's called self-control."

"You don't even realize, you're just a hairbreadth away from losing your mind." Quinn began to laugh, a high-pitched noise that made Deck want to put his hands around the man's neck and squeeze. "We all are, really. You'll come back to the fold, Lord Valoren," he taunted. He gave an exaggerated bow at the waist and a tip of his hat.

Deck did grab him now, grabbed him by the cravat and pulled the little bastard onto the toes of his boots. "What are you really doing here?" he asked through gritted teeth.

Quinn hung there, awkwardly suspended in Deck's grip. The cigarette flopped between his lips as he drawled, "I'm beginning to wonder that meself, old boy. Damned unpleasant out here."

Deck let him go and got more in his face. "No, I'm asking: What are you *really* doing here?"

A peculiar look appeared in Quinn's eyes. "What are *you* really doing here?" he answered softly, an edge of menace in his voice.

"You can stay, you know. You can stay. You're already going into withdrawal—we can finish weaning you off the addiction. Parliament isn't your only option. Nobody in Newgate knows exactly where you are." Deck added a little cruelly, "I doubt they'd send someone out here just to find you."

"I think you're underestimating them," Quinn whispered.

"I think you follow them blindly. You follow them because you don't know anything else anymore. You follow them because they tell you what to do, and if you don't they keep away the opiate. Am I right? Is that how it works? And if they keep away the opiate, then you can see your sad life, the pathetic shell of a man that you've become. You can't wait to get back, because you're starting to see too clearly. You'd have to choose your own way. Well, I'm not one of you. And I'll never be one of you." Deck suddenly wanted Quinn as far away from him and the Shadow Runners and their business as possible. Now. "You have fifteen minutes to be in the front lobby for that transport. Be on it."

With a lightning-fast motion, he brought the side of his hand down hard on Quinn's wrist. The dandy cried out and dropped his pathetic fag on the ground.

Deck pulverized it with his boot, then looked at Quinn, who seemed almost childlike in his distress. No snappy comebacks, no posing. Quinn's shell was cracking, and the man behind it was falling apart.

As the dandy got down on his hands and knees to scrape the remnants of the cigarette off the floor, Deck just curled his lip and stalked away. If the bastard wanted it bad enough, he could stick his face in the mess and inhale. Deck was done playing the diplomat. He was done tiptoeing around. It was time to make something happen here, and nobody was going to stop him from doing it.

It was obvious that Quinn knew too much. But it was also obvious that he'd always known too much. Deck keyed into a hidden door in the back of a janitor's closet and stepped into the war room, which looked rather like the inside of a submarine: Close quarters, dark, headsets, smart minds tracking the latest technology. Defense had been the last thing on his list, more because the Shadow Voice's communications couldn't wait than because he wasn't worried about danger.

Luckily, they hadn't needed a major defense until now, although Deck realized from the beginning that discovery was inevitable. He just hadn't counted on it being this soon. There was still time. The important thing was to get the Shadow Voice back online tonight, with feeds going to every possible corner of earth.

"Listen up, folks," he called to the others in the war room. "We need to begin immediate implementation of the two defense initiatives I spoke of at the meeting. Divide yourselves into teams and have one get started on moving the depot to another location and preparing a new mirage. The other team should put together a plan to recruit residents of Newgate for a militia. We'll need to have a system set up to vet these people, and to make sure they are true candidates for the revolution. I don't want any professional mercenaries."

His Shadow Runners immediately set to work, and Deck returned to the main control center. Jenny caught his attention there, standing up on the platform as Raidon worked on her security pass. She seemed restless. And there was something very small and solitary about the way she stood apart from everybody else. She looked a bit like a child staring through the window of a candy store. She looked like she wanted to belong but couldn't.

And frankly, it just wasn't the same belonging to something without her. The feeling he'd had when he knew they were on the same side, when they believed in each other—it was painful in its absence.

Raidon handed Jenny her pass, and she went straight for the door.

"Wait!" Deck crossed the room in an instant and put his hand on her shoulder. In spite of the turmoil he could see in her eyes, she didn't turn away, didn't shrug him off. It was a start.

"I gotta go take care of something."

Nice excuse. She still didn't want to talk. "You have somewhere pressing you need to be?" he teased gently. "I'd like you to see something. Are you willing?"

She looked toward the door almost desperately. "No, I—"

"It's important. Give me ten minutes."

She nodded, worrying her lower lip and barely making eye contact. He'd done a hell of a job on her, hadn't he?

He took her hand and led her to the war room and out the back of it, up a staircase. He unlatched the pop-door and climbed to the roof of the depot. She followed him up, and they stood there together, alone, with the desert all around them. The sand sparkled like millions of tiny colored gemstones. This far into the outback, the air was relatively unpolluted; it approximated the classic blue sky of old-fashioned picture books.

But Jenny's focus wasn't on the landscape; she walked along the roof, her attention directed down through the skylights in which Deck knew she could see the buzz of activity. In fact, she could see the very act of revolution taking place.

"This is amazing."

Irrationally pleased by her compliment, Deck felt almost ridiculous at the extent to which his heart swelled with pride.

"You really built this," she said, shaking her head in awe.

Liz Maverick

"They built it. I designed it and sent the funding along with the blueprints. It's nice to see their handiwork firsthand."

"I just don't get how you transmit the Shadow Voice if you don't know who it is or where it's coming from."

"The Shadow Voice supplies fiberoptic hooks, if you will, that we can absorb and grab data packets from. The hooks constantly change their vectoral location as a matter of security, and we have the technology to find them. It doesn't matter what, where, or who is supplying the data packets. We can find them without compromising the source. It's a more secure system for everyone and everything if we don't even try to find out."

"So you get the data—"

"We get the data and disseminate the information to every noncensored, unfiltered receiver our computers can find. Every single human being on the planet can access the Voice this way, even in countries where information is cleansed before the users can access it."

She nodded and continued walking the roof, peeking down through the glass where Deck's revolutionaries went about their business. She turned to him and blurted, "Deck, I've got something I need to say to you. I mean, I've done some bad things, you know, but—"

"Wait," he said, almost in a panic, suddenly afraid that he'd gone too far in the name of revolution, or simply not said enough to let her know how much he valued her. Or maybe he was just afraid of what she had left to say.

He should have spoken up before, even if he was scared, or if she didn't want to hear at the time. "Let me say this first. Jenn, I've played that scene over hundreds of times in my head. I would give just about anything to have that moment back, to do it all over again. I can't stop seeing your face, watching you fall, hearing you scream. I don't know . . . this isn't anything but me wanting you to know that I'm sorry. I am so very, very sorry that it happened the way it did. You're not the one that should die for all this. I'm sorry I forced you into it. These are my dreams. It should have been only my life in jeopardy. When we're done here, I want you to take everything I give you and go live the life you've always deserved."

Jenny looked stunned. She swallowed hard, leaning her head against the purifier pipe. "That means a lot to me," she said, completely choking up.

He reached over and stroked her cheek. "Will this business between us never go away? Is the damage irreparable? I know I don't deserve anything from you right now, but I'd like to know if it's possible you might someday forgive me."

She backed off. "I think I should go. . . ."

Deck looked up at the sky. She wasn't ready for these words. Forgiveness didn't come easy to Jenny. She needed time. Or maybe she just needed more from him. He held out his hand. "Let me show you just one more thing."

251

"I think I should go," she repeated blankly. "I'm . . . I'm tired. I was thinking of lying down for a while."

He silently pleaded for her to take his hand. "You won't regret it, I promise."

Chapter Twenty-two

As Deck led her back into the building and down the hall, all Jenny could feel was a horrible, welling shame. All of a sudden, it had become very, very clear that her justifying this big decision of hers, whether to go with Parliament or side with Deck and the revolution—it was no different than the moment she'd looked into Deck's eyes on that cliff and sensed his hesitation.

When did you start thinking of yourself as such a victim, Jenny?

She watched Deck punch some data into a computer. He looked at her with hope and excitement, like he was about to give her a precious gift.

He'd had to weigh his options, she knew now. There was a lot on the line. And she'd had to do the same. So, there wasn't really any judging to be done, was there? He'd apologized, and he was clearly agonizing over it.

253

How could she hold him to a higher standard than the one she held up for herself? It wasn't good enough to say that he started it, or that he'd done it first. That was a fool's game. God, it seemed as though she and Deck could never make it to safe ground before the world turned their relationship upside down.

"Sit here," he said, and maneuvered her in front of a large computer screen.

He leaned over her right shoulder and typed a few codes into the system. A graphic showing a world map appeared. Deck continued maneuvering through the mapped screens, drilling down. Jenny saw the world become more detailed, become continents, become countries and colonies . . . to the place of her birth in the UCE. She had no allegiance to the UCE. She hadn't spent much time there; she hadn't spent much time anywhere.

"Now let's go home," Deck said.

Dig he mean the slums where he'd found her, Macao?

And then he was scrolling through her life, the places where she'd been, moving with her father from one city to the next. All the places she'd told him about. And he'd been listening. She felt like he'd remembered and stored every word she'd said to him.

Live video streamed onto the screen. He zoomed into her district, down the streets in the neighborhood where she'd last been crashing. She could almost feel the mist on her skin and the scent of the place.

He took her right hand and placed it on the controls. She stared down at it, then moved the stick. She could see her favorite stores, the places she avoided, the side streets and alleys she knew by heart, and the rooftops—if she moved the joystick forward—the rooftops were buzzing with copters and hazy with smog.

She zoomed down and in even more. There were people on the streets. Into her favorite café, where she might meet an old pal.

And then she released the joystick and felt her smile fade away. The familiarity felt good to her, but when you zoomed from the big picture to the small, the reality staring you in the face was desperately, desperately sad. The hardship, the squalor—it was all there on the screen. And she'd been living that for how long?

Deck put his hand over hers and began to steer again. She looked over her shoulder and, when he smiled at her, she tried to smile back.

"We can make things better than this," he said softly into her ear.

He zoomed in to the sandwich man at Jenny's favorite stand in the market square. She saw his tight pinched mouth, the worry etched into his brow. The sadness. Always, the sadness. She remembered staring into his eyes just before this whole crazy mission began.

And she knew Deck was right. Things could be better if everyone took a stand. But it had to be together. Jenny had always felt so alone, had always felt that nothing she did could ever make a difference in the quality of her life. If there had been someone before who had fought this fight, she might already be living that better life. A revolution like this could have had the power to change everything for the better. It had to start somewhere. Someone had to take a stand. And the Shadow Runners and other groups like them—well, they were taking a stand.

Jenny jolted back from the computer and looked around her at a room full of people with hope in their eyes. They were crouched over computer screens, running documents back and forth, and the centerpiece of the room covering the giant front wall was a map of the world with green neon lights denoting communication hubs.

There were filtered, censored, and government-bugged hubs in red. Open underground hubs were in blue. Dots equaled thousands of connections per place. Thousands of connections reaching hundreds of thousands of users. More than that, even. And not users—people. People like Jenny herself, maybe sitting in an electric café with life going on all around and finally finding out how to make things better.

This was how you could gain control of your life. This was how you created a system where things weren't being taken away from you on a whim; this was how you prevented yourself from being at somebody else's mercy. This revolution was how you stopped being a victim.

And it wasn't just an idea in Deck's head. It lived and breathed. He was really fighting for something important. The revolution was real, and she wanted to be a part of it. If it wasn't already too late.

Jenny stood up abruptly and nearly toppled the chair over. "I've *really* gotta go."

Deck studied her for a moment, and finally said, "Just know this. I want you to be there in the room when we go back online, when the Voice of Freedom speaks. You have a security pass, now, and you can just come in as part of the team."

Part of the team. She liked the sound of that. "I'll try," she said hastily, and pushed in the chair. "I just need some time to . . . figure all this out."

He looked so disappointed. He was going to be a lot more disappointed if she didn't get the chip back in place before they went online.

"But thanks," she said, to soften the blow.

Deck touched her cheek. "We're going to get the Voice back tonight, and I just think that if you can see what revolution feels like, you'll understand what it is all for."

Jenny smiled and headed for the door. *I already understand. I just hope it's not too late.*

Chapter Twenty-three

Jenny ran down the hall toward the lobby and then made a sharp turn to take the long way around to the database room. She wanted to throw herself off the roof of the depot. Deck humbling himself before her like she'd never seen him do in his life, asking her to forgive him when she was the last person he should forgive—it made her sick to her stomach. If she actually pulled this thing off, and reverted the systems back to before she and Quinn tampered with them, she swore she would give Deck her trust for the rest of her life.

She used her new security card to enter the server room, and delivered a full-body blow to the equally surprised baby-faced janitor sweeping up the floor on the other side.

"Hi!" she said brightly, her blood pounding in her face. "Sorry about that. I was in a hurry."

"Hi," he said, frowning in confusion. "You're one of the new Runners, right?"

She held up her white security pass and smiled, feeling nauseated. "Yup. Deck said to go ahead and fish that thing out."

"What thing?"

She shrugged easily. "There's a part that got kicked under one of the machines I'm supposed to put back."

Baby-face looked where she was pointing and his expression relaxed. "Oh, okay. I gotcha. Go right ahead." He continued sweeping, turning the broom in tiny semicircles.

Jenny stared at his back for a moment, then bent down and got to work, figuring that the more obvious she made the whole thing, the less suspicious it would seem. She opened a couple of drawers and fished around until she found some wire from which she fashioned a hook.

She couldn't make contact with the box right away. On her hands and knees she kept at it, praying that when she did come up with it, the damn chip inside wouldn't be damaged. She'd tossed it in there as gently as she could, yet still hard enough to make it go far enough under the equipment to discourage Quinn from trying to retrieve it.

When she felt the wire make contact, she was practically ready to weep. Lying flat on her stomach, she gently nudged the chip toward her and picked it up.

She popped open the plastic box and held the tiny

chip plate in her trembling fingers, just staring at it. A little smudging marred the surface, but overall it looked, well . . . like a normal chip.

She glanced over her shoulder at the janitor and smiled when he looked back.

"Got it?" he asked.

"Got it." She took a moment to visualize what she'd done to remove it in the first place, then began to reverse the process. It didn't take long to maneuver the chip back into the exact same spot from which she'd pried it earlier. The casing around the chip was a little nicked, but otherwise none the worse for wear.

She popped the panel back on and allowed herself a sigh of relief. "All done," she chirped, bending the wire and tucking it back into the drawer. "See you in a few minutes."

"Yeah, see ya at the countdown," the janitor said, and gave her a friendly tip of his cap.

Jenny walked casually out of the room, shut the door behind her, and leaned against the wall. Done. It was done. She stared at her shaking hands. Well, not quite. She had to find Quinn and somehow get him to accept a deal. They could offer him everything Deck had originally offered her.

Oh, God. She still had to tell Deck about this. Everything was going to be okay, now, but she would have to explain to him what had happened and what she'd done and somehow make it square between them.

She headed back to the bathroom and splashed

cold water on her face, this time avoiding her reflection. Then she returned to the control center where the entire base had gathered. The tension was thick in the room. Near-silent, the entire base stared up at an old-fashioned sign hanging on the wall. The words were still dimmed, ready to proclaim ON AIR at a moment's notice.

Jenny scanned the room for Quinn as the Shadow Runners ran around purposefully like the old space teams ramping up for a shuttle launch. The Parliament dandy wasn't around, but Deck was, clearly enjoying the moment in the center of the storm. She caught his eye and he unjustly rewarded her with a broad smile.

A red light flashed. The transmission manager leaned forward into a microphone and began the countdown.

"Ten . . . nine . . . eight . . . seven . . . six . . . five . . . four . . . three . . . two . . . one . . ."

A pause, and then the light changed to green. "We're online. We are *open* for transmission."

A murmur ran through the crowd. Jenny watched Deck stare up at the world map looking as if he were about to jump out of his skin, but in a calm, controlled voice, he said, "Give it ten seconds once we start receiving input, then shut down so we can go in and double-check the firewalls and scramblers."

"Will do. Okay, circuits open."

The sound system crackled; the lights of the ON AIR sign flickered and then steadied; the very energy in the room itself seemed to surge, then a network of white lines began to light up in streaks across the world map.

"'Let us not be unmindful that liberty is power. The nation blessed with the greatest portion of liberty must in proportion to its number be the most powerful nation on earth. Do not be deceived by those who claim to hold you in their power . . . '"

A huge cheer erupted in the center of a euphoria that Jenny couldn't help but feel down to her bones. It could only be the Shadow Voice, the Voice of Freedom. Jenny had expected the words to flow over her like white noise. But she heard each, and she listened. And she felt.

"'Stand and prepare yourselves, for those who give up essential liberty, to preserve a little temporary safety, deserve neither liberty nor safety . . . '"

It was almost as if the Shadow Voice were speaking directly to her. She couldn't help wondering if Quinn was somewhere listening, too, and if so, if he'd come down enough from the opiate to be as moved by the words as she.

"'Tyranny, like hell, is not easily conquered, yet we have this consolation with us: the harder the conflict, the more glorious the triumph. What we obtain too cheap, we esteem too lightly; it is dearness only that gives everything its value . . . '"

It was something she couldn't ever remember feeling before: a sense of belonging to something bigger than just herself. Hell, even just the sense of belonging to anything was something special.

But this wasn't just anything. This was what it felt

like to care about a cause that you were willing to die for.

She caught Deck's eye through the cheering throng. Someone had put some music on, a trance beat with the Shadow Voice broadcast speaking over it. People were screaming, cheering, laughing, crying, jumping, dancing, going absolutely wild with joy.

She caught glimpses of their faces: ex-palace guards, onetime maids, former prostitutes and junkies, regular Joes seeking a better life, all come here, starting over as technicians and cooks and welders and guards and strategists all together in the name of a better life, working together for the betterment of themselves through the betterment of all. Jenny felt a smile burst right out of her.

Her whole life raced through her mind as she stared across the room at Deck, standing on his slightly raised platform and watching her through the crowd. He had an odd look on his face, as if he'd realized that her part in the mission was done. But then he tipped his head toward the exit, and suddenly Jenny couldn't get to him fast enough.

She pushed through the jubilant throng to reach him. Without a word, he drew her close, and, tangled in each other's arms, they barreled out through the exit doors into the empty foyer and down the hall. He led her to what was obviously the living quarters wing.

Deck fumbled with his smart-card, and finally managed to swipe the damn thing through the lock. They burst into a bedroom, and he picked her up and tossed her on the bed, then joined her, trying to wrestle her down and hug her all at once.

Jenny pulled him backward onto the bed, then rolled and straddled him. She pulled his shirt open and ran her palms over his chest, past the sleek muscles, the scars, licking and sucking and biting all over his flesh.

She could tell Deck liked it—he was more than ready; that much was obvious. She could almost feel his blood surging through him as he rolled over her, pinning her underneath him with her arms behind her head. "You're a tough one to nail down," he teased.

"I'm not exactly in the mood to play hard to get," she said, raising her hips and pressing herself up against his erection.

He swore and started ripping her clothes off her body. "I need to feel you, all of you this time." Shirt, boots, trousers, everything had to go. He worked quickly, intently, until he'd stripped both of them of every shred of clothing they'd worn.

And then as she lay there naked, tangled in the mussed up bedsheets, he just cocked his head. "My God, Jenny. You look very much like you've always belonged here," he said. His voice was husky. "In my bed."

"Mmm," was all she had a chance to say. He leaned down and took her mouth in a long, slow, hot kiss.

She felt his nude body against hers, all of him, and the warmth, the weight was so perfect, she couldn't quite allow herself to have it, to go forward, without . . .

"There's something I have to tell you," she murmured, her conscience tugging at the back of her mind.

"If it's not relevant to where I should kiss you, I'm not interested just now," he said, gruffly pulling away only to move lower down along her body.

Jenny laughed, and tried to get Deck to look at her. "I'm serious!"

He answered by pressing kisses up her inner thighs. Jenny gasped and tried to concentrate on forming a sentence. "Deck . . ."

"Ssshhh. Just let it go."

His hands slid up the sides of her body, and his mouth pressed a kiss between her legs, leaving Jenny shivering with want and more than willing to let go whatever he wanted gone. With his tongue, with his fingers, he was just delicate enough, just aggressive enough, to rocket her to the edge.

Jenny arched her back as pleasure sheared across her body. She eased herself down and then closed her eyes as if it would somehow help her save the moment.

Deck rose over her body without a word and cradled her to him, not rushing, just holding her. The sensation of his hot skin on hers, the hard press of his swollen flesh against her wetness; it made her feel such a part of something.

She cradled his head against her breasts and leaned down to whisper in his ear, "I want you to know how good it feels, Deck. What we have together."

He looked at her and smiled, then raised himself up and entered her, his cock hard and thick. He groaned with pleasure and tipped his head back as he filled her completely, then withdrew; taking it slow at first, before moving faster and faster within her.

He locked his gaze with hers, and his excitement was contagious. His body pressing against hers, the way he looked, the way he felt—Jenny felt herself veer to the edge again, raising her hips in uncontrolled response.

A blue light flickered in the dim room and began to flash. The light careened over Deck's body, but he didn't notice. His comm pack beeped, and it only seemed to spur him on. He cried out Jenny's name and slammed his body harder into hers.

But she didn't follow his lead this time. The comm pack continued to beep, and Jenny cradled Deck's face in her neck even as her heart sank without knowing quite why.

Deck groaned. "Not now."

But as he focused in on the blue light and seemed to comprehend what it meant, he froze. "Wait a minute. What the hell?"

Somehow, she just knew. *But I fixed it! I know I fixed it!* Jenny's throat seemed to close up, and a chill swept her body as Deck pulled away from her to answer the comm.

He stood there uncovered, his muscles rippling, his eyes gleaming in the strange light, and somehow Jenny knew he wasn't hers for much longer. Deck put the headset down and ran his hands through his hair.

"Raidon says there's been some kind of breach . . ." He looked completely nonplussed.

"What happened?" she managed to say, more of a hoarse whisper.

Deck hurried to dress. "The scrambler's been tampered with. The others think the signal might have been in the open long enough to have been traced. If that's so, at the very least, every antirevolutionary force in the world will eventually be coming to take this place apart. Look, I've got to get down to the control room."

Jenny felt the blood rushing from her face. "But I fixed it. I put the chip back."

Deck turned to look at her. "What did you say?" he asked. His eyes had gone cold.

And even though she'd managed to get some of her clothes back on, she'd never felt more naked in her life.

Chapter Twenty-four

"Was it you?"

The look on Deck's face was terrible, like nothing Jenny had ever seen before. She stared at him, willing herself to speak, but nothing came out.

"Was it you?" His fists were clenched at his sides, the muscles in his jaw throbbing. "Oh, God." He grabbed her by her bad shoulder, effectively holding her in place. "Did *you* do it? Did you mess with the system?"

"No. I mean yes. But I . . . It wasn't like that. I—"

"What was it like, Jenny?"

He was hurting her, but she didn't even try to make him let go. She wanted to feel the pain, as if somehow taking this from him would make everything square. But of course it wouldn't.

"It's not too late. Where's Quinn? We'll cut a new deal. We'll end this once and for all. We'll give him the key to your safehouse and the money and the visa and the, and the . . ." She just stopped talking. She sounded pathetic even to her own ears.

"Quinn's gone," Deck said tightly. "He went back with the last supply transport."

"What?"

"You heard me."

Jenny pushed away and struggled into her armored jacket. "I have to go after him."

Deck looked at her oddly, like he couldn't quite figure out whose side she was on. "He seemed certain you'd want to rest a bit more. But I can get you out on the next supply car."

Jenny slumped against the wall. She'd set this disaster in motion, and she had to figure out a way to stop it. She wouldn't give up. Quinn was just like everyone else in Newgate. If she promised him enough, she could buy him.

True, he could already have almost anything he wanted as a member of Parliament—as long as he was in Newgate. Could she get him out? Get him help for the FPs? She put her head in her hands and moaned a little. It didn't help much.

Deck hastily finished dressing and headed out through the doorway.

"Deck!"

"I don't have time for you." He slammed the door behind him.

Maybe he could have just punched her in the face. She realized she was still half naked, and it was off with the jacket, on with her underclothes, such as they were. Then she headed out the door after him.

There must be something she could do to make this right.

"Look, Deck, I can fix this. I mean, I thought I already did, but Quinn must have . . . He must have . . ." Her voice trailed away as Deck slowly turned around.

"What does Quinn have to do with this, exactly?" he asked.

"There's something I've been wanting to tell you."

He looked warily at her, as if he somehow already knew that whatever she said next would drive a wedge between them forever.

She looked him square in the eye. "I lied, Deck. Or really, I kept things from you. I had a history with Parliament. Quinn was putting pressure on me from the beginning, and then when we got here, he forced me to take that chip out. And I will admit that, for a moment, I wasn't sure what I wanted to do. I admit that. But I swear to you that I went and put it back, so the chip's okay, right? The chip's okay." She knew she was babbling, but she didn't care. "The main thing is that we have to get to Quinn and cut some sort of a deal. As soon as he gets back to Newgate, Parliament will know everything, and they will sell you to Kyber or the UCE and all this . . ." She swept her arm across the room. "This will be over."

He didn't move. He just stared at her. And then he put his hand out, and she thought he might strike her, but instead he grabbed her behind the neck and pulled her in close to him. She could feel his breath against her skin, his lips in her hair. And still she waited for him to strike.

271

"You stupid, stupid girl," he said. "The chip deactivates when removed because it contains information that might reveal the location of the Shadow Voice. This means that when we did the test, we were operating without a workable scrambler. And then . . ." He shook his head. "While you can congratulate yourself on successfully preventing Parliament and the rest of the world from using us to find the Voice, you have also unquestionably revealed the location of this depot. Even if we're lucky and no one was trying to hack in and get that information, we still have Lord Quinn on his way back to Parliament with a full report of the operations here, endangering the lives of every single person in this installation."

"I didn't know," Jenny said, faltering. "I didn't understand until it was already too late. I swear to you that I thought I'd fixed it. Have you ever put something in motion that you just couldn't stop? No matter how much you wanted to? Something you would give your own life to take back if you had a second chance?"

Deck had begun moving at a half jog down the corridor. Suddenly he stopped in his tracks and turned around. "Yes," he answered, almost a whisper. "The moment I let you fall. I still remember trying to reach you, and Raidon telling me to think of the revolution first, and God help me, for a few seconds, I did."

Jenny didn't move. She didn't dare say a word for fear of losing her grasp on the moment, on the shred of hope that maybe, just maybe, Deck didn't think all was lost.

He seemed to be studying her face as if to memorize it. Then he took a deep breath and shook his head. He looked incredulous. "These things don't just happen in a vacuum, Jenn. It's all part of a larger chain of events. It's incredible, but it traces back for years. I didn't save you from Newgate the first time around because I knew it's where I wanted to build this depot. I didn't get you out right away because I needed to use you for this mission. I made you hate me for it. I had Raidon bring you in and cut a deal so I could get what I wanted out of you. I made you hate me for it. I might have let you die falling down that crevasse. I made you hate me for it. And I guess it's all come around in the end. A gamble lost. I'm paying for all that hate I created and earned."

"I don't hate you," Jenny said haltingly.

"We're done, you and I. We have to be."

"No," she said in a whisper. "I'm with you now. I'm really with you. I understand about the revolution. 'Stand and prepare yourselves, for those who give up essential liberty, to preserve a little temporary safety, deserve neither liberty nor safety.' What the Shadow Voice is saying . . . I see now how it all pieces together. I thought I couldn't make a difference in anybody's life, much less my own. But together . . . I'm ready to stand up with you and fight for the revolution. For freedom. For you, I'm ready to . . ."

The look on Deck's face stopped her in midsentence. "You don't believe me? Or is it you don't believe *in* me?" she asked hollowly. A tear rolled down her face. Deck caught it with his fingers and brought it to his tongue.

"We reap what we sow, Jenny. We reap what we sow. We can't trust each other—we each can't put our guard down and totally open up for the other. Where's the point in that? You tell me you believe in the revolution now, and then you ask if I believe in you. All I know is what I see.

"In the big picture, you're not willing to sacrifice for me, and I'm not willing to sacrifice for you—so there you are. It's the game of who's going to die for what all over again. I wouldn't die for you, and you wouldn't die for me. And my first priority is to the revolution. You were right. Is there much more to say than that?"

A long silence clouded the air between them, and Jenny couldn't find any words to mend the breach.

Deck himself looked stricken, as if he were already wishing away his cruel words. Finally, he took a couple of steps backward and then stumbled away. He sprinted down the corridor, disappearing around the corner.

The disappointment in his voice nearly killed her. What was done was done, and she couldn't take it back no matter how much she wished she could. The fact was, her original intent had been wrong. But she hadn't expected to start believing in the revolution, to start believing in Deck himself, for God's sake. No one with her track record, with her past could have expected any of this to make sense.

How ironic. She finally believed in something, just in time to screw it all up. Well, she wouldn't surrender. She never surrendered. She'd figure out a way to make this right. And not just because the revolution mattered; because she knew in her heart that Deck loved her. And that just wasn't something she was willing to give up on.

"We'll travel light and fast this time," Deck called as he rounded up the people he needed. "I want horse-hybrids. I want a point person out front—someone who knows the trade routes by heart." He turned to Raidon, who looked as pale as the stucco walls. "You stay here. Let me go alone."

"I'm coming," Raidon said flatly.

Deck put his hand on his heavy's shoulder, and in a voice that betrayed more emotion than he'd heard from himself in a long, long time, he said, "I think it's time that you went out on your own. You are capable of more than just serving me."

Raidon didn't budge. If possible, he looked more resolute.

Deck shook his head. "What do you believe in?"

"I work for you, sir. What I 'believe' is irrelevant." But he said it without complete conviction.

" 'Deck,' not 'sir.' "

Raidon didn't fix the error. "Is there anything I can do for you, sir?"

Deck looked at the heavy, then shrugged and studied the ground. "No. There's nothing you can do to help me with this," he said bitterly. He chose a small stone and threw it away with a sharp motion.

"It's just that . . . well, people matter as much as ideas. More sometimes. Such a simple, simple notion, but I couldn't really see it. Not really. Individuals have to matter for a revolution to matter."

"You're speaking of Jenny," Raidon said, matter-of-factly. "You're in love with her."

"Of course I'm in love with her. But it's too late for that sort of business." He brushed off his hands and climbed to his feet. "Let's go get those supplies together."

Chapter Twenty-five

It felt strange walking through the front door of Parliament. It felt stranger still that nobody tried to stop them. They asked for Quinn, and apparently they were going to get him. Apart from being disarmed, nothing else was required. Up a stairway covered in yards of trampled red velvet, Deck followed the servant at a controlled pace. Jenny practically skipped in her haste behind him.

They'd been silent for most of the ride, Deck's mind processing everything Jenny told him about Quinn and the security breach at the depot. She didn't hold back anything, and he could have drowned in all the what-ifs and silly consequences her narration revealed. He tried to clear his mind to deal with Quinn, but it kept replaying the incident at the cliff.

He glanced at her nervously chewing on her trashed fingernails as they climbed the ratty staircase. It was as if they were both trying to weigh the relative differences between what he had done to her and what she had done in return.

Deck wondered if Quinn had already done his damage, revealing what he'd learned about the Shadow Runners to his masters. Or if he was waiting for them to present a better deal.

The servant led them down a hall and ushered them into a small bedroom. Deck was struck by the sparseness of it, decorated as it was with only the barest of necessities. A few token items seemed staged in the tiny space: a chipped china pitcher and basin in an oddly cheerful sprigged-flower pattern; a pair of opera glasses on a cracked, veneer-stripped bureau. On the nightstand, a frayed riding crop with a pretty silver and ivory handle. A set of long, ornately carved pokers leaned up against a fireplace containing neither wood nor ashes. A pair of well-worn slippers sat at the foot of a leather club chair. A small side table balanced at a precarious angle next to the chair. And then, above the door, an old-fashioned monitor was set to alert Quinn of any visitors.

Lord Quinn stood by himself at the window, looking dressed for a party in a surprisingly fresh fuchsia-and-green-striped satin waistcoat. But the party spirit itself had passed him by. The man played idly with his watch chain, standing in a haze of shifting dust highlighted by the ray of filtered light that shone through the one unbroken pane.

"Lord Quinn," Deck stated grimly, crossing his

arms against his chest, more to keep himself from pummeling the man than as a tactic of intimidation.

"What took you so long?" the man asked grandly. He didn't turn to face them, his concentration apparently occupied with using a penknife to peel the wrapper off a stick of pure opiate. He paused and smelled the drug as if it were a fine cigar.

"*What*, we asked, *what* could a member of the House of Han—or ex-member, as it were—want in Newgate? Prince Kyber's brother, no less! Did you come as an enemy," he asked languidly, waving one hand at waist level, "or an as *emissary?*" he finished, waving the other gracefully.

Deck didn't answer. He was afraid of derailing Quinn's train of thought, and there was too much to be learned. Too much more that he hoped the dandy would explain.

Quinn turned and gave him a long look. He appeared haggard, drawn. "No matter, consider it a rhetorical question. If you were an enemy, as a bastard prince who'd been mistakenly—it was *mistakenly*, wasn't it?" he digressed. "I can never remember if you really were responsible for scrambling your poor old man's brains. Most unsettling to completely lose one's faculties, don't you think? But I suppose that's not the point. As a bastard prince who'd been imprisoned and tortured at the hand of Kyber himself, perhaps you sought some sort of revenge. Your own brother—oh, pardon me, I should say half brother—took your father, your title, your dignity, and even what was once your destiny, no?"

"You exaggerate the case," Deck said tightly, working hard to control his anger. He was moving steadily toward the boiling point.

Quinn bowed his head slightly in acquiescence, placed his knife and opiate on the side table, and settled into the club chair. He crossed his legs, showing off his newly polished Hessians, and stared at Deck. "Perhaps. But the fact remains, you have lost your official place in the House of Han. What better revenge than to bring down his monarchy by joining an alliance following the word of the Shadow Voice, that which is mobilizing the most powerful groundswell the world has seen in over a thousand years of political history? Hmm?"

The Parliamentarian tapped one finger against his temple and continued, "But maybe it was the reverse. A trick. Maybe some of the rumor and innuendo coming out of North Han City were untrue. Or, as you claim, exaggerated. What if the world was only meant to *believe* you were an enemy of the House of Han? That way, you'd be the best possible choice to serve as an emissary of those whom others expected you to be working against. What if Kyber wanted his onetime holdings here in Newgate back, and you were here to examine that possibility? Everyone can be bought. We were sure you had a price, just like the rest of us. And who better would know your price than your own brother?"

Deck shifted in his seat, careful to leave his expression blank, to reveal nothing.

"I must say, my friend, you surprised me. You impressed me. I was certain it was the latter. We all

280

were. I was sent along to see what you really had in mind. I never expected you to be telling the truth, for God's sake, to actually reveal yourself as a Shadow Runner."

"Quinn, I want out," Jenny suddenly blurted out, kneeling at the lord's feet.

He looked down at her with genuine shock. "There is no out."

"Help us do the right thing. You saw what was going on. I know you heard the Voice; we all did. It had an impact on me, and I know it must have had an impact on you. They're good people there. It's a righteous cause."

Deck could hardly believe his ears. Jenny was pleading with Quinn in the name of the revolution? Jenny was using "us" in the context of the fight?

"Good people? 'Them's good people,'" he sneered. "We're *all* good people, Jenny. We all deserve more than we get. But not everybody can have it all. There's simply not enough to go around."

"I know you, Quinn. You're trapped, just like me. You have a chance to do something good here. To have your time here mean something. Help me make this right." She reached out and took hold of Quinn's wrist. The dandy's other hand moved absently toward the knife on the side table.

Deck tried to put his body between the two of them, focused on redirecting Quinn's attention. "Tell me what you want most in this world, Quinn. You said there wasn't enough to go around. Not enough of what? What do you desire most? Not for Parliament, but for you. Maybe I can get it for you."

"Parliament can already give me everything, except the one thing I truly want—to be rid of this damned addiction. And that, my dear fellow, is impossible." Quinn coldly detached Jenny's grip from his arm, and began to slice off chunks of opiate with his penknife again. "By the way, you do realize I've been systematically exposing you to this the entire time we were in the outback? You're about one major dose away from being me."

At his words, Deck gave a laugh, and waited for his hate to take over. Instead, he simply felt the rage begin to drain away, swallowed by the fear born of knowing the man might be telling the truth.

Quinn just stared at a chunk of opiate on the end of his knife. "By the time I returned here yesterday and walked through that door, I was so far into withdrawal, I thought it was possible I could die before ever saying a word to anyone about anything. It was the oddest experience, seeing Newgate, the Parliament Club, its members, everything through my own eyes." In a faint whisper he added, "It was horrible. The reality of this place is horrible."

"Did you tell them?" Deck asked between gritted teeth, trying desperately to remain focused, trying not to give in to . . . God, was it sympathy? For this man?

Quinn stood up. "Of course I did. I told them everything."

Jenny stumbled back. Deck just stood frozen in place. It *was* sympathy. And pity for this man, where he should have felt nothing at all except an obligation to put a bullet through the bastard's brains.

Quinn didn't seem to be taking much pleasure in

his success. His gaze was trained carefully on his knife, and in a very matter-of-fact voice he explained, "I told them all about you, Jenny. A true friend of Parliament. And I'm sorry to say they will not be honoring the terms of our agreement. While you have paid sufficiently for the murder of our man, you did not earn anything beyond that."

Deck stared down at the floor, searching the floorboards for a solution, some kind of answer to all this. "Lord Quinn, if Parliament is so opposed to the revolution, why didn't you stay longer, collect more information, try to buy off my people, attempt to send a dispatch, take pictures, whatever? Something just doesn't add up. I'll ask you the same question I asked you earlier. Why did you come?"

"Parliament cares about your revolution, of course. We keep our eye on potential uprisings. But we don't always jump to the conclusion that a shift in politics is necessarily bad—as you know, we are always open to our own advantage."

"Why did you encourage me to bring down the system, then, and then leave as if your job was done?" Jenny asked.

"Because I knew it would likely break any remaining bond between you and His Lordship. You were having an effect on him that I found quite counterproductive to Parliament's purpose."

"Which was?" Deck arched an eyebrow impatiently.

"Can't you guess? It's you, Your Lordship. My purpose wasn't to stop the revolution. My purpose was to reel you, Prince D'ekkar Han Valoren, into the heart of Parliament itself. We want you on our side—as one of us, so we can use you as leverage. You are a powerful man with a powerful name, Lord D'ekkar, in spite of your desire to bury it. Revolution is inevitable. You said so yourself. We've lain low in the past, thinking it was better for our survival, but the world is changing and the only way to create power and keep it, to avoid being overrun, is to roar the loudest and hit the hardest. You have the potential to be our 'kingpin,' if you will. A onetime member of the House of Han would certainly give us recognition among world powers."

"He would never work for you," Jenny said, her eyes narrow and focused.

Quinn gave a slow smile. "Not of his own volition."

"Did you understand what he just said?" Jenny asked. "His sole purpose was to reel you into Parliament. That first dose was an addiction seed, Deck. And after that, every exposure—the smoke in your face, the smell of it on his clothes . . ."

Quinn picked up a small remote control and changed his monitor's view from the entrance of his own suite to the foyer of the Parliament Club. The foyer was full of Parliament members dressed in evening clothes.

He said, "I'm to escort you down for the finale. I really should be finishing what I started."

Jenny's hand went automatically to her empty holster.

Quinn caught the movement and looked at her. "No point in killing me, is there?"

Jenny shook her head no, but raised her hand and

pointed her fingers in the shape of a gun, pantomiming blowing his head off.

"Really, my dear girl," Quinn said, raising his hands in mock surrender. His fingers trembled violently, at odds with his cavalier posturing. "I'm already half gone, you know. I was happy to tell them," he continued conversationally. "It made me feel important. It made be feel like I was in control." He laughed hollowly and turned to Deck. "Lord Quinn, useless second son, embarrassment of the House of Kobayashi. *I* brought down the revolution near Newgate." He thumped his chest. "Do you know how it made me feel? I understood usefulness for the first time in my life. And do you know what I discovered?"

Deck just stared at him.

"It's like the drug. When it's on, it's on. It's what beauty feels like. And then in the next moment . . ." He stared blankly in front of him. "You're nobody once more. Thank you very much, Lord Quinn. You've done very well, Lord Quinn. You can go now, Lord Quinn. We'll take care of things from here, *Lord Quinn*. I don't think you have any idea what it's like to have absolutely no control in your life, Lord Valoren. Jenny does." His thoughts seemed to wander for a moment. "So don't judge her too harshly."

He cut his blocks of drug into bite-sized pieces. "That's what struck me, you see, after the meeting. Kyber and Parliament, they are two sides of the same coin. Someone else calling the shots. What strikes me is that your revolution offers a level of personal control you just can't buy anymore. Dare I say it? Freedom."

Deck struggled against the sense that things were wildly spinning beyond his control. It was as if an electric charge hung in the air. And Quinn, for all his talk of powerlessness, at long last seemed to be the only one with the ability to make a move. "Quinn. I want you to think big here. Is there anything that can be done, now? No matter how tough. Is there anything at all that can be done? I will promise you anything you want in this world that I can do."

Quinn looked at Jenny. " 'Tyranny, like hell, is not easily conquered, yet we have this consolation with us: The harder the conflict, the more glorious the triumph. What we obtain too cheap, we esteem too lightly . . . ,' " he quoted.

"You *did* hear it," Jenny said, and then she suddenly reached out to Quinn with a startled "Oh my God." It was as if she'd just had some sort of epiphany.

"I'm no fighter. But nor am I a pawn," Quinn whispered, his eyes glowing as he drifted into a drug-induced haze. "I hope your triumph is glorious, indeed." He kissed the back of Jenny's hand, and looked up at Deck, locking eyes with him. "It's been a pleasure. Now, if you'll excuse me . . ." He never finished the sentence.

The chill of horror swept through Deck as Quinn placed a handful of the cubed hallucinogen in his mouth. The dandy chewed and swallowed quickly, a funny and sad half smile on his face. "There are some things you *can* conquer," he said cryptically, crumpling the drug's empty wrapper in his fist. "But not everything. At least I can say I was master of my destiny at the end. You did not get your final dose from me."

Then he settled back into his chair, his eyelids heavy, his eyes glassy.

"Quinn?" Jenny asked tentatively. "Quinn?" she asked again, louder.

Quinn didn't answer. He stared blankly into space, and a beatific smile slowly blossomed on his face. His breathing became shallower and shallower until he went completely still.

Deck knelt down and slapped the dandy's cheeks a couple of times, almost desperately. "Lord Quinn? We'll figure something out. There's always a deal to be made. It's not too late."

"Deck, stop. He's gone." Deck felt Jenny's hand on his shoulder. "It's pure opiate," she said. "He just jacked his brains out."

Deck closed his eyes. He didn't want to care, and really, if he thought about it, it could be said that it wasn't that he cared about Quinn—it was that what he saw in Quinn was something that could have happened to him. There had been a time after Kyber had imprisoned him and had him tortured that, when he came out of it, he'd felt like he was going a little crazy. He'd overindulged in drink, in drug, but somehow he hadn't let it consume him—and he'd had Raidon to pick him off the floor.

But this could have happened to him. He could have been Quinn, standing there wanting to die because the alternative was worse. And that was always tragic.

"Deck," Jenny said softly, tugging on his sleeve. "We've got to get the hell out of here. Now."

Chapter Twenty-six

Jenny left Deck's side and ran to the window. Her heart sank. The dandy's room was positioned on the far side of the Parliament Club, the side backed up closest to the giant concrete wall.

Her deal with Parliament? Gone. Her deal with Deck? Gone. And with it, any chance for a life with him. She looked at him, still kneeling by Quinn in disbelief. He was a dead man for sure if they didn't get out of here.

She glanced up at the monitor. The members of Parliament lining the halls had broken formation slightly, perhaps were discussing the delay. "Oh boy . . . Deck, are you with me?"

Deck ran his hand over Quinn's face, closing the man's eyes. He stood up and took a deep breath, and when he turned around to face her he seemed only a little frayed at the edges. "Yes. What's your call?" he asked, clearly working a bit to sound normal.

Jenny managed a smile. "We run. To be more specific, we jump from here over the, er, moat, if you will, and rappel down the wall."

This time, he didn't argue. "What do we have on us to pull this off?"

She rummaged in her bag. "Um . . . I honestly wish I could tell you there was a rope and two pairs of boot-knives in here. I've just got the one knife in my shoe on the right side, and the gauntlets, but the metal won't help us on concrete, anyway." She looked up at him. "What about you?"

He fumbled through the various compartments in his coat, then looked at her and shrugged. He pointed to the window. "Curtains. Tied together, there's enough fabric for a descent . . . and over there, a couple of fireplace pokers. If they're not too heavy—I don't know."

She glanced up at the vidscreen again. Members of Parliament were climbing the stairs. "Let's do it."

Jenny grabbed the fireplace pokers and tested their heft, while Deck yanked the curtains off the rod and tied them end to end. He worked quickly, winding the thinning, moth-eaten purple fabric around him like a toga.

"Lord Quinn?" someone called in a formal voice from outside in the hall. "Lord Quinn, are you ready, sir?" A pause.

Deck looked at Jenny, and then, without further hesitation, he climbed onto the windowsill and leaped to the colonnade. It was just over a deep, vast crevasse between the wall and the building; he slammed into the concrete and grabbed the head of the closest statue. It was too weak to hold his weight; a crack appeared along its neckline, and it began to give way.

Jenny held her breath as he quickly shifted his body and held on to the torso, while leveraging himself up into the thin space along the very top ledge between the two rows of statues. The head of the first statue broke off and fell, plummeting into the crevasse below. Deck braced his body and turned to face her.

She tossed first one, then the second poker like javelins over the crevasse. Deck caught each one neatly and then beckoned for her to follow.

With one last glance behind her, and, making a point not to look down, Jenny made a flying leap, arms wide, hair shearing out behind her. She aimed well, landing with her foot in the space between the two statues at Deck's right. He quickly stabilized her, grabbing her around the waist to prevent her from falling backward.

She took a deep breath, shaking her head in disbelief, and they turned around to handle the next hurdle. "Oh, wow," was all she could think to say, peering over the side down the sheer face of the smooth concrete wall.

"Raidon's out here somewhere," Deck said, unfurling the curtain and working to secure it around one of the statues. "That's why he didn't come in. But he can't help us until we get down."

They were positioned quite near the spot where Parliament had originally hunted them down. The arched column of Prinny's Place loomed just down the street. But on no contiguous side did another building butt far enough against this insane wall to jump. Jenny looked up at the empty sky. "Too bad it's a no-fly zone."

Down was the only way out. And the sooner, the better. From the balconies of the Parliament Club the cheated dandies crowded, pointing and jeering at Jenny and Deck as the two balanced atop what seemed like an impossible drop. It wouldn't be long before an envoy would come around below them.

It was down now, or never.

Deck focused on the rappel. Crouching on his hands and knees on the ledge between the two rows of statues, he surveyed the pitted wall for possible footholds.

Jenny looked at the Parliament Club nervously. People milled about everywhere, and also, as she'd feared, a group appeared to be mobilizing on one of the balconies, undoubtedly preparing to retrieve them. "They're arming themselves," she said to Deck. "And look down there. They'll bring out the hybrids soon."

Deck followed her gaze. They looked at each other. "There's not enough time," he said.

"What do you mean? Let's just go for it."

"There's not enough time for both of us to make the descent here and still have time to escape. One of us should rappel down, the other should take the pokers and will need to be creative...." His voice trailed off as the members of Parliament on the balconies dispersed, disappearing into the building. He stood up, wiping the sweat from his face. "Jenny, follow the wall toward the transit center and make your descent somewhere there. I need to go down here." He tugged on the knot anchoring his makeshift rope.

"We can both rappel down right here. I can make it right behind you."

"No," he said curtly. "It's time to split up. I'll go here. I've got to try to find Raidon, anyway. It's safer for you to keep moving and take another descent point. Just blend into the city somewhere. I've got to get back to the depot," Deck added.

"What?" He wasn't making eye contact with her anymore. And he was telling her to go. Alone. Jenny stared at him dumbly, trying to process that somehow this was the correct point at which they were to separate. Not to mention that, if he didn't come with her, if he didn't try to leave Newgate immediately, his life would be in serious jeopardy.

"I'm going this way, and you're going that way," he said impatiently. "I've got to get back to the depot as soon as possible." He checked his watch, seemingly unconcerned, while a hundred different emotions swirled through in Jenny's heart.

"You're not trying to be my decoy, are you?"

He was; but his look said he would never admit to it. "This plan makes the most sense. We're splitting up because it makes sense. You know it's me they really want anyway. If we stay together, it does nothing but jeopardizes your life. Look, I'm going to go to your armory for supplies to make up for what we lost on the trip out. I'll take a hybrid back. If you give me the GPS, I can find the same shortcut. I will be fine."

"Brilliant," Jenny sneered. She took his face gently in her hands, a part of her wondering if this would be the last time she'd ever feel his skin on hers, the last time she'd ever see him at all. "Look at me. Do you realize how many people are after you? Parliament's probably already sold your whereabouts to Kyber. Do you think he'll trust what you're doing here? And even if you escape for now, it doesn't mean anything. Trust me. If they don't kill you today, and you stay here, you'll be looking over your shoulder the rest of your life. The whole freaking world is going to be looking for you—*and* for your Shadow Runners. We've got to get out of here, out of Australia."

"No!" He reached around her, almost in an embrace, and rifled through her pockets. He withdrew the GPS device, which he dropped in his jacket pocket.

She let her hands fall. "No? What do you mean?"

He looked her square in the eye. "I mean no." The muscles in his jaw were working. He wrenched away from her. "This is how it needs to work. If my broadcasting activities here have been discovered, so be it. I didn't expect to be developing the militia side of the operation so soon, but it looks like we must build up a strong defense force—and a stronger security policy. The fact is, I've got to go meet Raidon before he launches another one of those glass-breaking infiltrations you pulled off last time."

He knotted the curtain at his waist, then edged himself around backward so that he was poised on the edge of the drop-off.

Jenny looked around wildly, but there was nothing she could do to stop him without putting him in danger of falling. He was playing this all off as common sense, but she could read between the lines. He was trying to separate them to give her more of a chance to get away.

Almost desperately, she said, "The smartest choice is to get off this overblown island to safety, where you can regroup and rebuild. Put someone else in charge. It's not like you'll be turning your back on the revolution. It's being smart. You've done what you needed to do to get the depot up and running. You're too high profile now. What you really need to do is disappear. Show up somewhere else."

He looked over her shoulder at the Parliament Club. "They're on the hunt, Jenn. Time to go. Give me your hand."

Taking a step over the edge, and now flat-footed at an angle on the wall, his full weight trusting the curtain, Deck reached into his breast pocket. He pulled out a dog-eared envelope that looked like it had been with him on the whole trip, to hell and back. He reached out and took one of Jenny's hands, uncurled her fingers, and placed the envelope in her palm. Closing her fingers around it, he said, "This is *my* battle. It's time for you to go."

Jenny stared at him, then slowly opened the envelope. She looked up at him, her voice cracking. "You've *got* to be kidding me."

She knew what it was without him telling her. It was a digital key—for a safehouse, currency, an exit visa, the access code for a bank account in Macao.

Jenny hastily closed the envelope and tried to hand it back. "You can't be serious. I can't take this."

Deck looked at her oddly. "Can't you?"

She winced. He wouldn't take the envelope. She put it down on the concrete at her feet.

He sighed, reached over the ledge, and picked it up again. "I'm not going to pretend that things worked out the way I wanted. I'm not going to pretend that I'm not disappointed in some of the choices you made." He paused and looked up at her. "Or in some of the choices I made. You did what you had to do to survive. That's how it works. I can't . . ." He choked up a little. "You deserve this."

"Deck—"

He grabbed her wrist, and the rest of her words were lost in her throat. "You deserve this. You earned it. Take it and go."

He'd made it clear. They weren't to be together. So it could only be a bittersweet victory in the end. Without Deck, she had no one to go to. And without this—she slowly took the envelope, her cheeks flaming—she had nowhere even to go.

He released her, his fingers lingering along the inside of her wrist. And then Deck bent his knees and pushed off from the wall to begin his descent. The curtain billowed out in purple folds.

Jenny watched the distance between them expand, trying to ignore the lump in her throat and the tears pricking her eyes. He could have stayed with her longer, making the descent somewhere farther down the line, farther away from Parliament. He was giving her more of a chance to get away. As soon as the gangers appeared, he would lead them away.

I hope somewhere deep down inside you know how much I love you, Deck. I should have told you, in spite of everything.

"Run, Jenny!" he called, though she could barely see him over the side. "Go home."

Run. It seemed it was what she did best.

Chapter Twenty-seven

Jenny picked up the pokers and started running between the two rows of statues. Shots were fired. A quick glace showed that some members of Parliament were swarming to the open windows, throwing ladders to the wall.

Debris, rock dust, and bullets sprayed through the air as she ran. Chunks of flying concrete, stone body parts, the pensive faces of angelic women and stoic men crumbled around her.

This wasn't going to work. She would either get shot or run herself right back to ground zero at the Parliament Club. No, thanks.

It was definitely time to get creative. And the only thing she could see dead ahead was a set of high wires hanging from a series of dilapidated communications poles. A short segment of wire passed just above the intersection of two sides of the Parliament Club wall, before continuing to the next support pole on the other side of the city street. Another flurry of bullets showered the wall around her. Never breaking her stride, Jenny tossed a poker out into the air. It struck the wires—no sparks, no charge, no nothing.

The poker disappeared, a metallic clang and echo ringing up through the crevasse as it landed in the street below.

The wires were dead. Not surprising, given they seemed to be part of some sort of obsolete communications system. Power wasn't distributed much aboveground anymore; it was too easy to find and sabotage.

A bullet *twanged* off the armored placket covering her lower leg. *Time to go.* Jenny studied the distance for a second, then, sticking the second poker down the side of her boot, she leaped into the air and grabbed the closest wire. Adrenaline streamed through her body as she steadied herself. Hanging on with one hand, she pulled the poker out with the other and flipped it up, laying it flat against the two wires.

It was a matter of faith to let go of the wire and grab for the two ends of the poker. Immediately, the poker started to slide along the two wires away from the wall. Jenny jackknifed her body like a lever, using all the strength she could muster to propel herself faster and faster away from the Parliament Club.

She slid rapidly toward the communications post at the opposite end of the wide street, and lifted up her boots to take the hit and absorb the shock. It was a simple matter to climb down the pole then, and quickly blend with the street crowds. On reflex, she looked around for Deck. Just a bunch of strangers. Was he with Raidon? Was he even still alive? Was he wondering the same of her?

Normally after such a feat, she'd feel a sense of triumph, a high. This time, Jenny dropped the poker in a gutter and just stood in the dirty street, giving in to tears. The passersby simply shoved past and crowded around and couldn't care less. She cried for the choices she'd made, the things she couldn't take back, the things she now understood, always too late, and the things she'd never have—even with what seemed like the world in an envelope in her hand.

Finally, drained and wary of attracting attention from the street predators lurking around her, she slung her bag over her shoulder and headed for the transport depot. She was quickly back in the immigration hall, milling anonymously in the crowd, pushing her way up the ramp against the huge wave of newcomers.

It seemed almost as if the key card in her pocket was a magnet, except that it didn't pull her toward freedom; it was trying to pull her back toward Deck and the cause. And just at the point where she might have actually let it, the inbound and outbound crowds were separated from each other by ropes.

The outbound side was pretty much deserted, and Jenny walked slowly on the near-empty ramp with only herself, a bleary-looking transport guard going for shift-change, and the visa-taker just up ahead.

She looked to her left at the inbound side, think-

301

ing of the beginning of the whole mess, when she and Deck were just starting the mission, and their relationship together—

Well, *that* was strange.

She shifted her messenger bag to the opposite shoulder and tried not to look obvious about staring. What she saw was strange in the sense that it wasn't normal to see a pair of fully uniformed royal guards from the Kingdom of Asia having a casual snack at a pocket-food vendor in the middle of the Newgate immigration hall. One was younger with a spanking-new flat-top, the other quite a bit older with a face pockmarked and burnt by the sun. Jenny didn't recognize either of them.

You don't want to know, Jenny. Don't go there. You're done. But she stopped in her tracks.

In spite of the fact that there were only a few travelers headed in the outbound direction, the visa-taker put his hands on his hips and called out impatiently, "Hey, do you have an outbound visa or not?"

"Um, yeah, I do. Give me a sec. I can't remember where I put it." She moved to the side by the ropes nearest the pocket-food vendor and the two men, put her bag down, and pretended to search.

"I mean, seriously, we should get hazard pay for this," the younger guy was grumbling, his mouth full of food. "Man, this smells like shit. Hey, what's the matter with you?"

The older man just shook his head.

"You know, my brother trained with the prince. Said he was a stand-up guy. This just seems weird."

Pointed silence.

"Can I read the orders?"

That got an answer. "You're kidding me, right? I think you need to be slapped upside the head. Want me to do it?"

There was a sullen "no" in response. Then, "Kyber doesn't support the revolution, does he?"

"Think of it this way. Revolution is okay if it weakens the enemy, but not if it weakens us. We've got to stay strong."

"Yeah, okay." The younger soldier shrugged. Jenny saw him glance up at the other man, then hesitate before asking, "We here to kill him?"

She held her breath.

But the older man didn't say; he simply wheeled around and smacked the kid on the back of his head. He looked about suspiciously, then in a forced whisper said, "You need to learn to keep your mouth shut, rookie. You don't need to know anything unless I tell you you need to know it. You got that? Just trust me when I say that if we do this mission right, Kyber is going to be very happy."

The younger guy rubbed the back of his head and nodded uncertainly. "Sure. I just don't really know what we're doing here, that's all. I mean, we're partners, and I don't get why I don't get to read the order. I just like to know what my job is."

But the older soldier had returned to his original stony silence. He crumpled an empty pocket-food cone and tossed it in the nearby wastebin.

Jenny kept her head down as they moved off. She glanced quickly over her shoulder, watching the pair

303

make their way through the thronging crowd toward the exit.

Well, this explained a bit more about the relationship between Parliament and Kyber's House of Han. She couldn't understand what Parliament had wanted from Deck. Leverage with Kyber was the logical answer, but why? For what? Whether Kyber thought of Deck in a positive or negative way at this point, Deck was still a potentially important political figure.

The visa-taker headed down the ramp toward her as she wrestled in her bag for her comm device. If Deck was still on the same frequency, she could warn him.

"I can't let you linger on this ramp," the visa-taker said sternly. "It's a security thing. Do you have a visa or not?"

Jenny pulled the key card out of her pocket and shoved it at the guy. She switched on her comm, and trying to keep the panic from her voice said, "Does anyone copy?"

In a drone that revealed he'd said the same thing a million times before, the visa-taker said, "Please note that you'll need to pass both security and immunizations screening prior to boarding. If you feel you cannot pass at this time, nor have the value to purchase completions or waivers, we suggest you attempt the trip at another time. Do you understand what I have said, or do you have any questions at this time?"

Jiggling her comm device as if doing so would

somehow produce better results, Jenny mutely shook her head in the negative. "Deck, copy?"

Nothing but static.

The man stamped her visa with an infrared handheld, then peered at his device. "You're 8675309. Odd numbers traveling to Macao today are being screened at Gate C9. Please proceed to the checkpoint."

Jenny acknowledged the guy by muttering a curse under her breath and switching frequencies. Moving on, she called in a few test patterns and picked up a few sidetracked comms, but Deck didn't answer.

At the next checkpoint, a grandmotherly woman smiled kindly. "Visa, please."

Jenny practically shoved it at the woman, her hands starting to shake as reality sank in. Deck wasn't answering. He probably had no idea empire guards were coming after him. They were much more dangerous than the Parliament rabble. And maybe he was already in trouble. Maybe he was—

"Bug check, dear." The elderly woman handed back Jenny's visa and pointed to a door leading to Disease Control Clearance. Only a few more hurdles before she could queue up for the ride home. Home.

Jenny managed a weak smile and started walking toward the door.

But this wasn't what she wanted. This didn't mean anything without Deck. She didn't want things to end like this, with him thinking the worst of her and giving her everything he'd promised anyway. She didn't want to walk through that gate and leave with everything falling to pieces behind her, in large part because of what she'd done at the depot. She couldn't live with that. Which was a strange, strange realization. Because she'd thought she could pretty much live with anything.

Jenny ripped the useless comm headset off and stuffed it in her pocket. She turned around. The only thing standing in her way was the elderly woman, who looked seriously alarmed as Jenny headed toward her. "Don't do it," the woman cautioned, grabbing Jenny's jacket sleeve. "You've already forfeited your visa. Whatever you left behind, leave it."

Jenny closed her eyes, sweat beading between her shoulder blades. It was still tempting to turn around. But without Deck, the visa meant nothing.

She'd thought for a while she'd earned the right to get away with anything and still have a clean conscience. But that was before she'd seen the other side. Now she understood what sacrifice really meant; she'd really looked into Deck's heart and seen what it meant to make a difference. And she'd felt what it was like to love and be loved, if only for a moment.

Maybe it was too late. Yeah, once more, maybe it was just too little, too late—but she was sure as hell going to try.

It must have been written on her face.

"You'll regret it. Turn around, sweetie, and just keep walking!"

"I can't!" Jenny cried in anguish, knowing full well this act could well be irreversible.

She yanked herself out of the old woman's grip and started back through the throng, fighting against her lifelong instinct to turn away and save herself.

The revolution needed her. It meant that she and everyone else who'd ever been held down, who'd ever lived on the streets, who'd ever spent years looking over their shoulders or scrapping for survival—they'd all have a better life.

And even more than that, Deck needed her. There would be no better life for her without him. No matter where she lived or what she did, it was meaningless without him. And if she didn't do something now, they'd get him. Whichever "they" got there first. He needed her.

Jenny hit the exit, and just started running down the street toward the armory. She reached the familiar building in minutes, though breathless and fairly light-headed. She pounded on the huge warehouse door. The armorer looked through the metal slot at the top, then shut it and opened the door a sliver of the way. She slipped in, and he quickly closed the portal behind her. "The two men. I was with them before. Still here?"

"Nope," he said. He didn't add more.

Jenny reached into her jacket and pulled out the envelope, which she opened with shaky hands. She put the key card on the counter between them.

The armorer looked casually down at the electronic valve in front of him, his face impassive. There was probably more than he'd normally make in a month. Maybe a year. He nodded at her. "If you want to catch them, you'll need to travel light on the fastest hybrid I've got. I'll give you as much ammo as you can strap on your back, but you'll want to err on the side of speed. Leave any extras with me. I'll hold them for your return."

Jenny swallowed hard. Deck was okay! Somehow he'd escaped the Parliament and found Raidon.

She swung her bag around to the front and pulled out just her canteen and a first-aid kit. She strapped a pair of knives to her thigh holsters, but hesitated when it came to the gauntlets. They'd come full circle, hadn't they?

"You want to trade those in for something else?" the armorer asked.

"Nah," she said softly, and slipped them over her wrists. "Sentimental value."

He tossed her bag in the storage shed and, just as she was about to turn away, her eye caught on something.

"What's this?"

"None of your business." He tried to shut the door in her face, but she stuck her boot in the crack. Two jackets hanging with button cuffs were monogrammed with the mark of the UCE.

Her heart started to pound. "These are hanging up front. When did they get here?"

He maintained an aggravating silence.

"If they aren't wearing uniforms, they're trying to travel incognito. I just gave you a lot of value. What do they look like?"

"Look, Jenny. I'm an equal opportunity guy. I deal one on one. You know I don't like that 'they went thataway' stuff. I tell you more than I tell most, but I try not to take sides. People want to buy my products, I sell 'em. Politics ain't my bag."

"You'll do this for me."

"Aw, you know I could crush you with my fist," he said pleasantly. "Don't try to play hardball now."

"You won't have any balls to play with if you don't tell me the truth."

He looked down and blanched. The metal points of her right gauntlet were aimed at his family jewels.

"Point-blank," she said. "Ouch."

He cleared his throat. "Okay. But just for you I say this. The UCE boys came in after your friends and asked a lot of really annoying questions. Tried to bargain me down on a set of spurs, if you can believe it. I wouldn't take them on at first. Until they said they also wanted a fast transport. They suddenly had the value, then." He shrugged. "I threw in the spurs for free. That's all that went down."

Someone was definitely going to get hurt today. Jenny just hoped it was the bad guys.

"Have you had any other visitors today?"

"Just you three groups. Your two guys, the UCEs, and now you."

"Have you seen any of the Asian Kingdom's men?"

"Not today, but maybe my luck will hold and they'll come in, too. Um, can you point that somewhere else now?" He motioned to her gauntlet.

Jenny snorted and moved her arm back to her side.

"Thanks. I'll get your ride." He opened the gated

309

door to the stables and led her to a black horse-hybrid that showed just the right amount of enthusiasm for exercise when the armorer helped her mount.

"What's its name?" Jenny asked, as she steadied the hybrid and turned toward the outback.

"Ned Kelly."

Great.

Chapter Twenty-eight

Deck reined in his horse. It reared up, whinnying.

Raidon looked over his shoulder and turned his horse back. "What's wrong?"

Deck stared into his heavy's eyes and shook his head. "I should have waited to make sure she passed through immigration safely. People have obviously observed her with me."

"I'm sure she's fine."

"What if Parliament . . . I should have waited long enough to see her leave with my own eyes."

"She's fine." Raidon nervously looked around at the desolate landscape.

"No, what if . . ." What if Jenny hadn't got on the transport on purpose?

Raidon seemed to read his mind. "Look, she's got a pocketful of currency and a key to freedom. She's not going to hang out in Newgate. Honestly, sir, I'm as worried about her as you are, but we both know by now that Jenny can take care of herself. If you turn back, it will be like riding into the heart of a wasps' nest. Think what we had to do to get out."

Deck had to work to steady his anxious mount. "I can't do this."

Raidon frowned. "You can't take the chance—"

He didn't have to. A rider atop a hybrid barreled toward them at full speed. A cloud of dust rose behind it.

Both men readied their weapons. And then Deck almost dropped his rifle, wondering for a minute if he was having some sort of opiate-induced hallucination. But Raidon's frown had transformed into an ear-to-ear grin, confirming what he saw.

It was a glorious sight. Red hair flying out behind her, riding her horse like a she-devil, Jenny was yelling at the top of her lungs. If the Shadow Voice's Paul Revere had been a woman, she would have looked exactly like this.

"The UCE is coming!" Jenny caught up to them, a whirlwind catching her breath.

Deck wanted to kill her for coming back. Almost as much as he wanted to take her in his arms and smother her with kisses.

"Deck, they know you're here. Parliament sold you out to everybody. And now you've got the whole world trying to find you. I'm not kidding."

Her horse reared and pranced. Deck grabbed the reins and reeled it in. "What the hell are you doing here? You should be halfway home by now."

She raised her chin. "I went. They were coming in as I left. Kyber knows, Deck. He's sent men out for you. I saw them at the immigration gates. They've taken the main part of the road we used the first time—we're just past the intersection, and they are no doubt going to be on our tails very soon. You don't have any more time left."

"Now, you listen to me," he said, trying hard to keep his voice calm. "You turn this horse around and you get the hell out of here."

"And then what?" she taunted. "Then you fight the bad guys by yourself? There's too many of them. Okay, it's not out of the question, but the odds are pretty bad. You've got Parliament trying to assimilate you, the UCE trying to kill you, and Kyber probably interested in arresting you for treason—assuming his men don't have something more evil in mind. That's not good! Let me do my part."

"Turn around and go home."

"No. I can't."

"Yes, you can."

"No, I can't. I turned in my visa."

Deck swore. She possibly could still bribe her way on. But, damn, she'd probably need more value to do it than was even in that envelope. "Why? For God's sake, why?"

"Because I care. Because it matters. All of it. I'm not just talking about the revolution. *You* are what matters to me, most of all, now. I don't care if I'm stranded here. I don't care if I sound like an idiot—I don't care if Raidon thinks I'm not good enough. I came back for you. The visa doesn't mean anything without you, Deck. I might as well be in Newgate as in paradise alone. I thought there could never be anything more important to me than my own security, my own stability, my own life. I never thought I could feel something strong enough to make me sacrifice everything I ever thought I wanted. I know we've made mistakes and wrong choices, like you said. But we're only human, after all. We've got so much to live for, and there's just no way I'm not going to see this thing through to the end with you, whatever happens."

He stared at her, trying to find the right words. "Jenny—"

"I *love* you, Deck," she said simply. "I love you."

"We've got company," Raidon blurted, pointing to a cloud of dust on the horizon.

Jenny steadied her horse. "What's the plan going to be?"

Raidon checked his weapons. "I've got a pistol with two cartridges, three range explosives, and a badass knife if it gets down to the nitty-gritty."

"That should be enough to get you both safely to the depot," Deck said.

Raidon and Jenny looked at him. She cocked her head and regarded him with narrowed eyes. "You're not about to pull some sort of I-care-about-you-so-much-I-can't-let-you-die bullshit, are you? Or am I getting this all wrong?"

Deck managed a smile. "I'm going to ride directly at them, take out as many as I can. You go with Raidon back to the depot. Someone has to lead them. Stay there until you can arrange with the other Shadow Runners to get a new visa. And as for right now . . ." He looked up, the pounding of their pursuers' hoofbeats sending tremors through the sand below them. "If any of these guys get past me . . . Jenny, you take them on. But you're going to go with Raidon first."

"This is suicide, riding into them alone," Jenny protested. "You realize that you're talking potential suicide. You can't be the one."

No, you can't *be the one.* Deck looked into Jenny's eyes and tried to remember what it felt like to be unsure about what was most important in life. He felt a clutching at his heart and knew it had nothing to do with fear.

"It's the best choice. You two need to make it back to the depot. I've already ordered the process of relocating the entire station, along with the mirage, to safer ground. Raidon, you can oversee the remaining logistics of that, and start mustering a small emergency militia." Deck spoke briskly, removing his communications headset and handing it to his heavy. "Channel 6. Take it."

He glanced up at Jenny, who was sitting atop her horse between the two of them looking rather crestfallen, stunned. He didn't blame her. "I love you" deserved something more than this, but there just wasn't the time.

Raidon fit the headset to his helmet. "Sir—"

"*Don't* call me, 'sir.' "

Raidon smiled uncertainly.

"You understand what I'm asking you to do?" Deck asked.

The sound of hoofbeats in the dunes became

louder and louder, and a funny look suddenly came over Raidon's face. "Yes, I do," he said firmly.

Jenny looked at him in surprise, and Deck managed a smile. Raidon didn't argue further. He didn't protest. He didn't claim his divine right, his moral duty to stay, to protect. He was ready. "You'll make a great leader. You've always had it in you. But I shall miss you, my friend." Deck held out his hand.

Raidon studied it, a slow smile creeping over his face. He took Deck's hand and in that moment seemed to release himself from all that had subjugated him to his liege. "We'll meet again, if there's justice in this world. Godspeed . . . Deck."

They ended the handshake as peers, and there was no doubt in Deck's mind that he was leaving his Shadow Runners in good hands.

He gestured toward Jenny and said, "Take care of her."

The heavy turned to her. "Ready?"

Seven horsemen were visible now, riding toward them, a cloud of dust rising up from where the horses' hooves furiously windmilled the sand.

Deck looked at Jenny. "Go on. Go with Raidon."

Jenny sat frozen on the back of her horse as it stamped and pranced, sensing the oncoming stampede. He took her hand. "Jenny, this was never your fight. It isn't your fight now. There's nothing to prove here. Not to me, not to anyone. They'll just kill you."

The riders were too close for comfort now, the colors of the Han guard and the UCE, and the silhouette of the top hats of several Parliamentarians discernible as well. How strange that they all would be working together. It was good to see that the revolution was a threat to them all.

Jenny looked back at them and started loading ammunition into her weapons, orienting them, and strapping them in place, accessible for a fight, obviously under some illusion that she was going to go with him anyway.

He swore as his enemies closed in and, sensing that Jenny might bolt after him, he flipped the reins away from her, over the hybrid's head. Raidon caught them on reflex.

"Go!" And without another look behind him, he spurred his horse and headed straight for his attackers.

Jenny watched Deck ride away, and she tried to grab the reins back from Raidon. She missed, twisted around in her seat, and called out Deck's name.

Desperately she turned back to Raidon, putting both hands on the reins and pulling with all her might. "Let me go with him. Please."

"Stop pulling so hard, or you're going to fall off when I let go."

She let up, and he just tossed the reins back over her hybrid's head.

"I don't take orders from Deck anymore," Raidon said with a smile. "And besides, if ever two people were meant for each other . . . Well, let's just say that you're equals in more ways than one. I owe you an apology."

"Thanks, Raidon. You know I'm going to miss you." She managed only a bittersweet smile before shots were fired. They both turned their horses, one in each direction.

Jenny looked over her shoulder. "You know what they say—there's the quick, and there's the dead. Let's make it a point to be the former." Her hands shook, and she clenched them tightly around her weapons. "See you on the flipside."

And then she was flying across the sand, Deck in her sights and still on his horse, thank God, a couple of enemies' bodies missing from atop their mounts, though.

She aimed at one of them and took a shot. Missed. She swore, cursing herself for not doing more target practice.

The enemy turned his rearing, stamping horse, his gun aimed at her for a point-blank shot, but he couldn't get one off as his horse bucked, surprised by a warning shout from Deck.

Jenny got up on her knees in her saddle and jumped, knocking the surprised monarchist off of his horse and down to the ground. His gun flew free and went tumbling into the sand.

They were equals now. Fist to fist, kick to kick, and any other street-fighting move he wanted to try on her. He backhanded her in the face, buying himself a little time to look for his gun while she raised herself up out of the sand and shook her head clear. Her bruised ribs were on fire as she staggered over to him and kicked him in the head with a perfect roundhouse. He went flying backward, but clearly wasn't down for the count.

From the corner of her eye, Jenny saw Deck losing

his battle with the balance of the attackers. Three remained standing. Three were out of the picture. But the trio, a UCE, a Han, and a member of Parliament, had finally managed to get the better of him, and they seemed to be arguing over him as they held him down on the ground.

Well, as long as they were arguing, they weren't killing. But Jenny's heart raced with fear, anyway. As her opponent recovered, crouching low in a wrestling stance, she knew she needed to finish this job and help Deck as soon as possible.

The glint of a UCE gun taunted her from the sand. She crouched down low, as if ready for another round of hand-to-hand, but as her enemy lunged she leaped to the side, grabbed the gun, kept rolling in a 360, and put a bullet through his forehead. She rolled around to face him once more.

He hit the ground, an expression of total surprise filling his face.

"I'm just giving him a sedative," she heard the Parliament dandy say. Jenny struggled to her feet in time to see him lean over Deck with a syringe.

"That's not a sedative, it's the opiate! Don't let him!"

"What the hell is going on here? This wasn't the agreement," the older Han guard said angrily. "You kill him, I'll kill you." He kicked the syringe away, and it smashed against his boot, the opiate spattering Deck's face.

"Get it off your skin," Jenny cried. She moved to help and was promptly bulldozed to the ground, her face mashed into the sand.

"You're the prettiest turncoat I've ever seen," a voice said. The Parliamentarian nuzzled the side of her neck, breathing in the scent of her hair. He closed his hands around her throat and began to squeeze, the foulness of his breath noticeable even as he choked the life out of her.

Jenny twisted and grabbed his wrists, but was unable to wrench free. Her eyes focused on her hands beating and scrabbling against the man's chest, the metal tips of her gauntlets glinting in the sun.

In the last moment, he bent his head to give her a final leer. She moved one hand to his neck and pressed the trigger on her wrist gauntlet. The hook burst out, embedding itself in his throat, and he reared away, screaming, blood spraying from the wound. Jenny prayed his hands wouldn't freeze around her neck in his final death throes. The moment he let go to bring his hands up to his own neck, she rolled to the side. Seconds later, his body slumped hard against the ground.

She lay still, struggling to breathe and watched Deck try to handle both the UCE soldier and the older Han guard. The UCE man held a knife to Deck's throat.

"We're not killing him," the Han was saying. "Nobody said anything about killing him."

The UCE sneered. "Listen, you can have the girl."

Jenny licked her lips nervously. Okay, then. At least she knew what she was dealing with. It was always helpful to know exactly what you were dealing with.

"That wasn't the arrangement I made with Parliament. They said we'd get the prince back."

"Well, in case you didn't notice, they were lying," the UCE soldier said. He moved his knife to scratch an itch on the side of his head.

"Right." But the Han held fast. "You want to make a deal with me, now that our third party is out of the picture?" he asked wearily, gesturing around to the bodies of the Parliament dandies.

The hybrids all stamped impatiently, spooked by the commotion.

The UCE soldier made a rude noise. He looked at the bodies of the Parliament members. "Damn prima donnas."

The Han was clearly struggling to stay in control of his emotions. "I'm okay with a new deal. All I know is that I gotta get him back to the Kingdom of Asia alive. The way I see it, you've got a dead buddy anyway; no one's gonna blame you if you don't get the guy. You can tell them whatever the hell story you want. You can have the girl and a nice chunk of value, but I get the prince."

"Nobody gets the girl except me," Deck said through his teeth. He roared out in anger and busted free, taking a nasty slice to his arm as he did so.

The Han went for the UCE, knife-to-knife. The two blades flashed and they staggered apart, one shiny red blade falling to the sand at their feet.

The UCE soldier grabbed his gun from his holster in an exaggerated motion, his eyes wide, his mouth gaping. He swung the weapon wildly between his three remaining threats—Deck, the Han, and Jenny, who still knelt on the ground trying not to black out, and not feeling like she had much threat left in her.

Her mind reeled. She slowly looked up at him, going borderline hysterical. Strange. The soldier was supposed to have an agenda. He was supposed to want Deck dead, so why didn't he just . . .

She blinked, focused in, and . . . Ah, because when you had about two minutes left to live, those two minutes belonged to you and you alone. No, the UCE soldier didn't have an agenda anymore; he had blood rushing from his gut and one last hurrah.

"One of you comes with me. You," he yelled at Deck. He aimed his weapon. Deck looked at Jenny. She looked back at him. Yelling out a war cry in unison, they leaped straight at the soldier. Deck aimed high, Jenny low.

As they took the man down, his gun discharged into the sky. Jenny mustered all of her remaining strength to hold his legs. And in the growing darkness of her last conscious moment, she watched Deck deftly handle the rest.

She had no idea how long she was out before she heard Deck's voice. "Jenn?"

She opened her eyes to find him kneeling down beside her. "You're still alive," she said hoarsely. "That's good." It was the understatement of the year, but she could barely speak, let alone get her thoughts together.

He reached out and wove his fingers through hers. "We did it," he said.

"You look like hell," she whispered hoarsely, flinching as it was painful to speak. "You're bleeding."

"You should see yourself." Her neck was probably covered in bruise marks; she could feel the lacerations on her face, neck, and arms.

"No, seriously. You're really bleeding." Rivulets of blood were seeping down his arm. "We need to get you some meds."

"It's not that bad. I'll take care of it in a moment."

"Damn." Jenny turned her head slightly, then stopped as the pain in her neck kicked in. She groaned and tried to sit up. She blinked, focused in on him.

Deck had to help her, and when he got her to a sitting position, he cradled her tight against his chest, smoothing his hand down her flyaway hair. "You're one hell of a fighter, you know that?"

She managed a smile. "I know." Then she glanced over his shoulder. The older Han soldier was tending to the rookie's wounds. The five other men lay dead on the ground. "Man. The body count just keeps getting higher."

He nodded. "We need to get away from Newgate," he said. "Not to mention that it's possible I ingested some of that opiate. It probably has the same half-life as plutonium, for all I know. My plan is to stay as far away as possible from Parliament until I can rid my system of the addiction seed."

"As far away from Parliament as possible is right where I want to be," she agreed. "As long as it's with you."

323

He kissed her on the forehead. "You asked me if I was going to pull that I-care-about-you-so-much-I-can't-let-you-die bullshit."

She nodded through misty eyes.

He lifted her up and carried her in his arms toward the horses. "That would be yes, I was. I am. And I will. So get used to it. I want you to be happy and alive. I love you, Jenn."

She lifted her face to his, and kissed him softly. "It's about time."

Chapter Twenty-nine

On the return trip to Macao, with an entire transport car to themselves, Jenny and Deck could have each had a full row of seats to lie down on. Deck wouldn't hear of it. He wanted her close, so they'd stretched out together for the duration of the journey.

Jenny sat up and leaned on her elbow. "You know, once we get to Macao, we can just keep going."

"Still running, Jenny?" he asked softly.

She frowned. "It's not me I'm worried about. Do you really trust Kyber not to bring you up on charges of treason? That is your plan, right? To walk straight back into the palace and have words with him? That's what you told those soldiers."

"I think making peace with him is the smart thing to do, though I admit what's between us won't die easy." He shrugged. "As for treason, I doubt it. There's definitely a lot of value in the idea of a mid-dleman between the revolution and the Kyber regime. If I'm wrong, then he's not really the man I knew as a brother."

"Well, that won't exactly be consolation for me," Jenny grumbled. "Whether Kyber gets involved or not, we've still got a lot of work to do. Just because we got the Shadow Voice back online doesn't mean it's over. The exact coordinates of your hub might be changed by now, but everyone knows at this point the Shadow Runners have cooked something up around Newgate . . . Hey, why are you smiling?"

Deck grinned. "Listen to you. 'We.' I can't tell you how much I like the sound of that."

"You better believe I said 'we.'"

"We is good. I like we. I sometimes think we must have been destined," he whispered. "Do you believe in destiny?"

"I suppose . . ." Jenny said, trailing her lips across his chest. "I suppose that depends on how things turn out." He could feel first her smile against his skin, and then the trill of her laugh.

"We'll, I've been thinking about that. Life, liberty, and the pursuit of happiness, Jenny. That's what it's all for. It seems I've managed the first two. I find that the only thing standing between me and the third . . . is you."

Jenny sat up and turned around to look at him.

"Marry me, Jenny," he said simply. "I simply cannot do without you. Revolution or not. You're the rest of my life."

Her lips parted in delight, and Deck took advantage by kissing her slowly. "Yes," she murmured against his mouth. "I wouldn't dream of letting you suffer."

Deck laughed and leaned back against the seat, shaking his head. He took her hand and tangled his fingers in hers. "You know, you never told me how you escaped Newgate the first time."

Jenny snorted and gave him a look. "I impersonated a cigarette girl. It took me a year just to save enough money for the bribes. I even got caught changing back into my street clothes, but I traded my freedom for the contents of the shoulder box. It was pretty hairy."

"You wore one of those little devil outfits?"

Jenny raised a finger. "Don't even think about it."

He tried to wipe the smile off his face without much success. "I think I could come up with one of those costumes," he said.

Jenny rolled her eyes. "I looked ridiculous, but I learned all the tricks." She leaned over and ran her finger over Deck's lips. "Welcome to hell, baby," she murmured in a sultry voice.

"It's definitely getting hot in here. And I have an idea." Deck looked around the deserted car.

"What?" she asked.

"Let's start a revolution," he said, pulling her close.

"Again? What, are you trying to kill me?" Jenny asked, snuggling in.

Deck kissed her once more and grinned. "Don't worry. Nobody has to die."